HIS SEDUCTIVE SPY

The Double Recall 2

Enjoy the seduction! :)

Lara Santiago

Lara Santiago 2012

EVERLASTING POLYROMANCE

Siren Publishing, Inc.
www.SirenPublishing.com

A SIREN PUBLISHING BOOK
IMPRINT: Everlasting Polyromance

HIS SEDUCTIVE SPY
Copyright © 2011 by Lara Santiago

ISBN-10: 1-61034-516-9
ISBN-13: 978-1-61034-516-3

First Printing: April 2011

Cover design by *Les Byerley*
All cover art and logo copyright © 2011 by Siren Publishing, Inc.

ALL RIGHTS RESERVED: This literary work may not be reproduced or transmitted in any form or by any means, including electronic or photographic reproduction, in whole or in part, without express written permission.

All characters and events in this book are fictitious. Any resemblance to actual persons living or dead is strictly coincidental.

Printed in the U.S.A.

PUBLISHER
Siren Publishing, Inc.
www.SirenPublishing.com

DEDICATION

To Raina James, friend extraordinaire.

HIS SEDUCTIVE SPY

The Double Recall 2

LARA SANTIAGO
Copyright © 2011

Prologue

"We may have a traitor." Paul Kelly mentioned this inflammatory information as blithely as he might comment on the weather.

Frankie Belle, intrigued, responded as he expected, but kept her focus straight ahead. "What makes you think so?"

"My gut."

"Meaning no proof whatsoever."

Out of the corner of her eye, Frankie saw a wisp of a smile register at the curve of Paul's mouth before he responded, "Correct." Amusement also registered in his tone.

"What do you want me to do first?"

"Find the traitor."

"And then?" Frankie turned her head and studied her employer's chiseled profile.

Paul gave her one sideways glance that told her all she needed to know before turning his head to fully face her and to bore his surly stare through her. She gazed back with equal severity. One of Paul's eyebrows rose slowly.

As was true of every government agency, there was a protocol for traitors and how they were dealt with. She only needed to know the degree to which he wanted the possible breach controlled.

"Right. I get it. You want me to stop them." Frankie broke the staring contest first.

"Exactly."

"Permanently?"

"No. I'll want information and the trail to the initiator."

"Right," she murmured again. "Stop them and bring them in for questioning." Her first instinct was to commit bloody mayhem against anyone threatening this covert agency. Jeopardy to anyone she worked with was like a threat to her person, and self-defense combined with a violent smackdown was justified.

"I've seen that look before, Francine. Rein yourself in. This is all supposition on my part. I don't want a full-blown investigative force formed. Just check a few things for me, okay?"

She hated when he used her given name, Francine. The nickname Frankie was more her style.

"But if it *isn't* just supposition?"

"Then I want to know where the information is going and who's buying it."

"I've done this a time or two before," she said tartly. "I rarely let you down. I mean, that's why you're telling me this in confidence, right?"

A faint smile surfaced on his lips. It disappeared like mist disintegrating in the harsh morning sun. "Yes."

They currently stood on the roof of the building where they worked. This was supposedly a safe area regarding any covert listening devices. Frankie didn't think anywhere was truly safe from prying ears. But the roof was better than most places.

"When do I start?"

"Not yet. But soon. A few questionable things have transpired, but nothing to raise a red flag all the way to full staff. If a threatening entity exists, I want them comfortable, at least for now. No need to let them know I suspect anything."

"Right."

"You're currently due for some leave, and you have training to complete. When you return, we'll discuss this further."

Frankie wanted to argue, but it wouldn't get her anywhere. Paul Kelly revealed information in his own damn good time.

The sudden fantasy of putting her boss in a headlock and forcing him to spill the details of his suspicions crossed her mind briefly, but Paul knew a few moves of his own. She'd seen him spar at the Protocol facility gym with Ken Davenport, another high level, yet under the radar, government agency leader. That particular battle had ultimately been a draw, but Frankie didn't want to embarrass herself by underestimating Paul's hand-to-hand combat skills.

"Enjoy your time off." The legendary smirk on his face was the norm for her boss, but sometimes, like right now, she wanted to clock him one.

"Time off? I'll be in combat training."

"Which you love. You can't fool me, Frankie. You were born to do this job."

"Right." *Whatever.* He was absolutely correct. And while she'd rather chew her own arm off than wait for more details on what Paul already knew about the possible traitor, pouting wasn't an option.

Pasting a false grin on her face, she added, "I will. Thank you very much. See you in a couple of weeks." *And by then I will have already done some research on my own regarding this possible threat.*

Paul clamped a hand on her shoulder before she could exit. "Before you go, the Protocol doc needs to give you a quick checkup."

"Why?"

He pushed out an exasperated sigh. "So you won't have to do it upon your return to the Protocol building. I want you ready to go the minute you get back from training."

Frankie relaxed and nodded. "Got it. Doc first, training vacation second, and mole hunt when I return."

"It goes without saying you're to keep the mole hunt to yourself."

It wasn't a question.

Frankie gave him an exaggerated eye roll in response. "I won't even tell you until you bring it up again."

"Good."

"One question. Now that Rachel is out of the program, will you assign me a new partner, or do I fly solo to look for this possible traitor?"

"As a challenge, you not only get a new partner, but you must keep her in the dark about the traitor."

"I see. A challenge. No problem." *Fuck.* Frankie turned to exit. Behind her, Paul laughed as she closed the door on his mirth. He knew she'd be pissed about the new partner. Her old partner, Rachel, had been removed from the program, and the truth was, Frankie hadn't wanted anyone else. She loved flying solo. However, that was not the Protocol standard procedure.

Off the sweltering heat of the roof and several flights down the service stairwell, she headed for the med lab in the east wing of the building with an optimistic attitude. Having a plan always lifted her spirits, and the minor irritation of having a new partner didn't dampen her mood.

Hopefully, the doc wouldn't have much to do. Probably just a routine check. Once she was free, Frankie decided she would sniff around a little and see if her "gut" reacted to anything in the recent mission archives.

If she could figure out what got Paul's radar up and his gut churning, she'd be ahead of the game when she returned to pursue the mole.

* * * *

Paul Kelly strolled into the Protocol Med lab ninety minutes after Frankie and he parted company. She'd gone straight to medical, so he was surprised to still see her there. In a separate glass-walled room, she reclined in the Protocol medical "chair," hooked up to several wires attached to her forehead, face, and chest. She was unconscious, or rather, she was being reprogrammed to be another personality.

When Frankie Belle wasn't kicking ass as Paul's very best Protocol agent, she was tucked away in a small town not too far away. Known as Daphne Kane in her alternate life, she spent her idle time as a file clerk for an insurance salesman who moonlighted as a used car salesman and managed his own lot of pre-owned vehicles. Benny was an idiot, but a harmless one.

He was about to turn and head for his office, but saw the technician put his hand on Frankie's chest, just below her collarbone, and stroke downward. *What the fuck!*

Silently, he entered the room and positioned himself behind the inappropriate technician. He was about to get a personal lesson in hand-to-hand combat courtesy of Paul's experienced fists.

"How is she?" Paul asked the technician hovering over her.

"Perfect," he muttered without breaking his focus on Frankie's serene face. He also didn't remove his hand from her cleavage.

Paul snapped his fingers next to the technician's ear. The guy jumped six inches in the air. When he settled, a scowl appeared on his pasty face. He tried to stare a hole through Paul before realizing his error. Once recognition lit his features, the tech turned beet red. "I'm sorry, Mr. Kelly. I didn't hear you come in."

The name on his white coat was Alden. Paul made a mental note to speak to the man's supervisor about his conduct.

"Stop gawking and pawing at my agents while they sleep and pay attention, Alden."

Alden's lips flattened as he turned his full attention on Paul. "What can I do for you, sir?"

"When will *Daphne Kane* be ready for transport back to Loganville? I thought she'd already be gone by now."

"Soon."

"How about we make it now?"

The tech's gaze slid sideways to Frankie's face before he answered, "She needs at least another hour in the chair."

"Why?"

Alden's expression shifted to belligerent. "Because, per your orders, Frankie stayed in her spy personality for longer than usual this time."

"Which is my prerogative as her boss. What's *your* problem?"

Alden pushed the center of his black-rimmed glasses up his nose. "I don't want her to end up like her former partner, Rachel."

Paul pushed out a long sigh and resisted the urge to throttle the high-handed tech. "That was different, and you know it." Guilt registered in his gut over Rachel momentarily, but Paul knew she was thriving in her new life away from the Protocol Agency.

"You asked, and I answered." Alden turned away to fiddle with the knobs of some medical equipment on the table next to the chair where Frankie rested.

"Do your job. Stop mooning over my agent and put her back in Loganville like you're supposed to." Paul stepped closer, crowding Alden's personal space. "And if I ever find out you put a finger on her again, I'll break all the bones in your hand before I have you fired."

Paul exited the med lab on a trajectory aimed for the department head's office. He fully intended to give Dr. Denton a full report on Alden's inappropriate behavior. Or he did until it occurred to him his mole problem could easily reside in the med lab.

Surely medical personnel with improper fixation disorders were prime candidates for traitorous activity. If he discovered a traitor in their midst, Paul planned a fate worse than death for the hapless individual. If the mole was being manipulated by someone else, he'd deal with that party just as harshly. But until then, and to ensure that it stopped, he'd hire a guard to watch over his female Protocol agents while they were "transitioned" into their other personalities.

* * * *

"You are so beautiful, Louise." He put his most sincere smile in place and brushed his fingertips lightly over the wrinkly tip of her sagging breast. Her smallish nipple came to attention. In college, his friends had called him Valentino because there wasn't a woman he couldn't persuade into bed.

"Really?" The quiet, desperate, hopeful tone in her voice was laughable. Valentino longed to snicker out loud and explain how brilliantly he was using her, but he couldn't. Not quite yet. Not until he'd finished this part of his plan.

Louise would be ruined over this liaison and of no further use to him once his plans were in full motion. He didn't care what happened to former government agent, Louise Bennett, once her function in this matter was completed.

However, for now he needed her cooperation. He needed her to bend to his will. He needed her to go against her faithful, good judgment and stay over with him tonight.

Valentino had lured her from her post so that another important part of his plan could be implemented. So far everything had worked perfectly. He longed to sing with glee at the ease to which all the female pawns in his master plan were falling to heel, but restrained the urge to declare his masterful prowess at least for now.

Louise stared at him as if expecting something. *Damn.* Had he missed something she'd said?

"What?" he asked in a dreamy tone as if he'd been lost in the moment of staring at her average face with rapture. The acting classes from his youth paid off regularly in this business.

"Do you really think I'm beautiful?" She trailed her hand from his collarbone to his chest.

"Yes, of course. Why can't you see your own beauty?"

She shrugged and a dim smile slid over her thin lips. Remnants of her cheap lipstick filled the cracks around her mouth. It wasn't that she was ugly, just extraordinarily plain. Truthfully, it was all he could do to get his cock to cooperate in fucking her repeatedly. His primary goal was to ensure she stayed away from home for as long as possible so as not to sound the alarm of her missing charge.

"I should probably get going…" She trailed off, rolled closer, and put her hand squarely on his chest.

Valentino closed his eyes, hugged her tightly against his body, and bore up to have sex with Louise one more time.

It hadn't been easy to get her involved to this level. She hadn't fallen into his arms automatically.

Early on, Louise had been extremely distrustful when he'd turned on his charm and tried to get her to go out with him. She'd said, "I know what I look like, what do you *really* want from me?" So he'd backed off, regrouped, and taken a completely different approach. This plan B effort was working out perfectly. One little change and voila, she was his love slave.

"Please don't go." He scraped his thumbnail over her nipple and she sucked in a lusty-sounding breath of encouragement. "Please stay with me just a little longer."

His cock throbbed, and blood pooled in his groin. Sex was sex, after all.

For his purposes in this matter, one wet pussy was pretty much like any other. Luckily, Louise wasn't ugly or distasteful…just so very average.

He closed his eyes and brought to mind the face of the hot, young flight attendant in first class on his recent trip to South Carolina from DC. He'd fucked "Tiffany" into her first membership of the mile high club in the tight enclosure of the airplane bathroom.

The young thing had insisted on his wearing a condom, and the mechanics of putting the damn thing on in such close quarters had been a test of Olympic gymnastics, to say the least, but ultimately worth it. The facilities rendered a slightly off-putting scent, but even that was not enough of a deterrent to stop him from blowing his condom-protected wad into Tiffany's cunt beneath her uniform skirt at thirty thousand feet.

The exhilarating memory enabled him to get one last fast rise out of his cock with which to mount Louise and further his plan to ruin the Protocol Agency once and for all.

Chapter One

Daphne Kane sprinted along the weed-strewn sidewalk as fast as her kitten-heeled shoes would carry her towards the door of the bank, which was seconds away from closing. Glancing at her watch, she put extra speed in her already precarious steps. She absolutely *had* to get inside that bank before it closed. Her job depended on it.

"Please, wait. Hold the door," she called to the back of a muscular man headed towards the same place also in a big fat hurry. She knew because he'd just passed her at a dead run. His work boot-clad feet being much more practical for sprinting, Daphne was left in his proverbial dust clutching the bulky bag her boss had summarily demanded she take to the company safety deposit box. The only good news at being left in the dust was that this man's butt was very nice to watch as he headed for the bank door.

She glanced down at the black and tan bag she carried and wondered why it was so vitally important.

"Get this into the safety deposit box at the bank or don't bother coming back to work!" Benny had screamed before handing her a pittance for expenses. After herding her out of the dingy, dusty file room at his insurance office, he'd tucked her into his car and bundled her onto a commuter jet at the municipal airport by mid-morning. Along with a ticket for a return flight home that evening on the same plane, she carried only her purse and the bulky bag.

The return flight home on Friday left at six sharp. She was already running behind schedule. If she was late getting from the bank to the airport, she'd be left all alone in a strange city without enough money for a hotel, or food for that matter, since the small commuter service only flew on weekdays. Then she'd have to beg her way onto the first early Monday morning flight back home to make it back in time for work.

Unless, of course, she failed to get to the bank on time. If that happened, she could take her time and stop off at the unemployment agency first. She didn't know why it was so imperative that she get this stupid package into his safety deposit box, but Benny would have a screaming hissy fit if she didn't succeed. And she didn't want to lose her job. Benny wasn't without his charms. He didn't chase her around the desk, and he paid her on time, even if begrudgingly. So she hurried along in her inappropriate shoes as fast as possible.

The delectable man who'd passed her reached the door and snatched it open before the bank employee could stop him. Daphne was too far away to hear their conversation, but it sounded like he was sweet-talking his way inside the bank. Good. If he got in, she was demanding entrance as well. She put her focus on his wide chest and continued running.

Two steps from the luscious man who'd passed her, Daphne tripped over something on the sidewalk and launched forward on a path towards the unforgiving cement. Clutching the patterned, black and tan bag close, she shot the other hand out automatically to break her fall. Instead of hitting the ground, she found herself swooped up in the arms of the man with the gorgeous, speedy reflexes. He straightened her up so fast she lost her balance and fell against his chest. Hard, firm torso exuding warmth like the heat from a potbellied stove met her in a full body contact from shoulders to knees. But his belly was not rounded, it was firm and wonderful.

"Thank you so much. I'd have probably split my head open if you hadn't caught me."

"No problem," he murmured in a deep, sexy tone. The sound registered in her core, igniting a long-ignored feminine desire. Settling Daphne against him, he angled his head toward the female bank officer standing in the door like a sentry. Her name tag said,

Edna Hodge, Asst. Manager.

Daphne absolutely had to get inside the bank and was prepared to say anything to accomplish her goal. "Hi. May I please come in? I've simply got to put this bag in my employer's safety deposit box or else face his wrath."

"I'm sorry. We're closed," Edna said without emotion in her voice. She didn't sound the least bit sorry. If a man had been closing the door, Daphne knew she might have had a better chance to sweet-talk him into making an exception on her behalf.

"Please. My boss said I was fired if I didn't make it in time to get this stuff inside there. I flew here on a plane, for gosh sakes. I didn't have the right address. I got lost three times in three different cabs. I'm all out of money, and I absolutely have to put this in there or I'm sunk. Couldn't you make an exception just this one time? I'll hurry. I promise you. If you'd just let me in."

Edna's eyes narrowed, and her mouth thinned. "I'm sorry, but—"

"Couldn't you make an exception and chalk it up to a random act of kindness or something?" The man still squeezing her torso had the most seductive voice she'd ever heard. Seriously, if she weren't focused on the fear of losing her job, she'd take an entirely different approach with this delicious man. Although, embracing as lovers separated by only two layers of clothing was sheer bliss. Daphne already planned to tuck this tidbit away in her memories to enjoy for years to come. Her life could use a little boost of sexiness, but first she needed to keep her job.

Edna was apparently also not unaffected by his outward charm. She cracked a smile.

Good job, Mr. Sexy Butt.

"Well, I really shouldn't." The assistant manager glanced over her shoulder quickly before turning back with a slightly wider smile in place.

Mr. Sexy Butt grinned at her. "Come on. Let her in. You'll have done your good deed for the day. And I'd personally appreciate it."

Edna blushed. "Well, I guess it would be all right. There are a couple of people still inside anyway."

Daphne breathed a serious sigh of relief, stretched on the tips of her toes to add height, and leaned forward in the arms of the attractive stranger. The too-quick kiss she planted on his gorgeous mouth in spontaneous gratitude made her lips tingle. "Thank you so much. You have saved my life and my job."

His eyes widened at her exuberant physical expression. "My pleasure." His delicious brown-eyed gaze seared a path to her soul as he spoke.

Daphne turned in his arms, gained her footing again, and squeezed past Edna. She slid into the foyer of the bank before the woman changed her mind.

"Do you need to come inside the bank as well?" Edna asked Daphne's yummy savior, who still stood against the outer door holding it open with his wide shoulders.

A big grin surfaced. "If I could, that would be great. I've got a poker game tonight, and I need more money than I can get from the ATM. I'm planning on winning big." He ended his plea with a wink directed at Edna.

Bravo. The bank official looked like she was about to swoon. Daphne resisted the urge to touch her fingers to her lips as the memory of his mouth sent a buzz along her sensitive skin.

"You might as well come in."

"Thanks, Edna." He touched her forearm and squeezed.

Edna released a sigh and motioned for him to enter. He had to slide his gorgeous muscular body even closer to Edna, who didn't move a single facial hair out of his way, forcing him to press up against her to get inside. He didn't seem to mind. Edna stood a moment and exhaled deeply before she locked the door behind him. Daphne didn't blame her. If she had another opportunity, she'd also go out of her way to rub up against the sexy man, again.

Once inside the bank, it became very obvious to Daphne that Edna wanted the man, and on any other occasion, she would have stepped back and let Edna have him, but not this evening. His scent alone made him worth fighting for. After what she'd been through today, she deserved a delicious man to soothe her wounded spirit.

She must be having some sort of out-of-body experience because Daphne, who was never forward with strangers, stepped into his personal space as soon as he got past Edna.

"I'm Daphne Kane." She held her hand out to him as Edna locked the outside doors behind them. "Again, thanks so much for holding the door open for me."

He grinned and grasped her fingers in one large hand. Squeezing firmly, he held on to her hand. "I'm Zack Mahon, and you're welcome. It's the least I could do since I left you in the dust on the sidewalk."

Daphne squeezed his hand and held on to keep his attention. "After we leave here, I'd like the opportunity to thank you properly. Do you have time for a drink before you go off to play poker?"

Before he could answer, Edna walked between them. She broke their hands apart in her wake to lead them through the second set of bank doors and into the cavernous bank lobby. "If you want into the vault, go over to the archway and speak to the clerk. He'll get your information." She whirled around with an expression of dismissal as if she'd just thought of something terrible and said, "You *do* have authority to access that safety deposit box, don't you?"

Daphne inhaled and gave her a bright smile she didn't mean. "Of course. I've been on the signature card since the box was opened. It was five years ago, as a matter of fact."

Edna pursed her lips together into a thin line which Daphne decided was very unflattering to her long, horsy face. The manager slowly lifted a stiff arm and pointed behind Daphne. "Well, go on then, we haven't got all night."

Daphne forced her lips into a smile and crossed in front of Zack toward the archway and the small, balding male clerk standing near it.

Zack's utterly devastatingly sensual scent lingered in her lungs even three long steps later.

"Daphne," he called. She whirled around and put an authentic smile on her mouth this time.

"I'll wait for you. Once you're finished with the box, come back here. We can leave the bank together."

"That would be great. Thank you." Daphne winked at him, noting that Edna's back snapped as straight as the section of quarter-mile racetrack her daddy used to lose his paycheck to each week when she was a child.

"By the way," Edna's disgusted voice broke in, "you have sparkly pink lip gloss smeared all over your mouth."

Zack chuckled and wiped a thumb across his bottom lip. Studying the dark, pink, glittery substance as if it were vastly amusing, he said, "There are worse things."

Everything single thing about Zack made Daphne's riotous heart somersault. There was a three-ring circus of butterflies bouncing around her insides. The innocent kiss she'd given him for helping her out had been from quick and spontaneous gratitude, but when she'd touched him, a spark flared deeply from her lips to the center of her body.

Daphne turned away to take care of her employer's business, but decided Zack might sport a lot more lip gloss in places a lot more interesting than his luscious lips before the night was over.

Well, he would if she had anything to say about it.

* * * *

Zack smiled at Edna, who only frowned in return. She was so obviously jealous of Daphne it was laughable. He needed to charm her before he left to secure the funds he needed.

He moved closer. "May I still get some money for my poker game?"

Edna's unhappy gaze followed Daphne over to where she now stood with the pip-squeak. The clerk was falling all over himself to help her into the vault and the safety deposit boxes.

"Of course, if you think you'll still need it?" Edna broke the stare and looked down at the floor.

Daphne would be his after they left the bank, but Zack was a notorious flirt. It wasn't a stretch to realize Edna needed some attention, too. For now, and to flatten her ruffled feathers, Zack pasted a sincere and suggestive smile on his face and aimed his rapt attention on Edna.

"Oh. I'll need it," he murmured. Taking a step closer, he watched as she blushed to her roots. "Poker night with the guys is something I rarely miss for any reason. Especially not for a girl." The now flustered bank manager pushed out a slow breath, nodded, and led Zack to the first window cashier. He followed very closely, and when she gestured to the bank teller, she was in good humor once again.

"This gentleman would like to get some cash from his account," she said.

"Yes, ma'am," the bland male teller said.

Zack reached out before she turned away and stroked her arm from shoulder to elbow very slowly. "Thanks, Edna. I really appreciate this."

She flushed as red as an end-of-summer tomato. "Of course. We like to keep *all* of our customers happy." Edna turned away and walked to the end of the row where tellers counted the end of the day's transactions. She disappeared into an office.

Zack withdrew a thousand dollars and thought up ways to spend it over the weekend. Dinner, dancing, and drinking, followed by a bottle of wine picked up for late-night toasts after a quick trip home. And breakfast delivery from his favorite restaurant scheduled for mid Saturday morning, if he got lucky.

Twenty minutes after they talked their way into the bank, Zack and Daphne exited together. She was able to get her items loaded into her boss's safety deposit box, and Zack had plenty enough money for the poker game he *wasn't* going to make it to tonight.

As he followed Daphne through the double set of doors and back onto the sidewalk where they'd met, Zack turned to the bank manager, smiled, and murmured, "Thank you for letting us in, Edna."

Edna's bright gaze snapped from the back of Daphne's head to scrutinize him. "You're welcome. I hope you have fun at your poker game." Her expression and tone dripped concealed envy. She obviously didn't believe he'd be playing poker tonight.

Zack turned his lazy smile into a toothy grin. He was fairly sure she was correct. He wasn't going to be playing any games tonight, unless they were with Daphne. "Thanks. I appreciate that you went out of your way."

Edna shrugged, scanned his body from face to knees and back again, and closed the door with a clunk. Her perturbed expression was clearly displayed not only in her frown, but in the stiff way she held her body. Dropping her gaze, she locked the door and disappeared inside without looking at him again.

Zack turned his focus to Daphne, the possibilities of the coming night, and how badly his buddies would razz him for missing tonight's poker game for a woman. Given the seductive sway of her butt, any grief would be worth it.

Five steps out of the bank, Daphne stepped into a sidewalk crack and broke the heel off her shoe with her next stride. He grabbed her arm and steadied her.

"Now what?" She took a wobbly backwards step, bent over, and wrenched the ruined heel out of the crack. His eyes strayed to the well-rounded curve of her ass. She turned to face him with tears welling in her perfect blue eyes.

"No sense crying over a broken heel." He grinned and ran a finger down her jawline.

The hint of a smile tugged at her mouth. "You're right, but it's not just that."

"What else?"

"The truth is, I've already missed my flight home. I have an open ticket to board any flight with an available seat leaving for my airport. However, the airline's last flight back home has already left, and there are no weekend flights. Now, I can't depart until Monday morning, maybe. I've got very little money and not a single credit card with me." She held up the shoe to eye level. "And now it looks like I'll be barefoot as well as homeless for the weekend. What else could possibly happen?" She tilted her head backwards and took a deep breath and exhaled loudly, twice. She then removed her other shoe, squared herself and took two barefoot steps away, studying the broken shoe.

"Not to worry. I can give you a ride."

She stopped dead in her tracks and whirled around, eyes wide, expression shocked. "What?"

Zack slowed and remained out of her arm's reach.

"I can give you a ride. How about to a shoe store?"

"Oh...um...yes. That would be nice, but—"

Zack took a step closer, and she halted whatever she'd been about to say. A slight frown encompassed her lovely face. What was up with this girl?

"I appreciate your offer, but the thing is, I don't know you. You're, in fact, a complete stranger." She leaned forward as if to impart confidential information and whispered, "Haven't you ever heard the phrase 'beware of strangers'?"

This was an unforeseen complication, one he knew how to deal with. His eyes narrowed. "If I showed you my identification, would it help?"

"Depends on the identification." She crossed her arms. Not uptight, but relaxed, like she was ninety percent convinced he was okay, but needed an extra something to push her over the edge from budding trust to complete faith.

Out of the corner of his eye, he caught a low beam of the fading sunlight in the west casting long shadows from the downtown buildings surrounding them. In fifteen minutes it would be dark, and he suddenly understood her caution. He nodded and reached into his back pocket, pulling out the FBI badge he carried for show. "Here is my badge. I'm really Zack Mahon. Does this make you feel better? Or do I need to show you my license, too."

She squinted and leaned forward to study his identification. He sucked in a breath, and a rush of her perfumed scent scuttled across his being and filled his lungs.

"You're an FBI agent?" she asked in disbelief.

No. Not really. What I do is too secret to explain.

"Yes," he fibbed. He *did* work for the government, but the FBI badge was his cover for the clandestine projects he participated in. He wasn't supposed to use it to pick up women. But this case was special. He needed to prove he wasn't a pervert, psycho, serial killer trying to lure her to her death. A fine line of distinction if there ever was one since he was still lying.

"How do I know this is a real badge and not a fake one you bought or stole?"

Hand on his chest in an affronted manner, he frowned. "I would never steal, but you have a good point. What can I do to convince you I'm not a thief?"

Daphne tilted her head to one side as if pondering what proof she would require from him. A big grin erupted suddenly. Combined with her intoxicating scent, Zack decided he didn't care what level of persuasion it took. He'd convince her to spend some time with him tonight.

"I have an idea." Daphne slipped one strap of her large purse off of her shoulder to open it and began digging around inside. After several seconds, she retrieved a cellular phone from the depths. Dialing three numbers, she dazzled him with a grin before her party answered. "FBI please?" She listened a moment. "Local." And then finally. "Thanks."

Zack sighed internally. This verification might result in embarrassment with his boss, Ken Davenport, but Daphne's wide smile made the future chastisement worth it.

"Yes, I'd like to speak with an FBI Agent named Zack Mahon, please." She squinted and added, "Oh, tell him it's Miss Daphne Kane."

He wiped a hand over his mouth and then casually settled both of his hands loosely on his hips. Staring at seemingly nothing, in fact, Zack covertly studied his immediate surroundings, which also included her luscious body, and waited for her approval.

Seconds later, his phone started ringing. Standard protocol for his unit operated like clockwork.

He reached into his pocket, extracted his phone, checked the small screen to verify who was calling, and flipped it open. "Agent Mahon."

A high-pitched female voice said, "Sir, this is the FBI central switchboard. I have a call for you from a Miss Daphne Kane."

"Thanks. Put her through." He grinned at Daphne and winked.

"Agent Mahon. This is Daphne Kane. I've decided to go ahead and meet with you after all. Are you still available to pick me up?"

"Yes, Miss Kane. I'll be there faster than you can say safety deposit box."

She grinned, and her perfect white teeth set in that luscious, wide mouth sent all sorts of wicked thoughts flitting along his brain pathways.

"Thank you, Agent Mahon. I'll look forward to the ride."

"As will I, Miss Kane." He lowered the phone from his ear and snapped it shut at the same time she did.

"Are we good, then?"

"Yes. Thank you for understanding."

Zack held out his hand. She grinned and placed her fingers in his. He walked down the sidewalk hand in hand with the most beautiful woman he'd seen in forever with a voice that made him want to kneel at her bare feet and beg for her to read out loud.

"Where to, Miss Kane?"

"Wait a minute. Not that I don't appreciate your offer, but don't you have a poker game tonight?"

"Yes. But no women are allowed to attend this particular game, and besides, I have a feeling I'd have better luck if I stuck with you."

"No women allowed? Isn't that a little sexist, given the age we live in?" She laughed out loud, and the sound resonated low in his belly. It also encouraged the beast in his pants to think wild thoughts about the coming evening.

"In my experience, women add a different dimension to a hard-core poker game when they're present."

"Distraction?"

He flashed her a grin. "Exactly."

"All right then. No poker. What should we do instead?"

He glanced down at her bare toes. "Why don't I take you to a shoe store close by, my treat, and then out to dinner? You'll feel better with new shoes on your feet, and a good meal in your belly won't hurt either."

"Shoe shopping and dinner with me instead of poker with the guys? You must be the only man on the planet who would make that choice." She leveled a sultry look his way. "Unless, of course, you expect something in return. Is that it? You're offering me the chance to prostitute myself for a pair of shoes and a meal?"

"Nothing so dramatic. I don't expect anything in return except your company. We can regard any purchases as a loan. Any sexual activity will be decided solely by you with no pressure from me."

"Oh really. No pressure. I don't believe that for a minute."

He shrugged. "Well, maybe a little persuasion. But I'd never make you do anything you didn't want to do. And I have a spare bedroom if your answer is no."

"Is that so? Well, that's a hard offer to turn down." Her manner was relaxed. She was softening.

"Let's go get you some shoes, and you can think about it."

Zack's libido silently chanted, "Let the persuasion begin."

Chapter Two

On the way out of the salon, sporting a dark red toenail color called *Valentino's Seduction* to compliment her new strappy, sexy shoes, Daphne felt Zack slide his hand around her waist to guide her to his truck. Before they got three more steps, she paused and put her hands on his chest.

"So…expensive shoes, luxurious pedicure, and on our way to a pricy dinner if my intuition about you is correct?"

"I like a good steak. You?" He moved closer, and she didn't stop him.

The scent of him greeted her before they touched. "What do you really expect in return?" she whispered.

"Nothing. I've enjoyed the evening thus far. How about you?"

Daphne hadn't felt this good in years. "How could I not?"

He shrugged. "Perhaps you think I expect you to sleep with me after I've filled your belly, but I don't."

"You don't want to sleep with me?"

"Oh, now, I didn't say that." His seductive gaze drilled to her soul. "However, any further action will be your sole decision."

"I've never been out with a man like you."

Zack slipped his other arm around her waist, leaned down until his lips caressed the shell of her ear, and whispered, "Define 'a man like me'."

"You know women's shoes better than I do, but you're obviously not gay. If I walk away this second without another word, you wouldn't follow me, harass me, or demand sex, would you?"

"Nope."

"You're interesting. You're a very careful man. You've been perfect all night, and after all the things you've done for me, I can't wait to get you into bed. In fact, I would follow you, harass you, and demand sex if you said no."

He leaned closer. "I'd say yes."

"I'll bet you would. See? You're very smart. You know women. You like women. You could have any woman, anywhere, any time. I think I'm half in love with you, and I don't even know anything about you."

"Not true. You know quite a lot about me. But is it enough?"

She laughed. "For an intimate evening?" He gifted her with a seductive smile and nodded.

Daphne considered what she was about to do before responding with a resounding, "Definitely. So what should we do next?"

Please say sex. We should have lots of sex. "Are you hungry?" he asked in a low tone and squeezed her fingers gently. Food, the last thing on her mind.

Daphne sent a wicked gaze straight to his soul and responded. "Yes, I'm very hungry, but not for dinner."

"Do tell?"

"Will you consider taking me to your place?" She pushed closer into his frame.

"Are you certain, Miss Kane? I don't want to get the wrong idea about your intentions."

She stopped walking and turned into him. She was tall enough that her mouth was at his chin when she tilted her head back. She had to restrain herself from licking him.

"Would you like to call the used car salesman asshole I work for and ask if I'm really his file clerk? Or would you rather take a chance on me, drive to your place, and start a private game of strip poker?"

"Let me think." Zack lowered his face to hers, pressed his lips to her mouth, and licked his tongue inside. She groaned and melted against him. Then she kissed him back.

Hungry tongues collided in a maelstrom of sudden passion, but before things got out of hand right here on the street in front of the nail salon, Zack released her lips and whispered, "I don't need to make any phone calls tonight."

"Good. Let's go."

* * * *

Zack's cock had gone from zero to sixty in the time it took to kiss her. He nudged her hips as if making a promise regarding their future, and was pleased when she promptly returned with a push of her own.

She hesitated and seemed to consider this for a long moment. Finally, a grin emerged. "Let me make a phone call to my aunt. I only have one bar left before my cell phone goes dead, and of course I didn't bring my charger with me."

"No problem."

She turned away to make her call. He listened in to the message she left. "Aunt Louise, it's me, Daphne. Mr. Benny sent me to Washington, DC to put something in his safety deposit box, but I missed my return flight home. I ran into an old college friend of mine to stay with, so I'm fine for the weekend." Zack heard her phone start beeping as if it were almost out of juice. "My phone is about to die, so I can't call back, but don't worry, I'll be back early Monday on the first flight out. Bye."

He put a smile on his face as she turned around. Her expression was pensive. Perhaps she had second thoughts about a lustful night with him after leaving the message to her aunt.

"What are you thinking?"

Her shoulders lifted slightly. "I'm pondering my expectations for tonight."

Zack nodded. She was likely looking for a way out. He'd oblige her. "I can take you to a hotel."

She crossed her arms. "I don't have any money."

"Well, luckily I do since we talked our way into the bank earlier. I can pay for it for now, and you don't have to feel compelled to pay me back later either. It's my treat." He gave her a sidelong glance before turning his attention back to the traffic in the street and the star-strewn, dark skies.

"No. I don't like being beholden."

"Beholden? That's a word you don't hear every day. It can be a loan. I don't expect anything sexual in payment, you know."

Out of the corner of his eye, he saw her turn toward him and stare. "Do you really have a guest room at your house?"

He glanced at her hopeful expression. "I do."

"Would you let me come home with you? I won't get much safer than an FBI agent."

He grinned. "Safe is a relative term. What makes you think you'd be safe with me?"

"Your eyes mostly. You come across as very trustworthy. You helped me out with no consideration for yourself at the bank and the shoe store, but also, your soothing voice makes my stress level lower with every word you speak."

"Soothed isn't the same as safe, you know."

"Well, I'd be safe enough for my needs."

"Great segue. Let's talk about your needs." Zack took a step closer. "What are your expectations, now that you've had time to ponder them?"

"Well, I rarely get out of my ho-hum existence back in South Carolina, and I believe I *need* a little adventure. Honestly, I want to experience something out of my ordinary life."

Zack's libido came up with several possibilities. "You're going to have to be specific. I do not want to misunderstand."

"I haven't been with a man in over three years. I'd like to have sex with you. Is that specific enough? And are you even interested in me?"

Zack's grin went wider. "Yes and oh, hell yes."

"I'm in an interesting mood. I want to experiment. I want to try new things. I want to try several different new things."

"If you don't stop talking, I'll have to pull you into that alley and begin the foreplay before I get you back to my vehicle."

Her exuberant laugh made his already sizzling blood pulse to the boiling level. Her voice made his dick stiffen with every word she spoke. He'd be able to hammer nails into concrete with his cock by the time they got to his house, and likely he'd have to be careful when he entered and exited the truck not to hurt himself.

"Foreplay? Wow. The few inadequate men in my past didn't know that word. I don't know what you've got in mind, but you already rival every man in my past. This *will* be an interesting night."

Zack laughed low and deep from his chest. "Oh, it'll be more than interesting if I have anything to say about it. We're going to have such a great night, Daphne, you won't want to leave to go back home."

"Not to get too far ahead of myself, but does the weekend come with a ride to the municipal airport early Monday morning?"

"Of course."

"Thanks, Zack."

"No problem."

"And I promise I won't go all *Fatal Attraction* on you. I have this weekend to do whatever I want before I return to my sad and boring life."

"First of all, I'm not married, so you won't have to whip out a butcher knife or slaughter a rabbit. Second of all, why do you think your life is sad and boring?"

"I'm paying the price for my shortcomings."

"Sorry. I don't see that you have any."

"They're invisible, but they do exist."

His eyes narrowed. "Explain."

"Okay. Here's the short version of my sad life. A long time ago I fell head over heels in love with a man. My aunt Louise didn't care for him, but I decided to marry him anyway. We planned a big, expensive wedding, but a few days before the ceremony, we found out that I'd never have children. He told me it didn't matter, but then he left me standing alone at the altar with three hundred guests. In the note he sent a week later from the hotel address where we were supposed to have honeymooned, it turned out being childless mattered more than being with me."

"I'm sorry, Daphne. That's a harsh life lesson."

"Yes. But I survived wiser and more jaded. I had no money, so I moved in with my aunt. She helps keep me balanced when other men try and convince me they're serious."

"Has that ever happened again?"

"No. I keep things pretty simple."

"What do you do?"

"I work for a guy who's an insurance agent part-time and a used car salesman full-time. It doesn't get any more pathetic than that. Unless, of course, he starts taking night classes as an ambulance-chasing lawyer, then he'll have the trifecta of sleazy jobs nailed down. And I'm his lowly part-time file clerk. What does that make me?"

"Seductive."

"So I see the foreplay has begun."

Zack laughed. "Trust me, when I start, you'll know. But I mean it about your voice. It rolls over me in the best way possible. We haven't met before, have we?"

She grinned. "No. I definitely would have remembered you."

He took a half a step closer. "Your voice makes me think of sex," he said in a low seductive tone.

"Then I can't wait to get you alone and in a more private venue."

Yes. Then I can seduce you thoroughly and completely. He glanced over one shoulder as the noise of the evening traffic intruded briefly before he then focused back on her face. "Me either. Let me take you to my home."

Now that they'd established the plans for tonight, he slung his arm around her back and hauled her to his side as they walked with a purpose to his truck.

Zack opened the passenger door and helped Daphne climb inside. Once settled in the seat, she reached out and put her hand on his cheek in a gentle caress, so he kissed her again. This time, the exchange was soft and sweet instead of demanding and persuasive. It was time to get her home and relieve the sudden ache that had just shifted from his cock all the way to his balls. He released her lips reluctantly and closed the door.

With his thoughts on Daphne, he might not have noticed the sedan as he rounded the back of his vehicle except that he was double-parked three cars down, causing some motorists to honk and pass angrily. *Idiot.* Without staring at the driver, but noting his features out of the corner of his eye, Zack moved the rest of the way around his truck quickly and climbed into the driver's side.

Headed for home using the quickest route he could think up, Zack noticed the sedan start to tail him almost as soon as he straightened his vehicle into Friday night semi-rush hour traffic.

"So tell me, does your asshole boss have any reason to assume you're 'his woman' in any kind of romantic sense?"

She wrinkled her nose. "No. Not at all. His wife is a possessive southern belle. She'd cut his dick and balls off together with one swipe of a rusty, dull knife if he ever even dreamed about another woman. It's possible she's already done so and displays his family jewels proudly on the mantle at home, but I've never been to his house to verify that. Why do you ask?"

Zack winced at the visual, chuckled, and glanced in his rearview mirror at the sedan two cars behind them. He noted the plate number to look up later. "No reason. Just want to make sure no one will come after me for having my wicked way with you tonight."

She laughed. "You're going to have your wicked way with me? How intriguing."

"Maybe I will." He glanced over at her, winked, and added, "But only if you say please."

Her hand landed on his thigh and squeezed lightly before another heartbeat went by and brought his cock to rapt attention. "Please, Zack."

The sultry look accompanying her plea tightened his groin with urgent speed. His dick reached out for her, but his jeans stopped the progress. It was time to put his badass spy skills in motion, ditch the car that followed them, and find some quiet place to discuss intrigue and defiling. He turned right down a quiet street without signaling and took an immediate left into a parking structure beneath an office building.

Instead of getting a ticket to park in the basement garage, he twisted the wheel sharply and took another quick right into an alternate exit.

The one-way road led him beneath the length of the building and around to the loading area. Zack shot out of the building's cover and wheeled to the left, where several delivery trucks were backed up to the dock. The sun's last arc of brilliance had already long ago dipped below the skyline as Zack goosed the gas pedal and hauled ass past the darkened loading area. With one final hard right, he sped down another narrow alley, confident that he'd lost the sedan following him from the bank.

He'd used this path to lose a tail once before several years ago. Good to know it still worked. The alley he drove through was a tight squeeze for his truck, especially considering how fast he was going, but he didn't want anyone to follow him home.

Zack maneuvered his getaway very well in his favorite truck. Dodging trash bins and rubbish, the mouth at the end of the narrow passage approached quickly. A quick rearview mirror check revealed no one following him. He slowed and nosed out into traffic, taking another right after yielding to the cars on the road. The sedan he'd seen didn't come down the alley behind him and wasn't anywhere in their vicinity. He turned onto the street going the opposite direction of his place to ensure they were completely alone.

Taking the complicated way to his house, Zack ensured they arrived without an escort. He should probably take the time to run the plate from the idiot tailing them, but found his interest was divided. He wanted to explore Daphne more than he wanted to discover who'd been following him. He made a mental note to check on it Monday after his trip the airport.

Zack lived on a quiet residential street off the beaten path because he liked privacy. He slowed his truck and scanned the yards along the way to his house. He'd purposely found one at the end of the cul-de-sac. And he spent a long while trying to find one that had a single-story front with a two-story back of the house designation. The front of his house looked slightly neglected, but anonymous, and mostly it seemed to deter visitors.

"This is your house?"

"Yes. Surprised?"

"A little. From the outside it seems like the middle-class American dream with a touch of overzealous and slightly neglected landscaping. So is it bachelor pad chic on the inside?" Her giggle was music to his soul. She touched him in ways no other woman before ever had.

"It's a house. It serves my purposes very well."

Wary of her possible motives and visceral impact, Zack found he still lacked the common sense to disengage. His past was littered with disappointed women. There had been women who wanted to tame him and put him in a little suburban dream house with two point five children. He wasn't interested in that life. Far from it. He was more the love-them-for-awhile-and-leave-before-it-got-too-serious type. He rarely went anywhere with women who didn't understand his philosophy up front. Daphne was different. Perhaps he'd relax his strict standard. He'd already given up poker night. The first step in a steep slide down the slippery slope of concern to avoid a relationship.

Inside the house was much different from the outside in looks and money spent to maintain. He'd spent a shitload of his hard earned dollars to customize it to suit his lifestyle. Daphne was hopefully about to enjoy the custom king-sized bed he installed before moving in.

Zack turned into his driveway and went straight for several car lengths. The drive went along the side of his house and through several curves leading to the rear yard where his garage was. To the right of the garage was the lower story of his deck. He had a hot tub there for private parties. Zack pushed a remote, and the left side garage door slid silently upward, disappearing into the opening. A light came on as he drove into his oversized space.

Inside, and on the right side of the garage space, was a rental car he'd never seen before. *Shit.* That meant his sometimes-roommate Jeff Coleman was in residence. He suddenly remembered a message from Jeff that he'd almost ignored in favor of getting to the bank on time. He'd sent Jeff a return text about his poker game and then forgotten about it.

Jeff's infrequent visits were rarely problematic. In fact, they often shared women on the extraordinary occasions they were both here at the house and in the mood for that particular pleasure. But Zack didn't think Daphne would consent to a threesome without expecting one in advance. Even if she was "letting her hair down" this weekend.

She wasn't his usual conquest in the battle of the sexes. He wasn't sure he wanted to share her even if the opportunity revealed itself. Maybe. The idea of Jeff bringing her to pleasure while he watched was an intriguing fantasy.

A flash of Jeff touching Daphne slid across his frontal lobe and his cock throbbed. It didn't matter anyway. Daphne would never consent to a threesome, would she?

No.

He put it out of his head and focused on the coming night with just the two of them. Paradise in the making.

Zack exited his vehicle as Daphne did the same on her side. He hit the button to close the garage door, and soon they were ensconced in the quiet space.

"So far so good."

"What do you mean?"

"Your space is nice. Not too clean. So that's good."

His eyes narrowed. "What's wrong with too clean?"

"Everyone knows serial killers and weirdos are ultraclean." A wide grin appeared, dimpling her face, and lit the dim garage space.

"Right. I'd especially hate to be a called a weirdo."

Zack rounded the rental car and headed for the door inside his house. He twisted the handle and held it open for Daphne to enter. Directly inside was a long staircase leading to the upstairs on the left and another closed door straight ahead leading to the space where Jeff lived when he was here.

Daphne passed by him and rounded the corner to head upstairs. Her fragrance trailed after her and impaled his lungs with the promise of hours of satisfaction. He watched her shapely ass as she climbed from the basement to the first floor. They stepped into the kitchen and the scent of food replaced Daphne's unique smell.

Dressed in casual clothes, Jeff was bent over in the process of taking a pan out of the open oven. Oven mitt on one hand, he grabbed a cookie sheet out. Small food was scattered across the flat surface. He placed the flat pan on a trivet centered on the kitchen table, and grinned as they entered the room.

"I thought you were playing poker tonight."

"I found something better to do."

Jeff's gaze slid to Daphne. "I see that." He shifted his gaze back to Zack, and his unspoken question was clearly expressed. *"Are we sharing her tonight?"*

Zack shook his head slightly, and Jeff nodded imperceptibly in return. They had an understanding. Some women were for sharing. Others were not.

"Daphne, meet my sometimes roommate, Jeff. Jeff, this is

Daphne."

"Good to meet you." Jeff nodded once, but didn't approach.

Daphne smiled. "Likewise." Jeff gestured to the pan covered with small appetizers. "Are you two hungry?"

Daphne walked to the table. "Starving."

Jeff grinned at her again and reached for one of the tarts. He picked one up with two fingers and held it to her lips. "Blow on it first. It's hot." She leaned forward, pursed her lips into a tight circle, and blew on the food. After three such air currents over the tart, she leaned forward and ate the treat from Jeff's fingertips. It was the sexiest thing Zack had seen in quite a long while. Maybe he *could* talk her into a naughty night with two men. But first, he needed to be a gentleman and show her to the guest room.

Daphne chewed the appetizer and soon moaned in appreciation. "Delicious. Wow. Where I come from, men don't know how to cook much."

"I've been a bachelor for a while, and I've discovered that the best way to a woman's libido is often through her mouth."

Daphne laughed. "Funny. You're a funny guy."

"Thanks. Here, let me make you a plate." He picked up a small round plate from the table and put several appetizers on it.

"Here you go. Enjoy."

"Thank you." She picked up a stuffed mushroom, popped it into her mouth, followed closely by two more bites of another tart.

Another appreciative moan escaped from her throat, and Zack realized he should get her alone as soon as possible. She crossed the room and deposited the empty plate in the sink with a smile.

From downstairs, the sound of Jeff's private door opening captured his attention. What sounded like two people ascended the stairway from below.

The doorway to the kitchen soon filled with a very busty brunette woman. She came in, followed by a second brunette equally endowed and scantily clothed.

"Jeff," the first exclaimed in a giggling voice, "what's taking you so long? We're hungry."

"Ladies, this is my roommate and his friend. I stopped to chat. I'll be right down with some nibbles for us."

Daphne stepped closer to Zack. He snuggled his arm around her and squeezed. "We'll let you get back to your guests."

The two dark-haired women giggled all the way back down the stairs. Jeff grinned again. Zack knew he'd be engaged all night, so no threesomes would be possible anyway. And that was just fine. He'd take care of Daphne all by himself. If she still wanted him to provide some adventure and foreplay.

"I'll leave you a plate warming in the oven for later." Jeff turned and removed another tray from the oven.

Zack nodded. "Thanks."

"And I'll even make breakfast in the morning if you're interested."

Zack nodded. "Have a great night."

"You, too."

Centering his hand in Daphne's back, Zack pushed her to the door on the far side of the kitchen leading to his domain. He had three bedrooms upstairs, one of which he used for an office. The door at the end of the hallway housed his master suite. At six foot four, he found most standard beds a difficult and uncomfortable fit. The custom California king in his room was uniquely constructed to his personal specifications and very comfortable. Zack was anxious to show her his bed, but first he'd offer her a safe haven. She deserved to know she had an out if she decided not to engage in his sexual foreplay and prowess.

Before showing her his room, he opened the last door on the left.

"This can be your room, if you'd like."

Daphne looked inside the Spartan guest room and shrugged. "I thought I was sleeping with you."

"I don't want you to feel obligated. You can have your own space if you want it." He slid his hand up her spine, ending at her neck where he massaged lightly until her head leaned back.

"That feels really good. Very relaxing."

Zack leaned in and kissed her neck lightly. She moaned, and his cock throbbed once in reply. "Relaxing is where it starts."

"Where what starts?"

He put his lips to the shell of her ear and whispered a single word, "Foreplay."

"Oh." A shiver rippled down her body in response.

Encouraged, Zack continued, "I call this light foreplay."

She laughed. "I can't wait until the heavy foreplay starts."

"Excellent." Zack reached up and cupped her breast, thumbing her nipple through the soft fabric of her shirt. The sound she made was so seductive, it was a wonder his dick didn't burst through his zipper.

He cupped the back of her head and kissed a path from her cheek to the corner of her mouth. Flicking her nipple again, Zack centered his mouth over hers before connecting with her lips in full, commanding seduction mode. She fell a few inches backward against the wall, taking him with her and never once breaking the kiss.

Zack pressed into her, pinning her to the wall next to his room. He licked his way into her mouth, where she surrendered to him in a delicious way. He teased her with the tip of his tongue until she licked back, and soon they kissed hungrily, passionately, with a healthy dose of aggressiveness. Just the way he liked it.

Daphne, while at first seeming on the shy side, warmed to his overtures. He squeezed her breast again, and she moaned into his mouth. Her nipple hardened against his palm through two layers of cloth. He pressed his hips into her belly. She couldn't possibly miss the size or intention of his cock burrowing into her.

"I definitely want to sleep with you," she whispered. "Now would be good. Or we don't have to sleep."

"We won't." Zack pulled her against his chest and led her to his room without releasing their close embrace.

Chapter Three

Once inside his room behind the closed door, clothes fell from their bodies to the floor like autumn leaves escaping a tree in a brisk wind. They shed articles of clothing with a speed born of desire.

Before he removed his pants, he slowed down only long enough to pull his spare gun from the ankle holster and tuck it away with his fake FBI identification into his dresser drawer.

Daphne watched with interest. "So you have a backup gun on your ankle. Is that a required for a federal agent?"

He laughed. "Perhaps. And now you know where my secret weapon is located. I'll have to use my charms to erase your memory."

"No need. I don't even know how to shoot a gun. And besides, the only *weapon* I'm interested in is located behind your pants zipper."

"Good answer." He kissed her, and their clothing continued to fly in every direction.

By the time they'd crossed the room to his bed, they were naked, clenched together and engaged in a vivid, sexy lip-lock.

Daphne's arms were wrapped firmly around his neck. Her sweet tongue tangled with his in aggressive abandon. Zack slid his hands down her body until he hooked them beneath her thighs. Lifting her up, he spread her legs apart until she locked them around his hips. His cock was trapped against her pubic bone and pulsed in delight with each sexy sound that erupted. He secured one arm around her waist and rubbed her soft butt with his other hand until he changed direction and put his hand between her legs to assess her readiness-for-sex level. Forefinger grazing her pussy, he determined she was already dripping wet.

She made an unexpected moan when he slipped his finger inside her body. But it sounded like she enjoyed it, so he went deeper. Her grip tightened around his neck when he pulled out and brushed across her clit.

Zack broke the kiss. "So are you ready to get started on that foreplay?"

"Foreplay? I'm ready to have sex. Or couldn't you tell?"

He nodded. "You are very wet, but we're so far away from penetration. You see, I have lots of foreplay to get through first, so be patient with me."

"I'll try." She blew out a long sigh. "So what's first?"

Zack walked to the edge of his bed and bent over, placing her in the center. "Close your eyes."

"You aren't going to tie me up, are you?"

Zack climbed onto the bed beside her. "Not yet."

A nervous laugh escaped before her eyes drifted closed.

Zack kissed her mouth lightly once then stroked a nipple with one finger. He replaced his finger with his mouth and sucked the pebbled tip between his lips. His hand moved to her other breast as he feasted on the first nipple, licking and teasing the tip.

Her breathing increased until she was panting and moaning with each pull of his lips.

"That feels so great, Zack." Her whisper sent his libido into the red zone.

"I'm glad to hear it."

"Are you sure it isn't time for sex yet?"

"Positive." He kissed a path from her breasts to her stomach and circled the tip of his tongue around her belly button.

She giggled and writhed. "I'm ticklish there."

"Good to know."

Zack kissed further below until he buried his face between her thighs and licked her clit with a firm stroke.

Daphne sucked in a deep, shocked breath and moaned something inarticulate.

He pressed his palms to her inner thighs and opened her legs to make his oral foray easier to accomplish. He thrust his tongue deeply into her wet, slick pussy, and another unintelligible groan sounded from her throat.

Zack loved foreplay. He especially adored oral foreplay. From the sexy noises she was making, it sounded like Daphne liked oral foreplay, too.

After lapping up her intoxicating flavor, he swirled his tongue around her clit a few times until she started writhing and making shrieking noises. He slid two fingers deeply into her pussy and sucked her clit between his lips to bring her off. Five seconds later, her back arched, and a lovely low scream of pleasure filled the air.

Her pussy clamped on his fingers rhythmically, signaling her first orgasm of the evening.

Still panting, Daphne flattened on the bed. "What was that called again?"

"Foreplay."

"I *love* foreplay."

Zack chuckled. "Me, too." He kissed a path from her inner thigh to her belly, tickled her again, and moved to rest his head on her perfect breasts.

Daphne tightened her arms around his shoulders in a hug. "What's next?"

"Sex."

She giggled. "I can't wait."

"Me either." Zack slid up her body further and burrowed his face into her throat. She kissed his forehead. "So…what would you think about turning over onto your stomach?"

She was silent for a slow count of ten. He was about to retract the question when she responded in a low, sultry tone. "I've never done it that way, but whatever you want. I'm all yours." She leaned her face close to his, kissed him again, and rolled over onto her belly.

Arms bracketed over her head on the pillow, Zack studied her backside. It was as beautiful as her front side. He ran a hand from her neck to her shoulder blades, down her spine over her ass, and back to where he'd started. She released a sigh, and he could see a smile shape her lips, but otherwise she didn't move. She waited. Anticipated.

Zack got a condom from his bedside stash and put it on quickly. He rolled over and snuggled up next to Daphne for a minute and kissed her shoulder. He got on all fours and positioned himself on his knees between her open legs. He slipped his hands beneath her hips. Lifting her butt in the air to the level of his rock-solid cock, Zack rubbed her ass a few times.

"Are you ready?"

"This seems a little naughty, but I love it. I'm ready."

"You've really never had sex in this position before?"

"Nope. Purely vanilla missionary sex is all I know."

Zack grabbed her hips and pushed his cock into her pussy a few inches. "I like this sexual position because I can go very deep." He pushed in all the way to prove his point. She sucked in a deep breath, but the smile remained. He reached around and fingered her clit. "And best of all, I can touch you while I thrust."

A groan of pleasure escaped. "Great idea."

Balls deep in her exquisitely tight pussy, Zack paused. "You're really tight." He pulled out and quickly thrust inside her pussy again as deeply as he could, and another low groan escaped from her.

She turned her head to the side, and a long sigh erupted. "And you're really big."

Zack stroked a finger across her clit a few times. "Does this feel good to you, or do we need to head for vanilla land?"

"It feels amazing. I'm never going back to vanilla land again."

"Excellent." He smiled and pulled halfway out to begin thrusting forward in earnest.

Each push into her tight pussy tested the capacity of his dick to withstand the grip without erupting like a teenager with his first girl. After a few thrusts, she picked up his rhythm and pushed back against him as he thrust forward. Zack went even deeper. Tighter. It was exquisite torture to keep from climaxing with each stroke inward, but he did. He longed to feel her next orgasm squeezing his cock to superb release.

Zack rubbed her clit a little faster as he pounded inside her tight pussy and experienced the most acute pre-climax pleasure he'd ever endured.

Daphne panted, and after what seemed like a hundred strokes, she gripped her fingers into the pillow, buried her face, and let loose a rapturous-sounding scream. The muffled shriek came on the heels of her blissfully pulsing orgasm.

The first rippling grip of her pussy caught his cock all the way embedded. The sensation was more powerful than any in his past. Perhaps it was her innocent curiosity to try a new non-vanilla position. Perhaps it was her unique scent or her seductive voice, but Zack released his pent-up passion with a vengeance. He pulled out a quarter of the way and blistered the end of his dick inside the condom with his hot, shooting cum. He slammed into her pussy all the way and hoped his protection would hold as rapturous release filled him from groin to heart to head in seconds.

He lost the feeling in his legs as he tried to recover from the best fucking orgasm he'd ever had. A groan escaped his lips in a satisfied rush. Zack slumped over her back and pinned her to his bed. She trembled beneath him.

"Am I crushing you?" he managed.

"…hmm…a little bit…"

Zack took all of his limited reserves to shift to one side, taking her with him to remain deeply connected. He slung one arm over her and snuggled one under to embrace her torso hard to his chest.

"That was fucking amazing." He kissed the back of her neck, and she shrugged her shoulders as a giggle escaped.

"I agree. *Fucking* amazing." She giggled again. "You made me say the F word. And I very rarely curse."

Zack laughed and nibbled her earlobe. "No. I made you *do* the F word."

"True. And it was…indescribable."

"Fucking amazing sums it up for me." Zack put his hand over her breast and played with her pert nipple.

"I had two orgasms tonight." She twisted her head as if to ensure she could see his face before adding, "Two!"

"Well, I guess I'll have to try harder next time and ensure you have three before I let loose."

She put a hand to one cheek. "I don't know that I'd survive three."

"We have the rest of tonight, all weekend to try and find out." Zack kissed the fingers resting on her face.

"I'm so relaxed now I don't know if I can stay awake. I'll try." A moan of pleasure slid from her throat and warmed his heart. He loved the sound of a well-satisfied woman all soft and warm in his bed.

Zack pulled his cock from her and excused himself to the bathroom. When he returned, Daphne slept so soundly, she didn't rouse when he put her under the sheets.

He nestled his body close and shut his eyes, not expecting to sleep, but he did. He didn't usually relax fully when a new woman was sharing his sheets. Tonight, for whatever reason, Daphne allowed his guard to slip into neutral until he drifted off to blessed dreamless slumber.

His eyes opened almost exactly three hours later. He saw the red glow of the bedside clock's digital numbers, and for a second he couldn't remember where he was. Zack sat up, and Daphne stirred beside him with a soft murmur, still deeply asleep. *Fucking amazing.* He ran a hand down his face to shake from the unexpected nap, and glanced at his bed partner.

Daphne was lovely. Beautiful. Enticing.

He stroked a hand along her spine all the way to her ass. Slipping his fingers between her legs and then inside her slick pussy lips, Zack ascertained that she was still very wet and inherently fuckable. He wanted her again with a desperation he wouldn't have expected so soon after his earlier, and very powerful, release.

His cock came to rapt attention as if he'd gone celibate for a year and this was his first opportunity for satisfaction.

Zack leaned down and kissed Daphne's shoulder. He stilled his intimate touch only long enough to turn her over. He latched on to one nipple and sucked it into his mouth. Rolling the hard bud over his tongue earned him a long sigh from her parted lips.

He stopped only long enough to sheath his cock in latex before proceeding to place his mouth on her other nipple. Another contented-sounding sigh escaped from her lovely mouth.

Zack sent his hand down to rub her clit while he alternated his mouth on each peak. It only took a few minutes before her eyes opened. He released one nipple and kissed a path to her lips. He licked inside her mouth and continued stroking her clit with the same cadence.

A moan vibrated between them. Zack released her lips, but didn't stop rubbing her clit. "Zack." The whispered murmur of his name from her mouth made his cock pulse hard with sudden desire.

He whispered, "Daphne," in response and pushed two fingers into her pussy, resuming the steady stroke to her clit with his thumb.

Her arms slid around his neck, pulling him closer. Zack kissed her lips again, and her warm response, complete with her tongue sliding into his mouth, made his dick jerk with a desire to fuck. Soon. He'd sink his cock all the way to the end of her pussy very soon.

Zack shifted his body on top of hers and lost contact with her clit as he covered her completely from neck to knees. His cock nestled at the apex of her thighs, ready and waiting to fuck blindly. He tempered his lust and pondered momentarily which non-vanilla sexual position he wanted to try next.

He pulled his lips from her and stared deeply into her eyes. "I want to see your face when you come this time."

A grin erupted. "Okay."

Strands of her hair spread in a fan of warm color behind her head. Ambient radiance from the bathroom light he'd left on earlier shone on her lovely smiling face. The scent of sex flavored the air and made his cock tighten and get even harder.

Zack shifted to his knees, squatted on his heels, and pulled her legs apart with his hands. Her thighs rested on the tops of his legs until he lifted one, straightened it, and placed her calf against his chest. He pressed a kiss to her ankle and slid his hand down the length of her long leg to beneath her ass.

Lining his cock up with her pussy, he inserted his dick inside an inch or two.

"Want to take a walk on the wild side?"

Daphne's eyebrows went straight up. She glanced at her leg resting on his chest and whispered, "I'm already there."

Zack pushed his cock forward another couple of inches into her pussy. "Good. Then touch yourself. I want to watch you climax."

"W…what?"

He grinned at her puzzled expression. "Put one hand on your breast and play with your nipple. Place the other between your legs and stroke your clit while I fuck you."

Chapter Four

Daphne rested in a virtual stranger's bed with his huge cock embedded in her body. Zack watched her face with an intensely lustful gaze. He waited for her to "touch" herself. It was so shocking, she stilled everything but her breathing.

It wasn't that she hadn't ever done this in the privacy of her own room deep beneath her covers, but she'd certainly never ever had an audience while she did so.

"Touch myself?" She hated to sound so stupid and inexperienced.

"Yes." Zack smiled and pushed his cock inside her body all the way. "Trust me. It will feel very good."

"But I've never…" She couldn't even finish her own sentence. Of course she had, but had never admitted it. And had certainly never thought about doing it in front of anyone. Her cheeks felt blistered as she contemplated his request.

He drilled his unrelenting gaze into her eyes. "Do it."

Daphne remembered the phrase, she'd already agreed to "take a walk on the wild side," and her curiosity took over. What would it be like for him to watch her while she…fingered herself? *Exciting.* Heart thudding in her chest, she slid her fingers between her legs and found her clit. She stroked the sensitive bundle of nerves only once, and the pleasure was almost unbearable.

"Watching you do that is so fucking sexy," Zack murmured from above. Her eyes slid open partway to see him watching her hand work between her thighs as he pushed his huge cock all the way inside of her pussy. He nodded his head once at her other hand. "Now play with your nipple."

She reached up and cupped her own breast and ran her thumb across the pebbled tip. Zack licked his lips, and she almost stopped breathing. The sensation was visceral and vivid, as if she could feel his gaze burning on her clit and her nipple adding heat to the already intense feeling. It was as if every nerve ending in her entire body had moved to either her clit or her nipple in order to be stroked and pleasured by her own hands. The sensation of his wide cock buried to the hilt only added to the exhilaration of the experience.

Zack made a low, sexy noise in his throat and picked up the pace of his thrusts. Deeper and deeper, his cock struck the sensitive wall at the end of her pussy to more shuddering bliss. Her eyes slid shut briefly as rapt waves of pleasure filled her being.

"Open your eyes, Daphne," he whispered urgently. "Watch me fuck you. Feel my cock drill all the way inside your pussy."

His coarse words thrilled her neglected libido. Her eyes popped open and went to where their bodies were joined. As his cock entered and exited her pussy fast and hard, she saw her finger rubbing her clit with furious, single-minded strokes.

The pungent scent of sex filled the air around them when she took a breath, and seconds later Daphne fell over the cliff of orgasmic oblivion in a sudden rush of pulsing climax. The force of her release stole her next breath as her shoulder blades lifted off of the sheets when her back arched.

"Daphne!" Zack's urgent tone voicing her name came one solid stroke before he pierced deeper than she'd previously thought possible. Her body warmed inside with the deep thrust. He growled a satisfied sound, and his body went stiff.

Her eyes slid shut as waves of pleasure rode up and down her body. Zack pushed her leg off of his chest and fell forward until he covered her with his sweat-soaked torso. He planted rows of soft, wet kisses along her throat, neck, and jaw until she giggled from the tickle of his scratchy face and shrugged her shoulder to stop him.

"Do you know what that was?" she asked.

Zack stopped kissing her and cleared his throat. "Even more fucking amazing than before?"

"Dang skippy it was."

He slipped his arms beneath her and hugged her tight. Daphne circled his shoulders with her arms and embraced him in return. She kissed the side of his face and knew she'd never felt so good after a sexual experience in all her life, with the exception of the last time they'd had sex.

Walking on the wild side might be very addicting. At least with Zack it was something she wanted to try again.

He disengaged from her and shuffled into the bathroom to clean up. Drowsy and overly satisfied yet again, she dropped asleep before he returned to bed wondering what other pleasures resided on the wild side and how many of them she'd have time to try out before her return flight on Monday morning.

* * * *

At nine o'clock on Friday night, Ken Davenport was unhappy to still be crouched over his desk working on a quarterly manpower report. Stifling a yawn, he closed the document and shut down his computer even though he wasn't finished. He was bone tired. Tomorrow was another day, although he hated working weekends even more than he hated late Friday nights.

Plus, he had plans for later on. There was a satisfying arrangement he refused to disregard because the thrilling agenda gave him a new lease on life. He mentally patted himself on the back for getting away with the secret ploy for so long. Those closest to him, still had no idea that he was sneaking around, and he planned to keep it that way. Whatever the cost.

The shrill ring of his office phone startled him. Damn it. Now what? He almost didn't answer, but since he hadn't signed out of the building, operations knew he was still in here.

With a weary sigh, he picked up the handset. "Davenport."

"Sir, this is the FBI central switchboard. There's been activity from one of your agents, however, we don't show him currently assigned to an FBI case."

"What activity and which agent?"

"There was a phone call put through central switchboard to confirm Zack Mahon was with the FBI."

Ken's eyes shut. "Who was asking?"

There was a slight pause. "It was a Miss Daphne Kane. I couldn't find her name on any active federal cases either. The dialogue between them suggested he was about to pick her up and drive her somewhere."

He rolled his eyes. If Zack was using his ID to pick up women again, Ken planned to kick his ass. But there was no need to involve the FBI in his agency's private business.

"I authorized it. Put it under civilian contact inquiry." That was a general catch-all account for insignificant details of the various jobs they worked.

"Yes, sir. However, I'll need a designation report signed with the justification section filled out."

"You need it filled out and signed tonight? I'm on my way out the door. Just put it in an inner agency office package and I'll take care of it Monday."

"Thank you, sir. I'll look for it Monday."

"Good night." Ken rolled his eyes again and hung up the phone. He hoped Zack was having a fun weekend with Miss Daphne Kane because come Monday he'd pay dearly for his misuse of government credentials in a big way.

Ken put a hand on his office door and paused. Why did the name Daphne Kane sound so familiar? Was she listed on an old case file of Zack's? Could she be a threat? It was probably nothing, but his gut registered an uneasy feeling. Ken turned back to his computer to check a few private sources to learn the identity of Zack's "date" in case his agent was in a different kind of trouble.

* * * *

Daphne's eyes slid open several hours later. The rush of new memories in her sexual repertoire crowded her mind. Light sifted through the edge of the curtains hiding a window on the wall next to the bed. Her body felt like melted honey spilled on a blistering sidewalk during the hottest day of summer.

Her next realization was the salacious fact that she was completely naked beneath the silky sheets. *Shocking.* She'd never slept nude before as a practice.

A grin shaped her mouth in further memory of all the wonderful wickedness from last night. This weekend was certainly more exciting than how she usually spent her time away from work. A popping noise from somewhere else in the house caught her attention.

The sizzling scent of bacon filled the air, and her stomach growled in desire for food. They'd discarded dinner plans at her request for a night of decadent pleasures. She didn't regret a single minute, but right now she was starving. Before all the sex, Zack's roommate, Jeff, had mentioned making breakfast. The aching rumble from her belly prodded her to seek sustenance.

Slipping from the bed carefully didn't seem to wake Zack. Facedown and turned away from her, he didn't move a single muscle with the exception of the rise and fall of his torso from quiet breathing. She took a few steps and tread across the clothing they'd discarded the night before. She scooped up the first item in front of her, which turned out to be Zack's button-down shirt. She slipped her arms into the oversized garment and rolled the sleeves up to see her hands as she made her way to the bedroom door.

She tiptoed down the hallway and buttoned the shirt she wore along the way. At the end of the hall, she pushed the door to the kitchen open. A blast of coffee, bacon, and cinnamon hit her square in the lungs with her first inhale of kitchen air.

"Whatever you're cooking smells divine."

Jeff whirled as if in surprise, the spatula in his hand shifted forward as if to defense mode, and the look on his face suggested that it was a good thing he hadn't been armed with a weapon.

"Whew! You surprised me. Zack makes a lot more noise when he stumbles in for breakfast." His engaging accent sounded slightly southern, Texas maybe. He grinned suddenly and motioned her forward. "Want a cup of coffee?"

"Yes. Thank you." Her stomach growled, and Jeff's grin widened.

"Excellent. A hungry someone." He pointed to the table. "There are some cinnamon rolls there on the table to get you started. I'm almost done with the bacon and eggs." He opened a cupboard next to the stove and pulled out two large coffee mugs.

"Thank you." She crossed to the table in the center of the room as he grabbed the coffee carafe's handle. She seated herself facing away from where he worked at the stove.

"How do you like your coffee?"

Over one shoulder, she said, "Sweet and light, please."

He laughed. "As I suspected, sweet and light just like you are."

Daphne's cheeks heated at his words. She hadn't spent so much time around such overtly sexy and desirable men in well…ever. And compliments were something she wasn't used to either. Tilting her head down, her hair slid forward, blocking the majority of her view, and gave her a great hiding place for a minute.

Jeff rattled around in the refrigerator and on the counter fixing her coffee as she watched him covertly through the curtain of her hair. He was very attractive and the complete opposite of Zack. Jeff was whipcord lean, fair-skinned, with light eyes, where Zack was big, muscular, and dark in both skin and eye color. Jeff wore khaki slacks and a simple, white button-down shirt. Even after her delicious foray into the wild side of sex all night long with Zack, Daphne noticed that Jeff looked pretty good this morning, too.

The idea that Jeff had spent the night with two women popped in her mind and intrigued her very much. Did he have the stamina to satisfy two women like Zack had satisfied her last night? Likely so. And he cooked. She pushed out a quiet exhale in silent salute to his many desirable attributes.

Jeff grabbed a spoon from a drawer, closed it with a tap from one hip, and dropped the utensil in the mug before she turned away to keep from being caught staring at him. He leaned over her right shoulder very close and placed the doctored coffee in the center of the placemat before her. He was so close, his stubbly cheek brushed her head. She heard him inhale as if he took a deep lungful to sniff the scent of her hair. He made a moaning noise like he enjoyed what he smelled. Daphne inhaled, but she could only smell the light residual cologne from Zack's shirt along with his personal scent.

She didn't know what possessed her to speak. Perhaps it was the need to explain her general morning disarray. "I haven't even showered yet. I probably smell bad."

Jeff leaned even closer, grabbed her hand, and brought the tips of her fingers to his lips for a light kiss. He then inhaled deeply. "No. Not at all. Actually, you smell like faint perfume and gratified woman."

Realizing he had a hold of the hand she'd "fingered" herself with the night before during her amazing walk on the wild side, Daphne snatched it away. She felt her cheeks heat in embarrassment that Jeff might know what she'd done last night with Zack. Again her mouth uttered the words on the tip of her tongue without thinking them all the way through. "I think you're a very bad boy, Jeff."

"You're absolutely right." His sexy grin slid into place. "I *am* a very bad boy." He grabbed her hand again, slipped "that" finger between his lips, and licked the tip of it with his warm tongue before she could stop him. "Meanwhile, you smell fantastic and taste even better."

How had this conversation progressed so far afield from coffee and breakfast to licking and sexual overtures?

She pushed out a panicked breath and eyed the doorway leading to Zack's room, wondering if she should forgo breakfast even as the siren wisps of delicious, fragrant, hot coffee assaulted her nose.

Daphne didn't operate on the same level as the wild and wicked girl she was last night. She tried to pull her hand from his, but he held tight and his gorgeous grin intensified. He sandwiched her hand between both of his and squeezed gently. His eyes said very clearly that he wanted her for more than just a breakfast companion.

Heart pounding a staccato beat, Daphne tried to stand. She made it halfway up, and Jeff moved even closer. He rested his face against her head and made a humming noise of appreciation. One of his hands went to her torso, dangerously close to her breast. Panicked and trapped, Daphne's body went completely stiff. "Please let me go."

Jeff immediately released her hand and took a step back. The instant half-puzzled, half-contrite expression covering his features said he regretted letting things go so far. "I'm sorry. I didn't mean to come on so strong. I thought you were playing with me. I thought you..." He shook his head once, lifted his hands in a surrender pose, and left the last sentence incomplete. A disappointed smile graced his lips. He took another long step away and returned to tend the bacon sizzling on the griddle behind her.

"I'm sorry, too. I didn't mean to *play* with you inappropriately. I'm sort of new at all this. I'm trying some different things this weekend. However, flirting with a new man after sleeping with a veritable stranger the night before is a little much for me so early in the morning."

"I promise not to engage you further. Sit and I'll bring you some food in a minute for complete absolution of my blatant and unwelcome flirtation."

Daphne stared at the steaming coffee mug on the table. "You made me coffee the way I like it, so I forgive you. Feed me some breakfast and we can be best friends."

A quiet laugh came from behind her as she eased back into the chair.

"Done. Thank you."

Daphne wrapped her fingers around the coffee mug, lifted it, and took a sip of the best coffee she'd ever tasted in her life. She moaned into her cup after the second sip, and the spatula Jeff had been using on the bacon clattered across the floor.

"Sorry. The coffee is really good."

After retrieving the fallen utensil to drop in the sink, he opened another drawer and grabbed another turning spatula. "I'm so glad you like it." The tone of his voice suggested that he was very impacted by her moaning. How interesting.

Another sip brought another unanticipated moan. She inhaled deeply to quiet her riotous feelings. She shouldn't take advantage of him, but the idea that she was so desirable to more than one man in such a short span of time was like an aphrodisiac.

If she spent the rest of her days living a quiet little life in Loganville, South Carolina, the entirety of the entertainment there would never equal the exhilarating few hours she'd already spent in Zack's house.

"I made bacon and southwestern scrambled eggs." Jeff slid a plate in front of her. The eggs had chopped red and green peppers and cheese on top. The aroma alone made her want to groan in ecstasy, but she'd already made enough noise for Jeff. Time to tamp any yummy noises down a notch.

"It's perfect. Thank you very much."

He grinned and seated himself next to her with another plate for himself. After a few bites of the best breakfast food she'd eaten in a long while, Daphne downed some more coffee and tried to get her feelings under control.

"So how did you and Zack meet?" Jeff asked between bites of bacon.

"At a big bank downtown." She took another long sip of coffee. "He helped me get inside when they were about to close the doors for the night. If he hadn't been there, I'd be in a lot of trouble right now."

Jeff nodded. "Zack is all about the damsel in distress. Usually doesn't work out for him, though."

"Why not?"

He shrugged and made a face like he'd said too much already, but replied, "The thing is, women tend to get way more attached to him than he's able to reciprocate."

"Ah. The clingy types, huh?" She took a bite of eggs, which were divine, as Jeff nodded.

"Oh yeah. Clingy to the point of being hermetically sealed to his body until he peels them away crying."

"Well, he's very nice to be with." Her gaze cut to Jeff, with an accompanying heat to her cheeks regarding "being" with Zack. "I can certainly see the attachment, but I've got to go back to my real life Monday morning early, so he's safe with me."

Jeff winked at her and munched on a slice of crisp, perfect bacon. "Of that I have not a doubt."

"May I ask a personal question?"

"Sure."

She hesitated. "It's *really* personal."

He grinned. "Noted. Go ahead."

"Did you actually sleep with those two women last night?"

A chuckle escaped, and he sent a gaze directly into her eyes. "Yes, I did. I'm a very bad boy, remember?"

"And if I'd been interested, you would have had sex with me this morning, too, is that right?"

He swallowed hard. "Yep." His gaze slid to her hair, back to her face, and lower before snapping back to her eyes. "We wouldn't have even had to leave the kitchen."

Daphne's eyes widened. She focused her attention back on her plate momentarily until an intriguing question surfaced and spilled out. "Have you and Zack ever…" Daphne paused and decided she couldn't complete the question. It was none of her business anyway.

"Shared a woman?" His grin came shining out as he finished her thought and answered the question with an exuberant, "Yes."

"Really? More than once?"

"Lots of times. Is this something you're interested in, Daphne? Because if you are, it would be my pleasure."

"I'm not sure. How does it work?"

"Oh. I'd so much rather show you." He didn't make a move, but his gaze drilled through her.

Whoa. What am I doing?

"Two men in two days isn't exactly my style or something I'm comfortable contemplating just yet."

Under his breath, she heard his sing-song tone chant, "You don't know what you're missing."

Daphne laughed. "I'm not saying I'm not interested. I just want to know the mechanics of it. What happens with two men and one woman?"

"Did you talk to Zack about this already?"

She shook her head slowly back and forth. "Why?"

"No reason." He folded his hands in front of his chin and commenced speaking as though he were a college professor trying to ensure she understood his sex lecture. "'It' is usually called a threesome or ménage à trois. It involves three people having sex at the same time. It can be any combination of men or women. In the past when Zack and I have shared a woman, very simply, we pleasured her. Zack and I both like to watch the other give satisfaction and delight to the woman involved. Sort of like live-action porn."

"I see. So what would I be required to do?"

"You'd be required to enjoy the two of us. And let us do whatever we wanted."

She mulled this over for a minute. It sounded intriguing. "So…it doesn't hurt, right?"

"Of course not. Only pleasure. I've never participated in the whole pain-pleasure thing." He shrugged. "It's just not what I'm into sexually." Another smile erupted as if the fact they were still talking about this subject was amusing. "And so far as I know, neither is Zack. In case you wondered."

Daphne released a breath she hadn't realized she held and took another sip from her mug. The sweet creamy flavor of coffee slid down her throat as the mere idea of sharing a sexual relationship with two men made her cheeks heat in anticipation.

Do I have the courage to act on this desire?

Before she could ask any more questions, a noise like a cattle stampede erupted from the direction of Zack's bedroom hallway.

Seconds later, Zack came into view. He looked like a half-mad, disheveled sexy beast, and her core pulsed in desire at the mere sight of him. Her cheeks heated in memory of all the wicked things they'd done the night before, along with the current topic of sex for a breakfast conversation.

A glance at Jeff and she knew he wouldn't say a word unless she brought it up.

"Mornin', Zack, need some caffeine?" Jeff asked. His tone sounded very amused.

"Yep. Thanks."

Jeff stood and headed to the coffeemaker. Zack settled in the chair next to Daphne's and grabbed her hand. He kissed her palm once, winked at her, and rubbed his other hand over his head as if to hasten his wake up. His gaze slid to Jeff and the imminent coffee on its way to him.

Daphne wanted to kiss him and hug him and drag him back to bed. Then, without warning, the idea of Jeff joining them slid stealthily into her mind. Her heart started pounding so hard she wondered if the others could hear it.

"Here you go." Jeff deposited a large mug of black coffee in the center of his placemat.

"Bless you."

He took a large, loud sip, and Daphne blurted out, "We've been talking about threesomes and ménage à trois."

Chapter Five

That Zack didn't choke on the hot coffee sliding down his throat at her surprising statement was a testament to his inability to think coherently without caffeine first thing in the morning more than anything else.

Daphne looked like a rumpled sex kitten in his shirt, and he could still smell her juices on his fingers. If Jeff hadn't been in the room, he might have given her a more exuberant greeting.

She'd uttered the words, "ménage à trois" and his brain froze trying to think of another meaning. Surely she didn't mean the obvious ménage. Then again, what else did it mean?

"Let him get some coffee into his system," Jeff said with a smile. "Then he'll be more able to form an affirmative response. Want some eggs, Zack? I hear they're referred to as brain food. You look like you could use some right about now."

"Eggs would be a good idea." Zack turned to Daphne. "I'm glad to know I didn't scare you off last night. When I woke up alone in bed, I wasn't sure you'd still be here until I saw your clothes where we left them."

The ripple of her unexpected laughter powered a sensation beneath his skin like a low, pleasurable vibration. Elbow on the table, Daphne placed her chin on her palm and said, "Beyond the fact that I don't have anywhere else to go, I loved last night. It has definitely been an education."

"Sounds like you and Jeff moved on to a more sophisticated plane of learning while I slept."

"It was just talking, but I'll have to admit, I'm intrigued."

Zack took another long gulp of coffee. "What would it take to go from intrigue to action?"

She shrugged. "More information, maybe."

"I'll tell you everything. And trust me, I don't say that too often."

Daphne glanced at Jeff. "No pain, right?"

Both of them shook their heads in unison.

"Okay, then after breakfast, I'd like to try it once."

* * * *

With the goal of taking down a well-funded and classified agency, Valentino knew his plan had to be carefully thought out. He'd organized and planned every detail to destroy the Protocol Agency, all the way down to the hair on the gnat's ass, and yet, the initial step of his plan hadn't gone according to his carefully mapped out plan.

The bank employee he'd seduced and trusted to arrange the capture of Paul Kelly's best spy, Frankie, had instead fucked everything up royally. He'd gone over and over the plan, but even acquiring the sexual loyalty of the bank's assistant manager hadn't worked in his favor. She hadn't been able to think on her feet when another bank patron had interfered with his masterful plan to keep "Daphne Kane" in the bank until Valentino and his carefully selected group of mercenaries got there to rob it.

Although, he now knew the identity of the interfering patron and, while coincidental in the extreme, Valentino was delighted to learn that a member of Ken Davenport's team was involved. Valentino planned to shoot Zack Mahon at the very first opportunity. Damn Edna and her stupidity of letting what she considered a "very attractive" man into the bank with Daphne.

Valentino would have to arrange a hasty airport pickup on Monday morning. A fucking nuisance since she should already be in his custody and paying the price for Paul Kelly's continued commanding audacity. Then again, the new twist at having a member of Ken Davenport's agency also involved forced Valentino to stifle a giggle of glee at the convenience of killing two birds with one stone.

Or rather, the taking down of two covert agencies with his one masterful plot of vengeance.

* * * *

The sound of water running in the master bathroom's shower signaled the beginning of Daphne's first sexual interlude with two men. Heart thumping wildly in her chest at the mere idea of this event, Daphne admitted that she could hardly wait to get started.

Once it had been established that she was willing to play this sensual game with the two of them, she was led into the bathroom. The only ground rules had to do with an established word for them to stop everything if she became uncomfortable.

"Why?"

Smiling gently, Zack whispered, "Because I know this is your first time with two men, and I want to give you an out. If we'd done this before, we might not need it. I want to ensure you're not unduly persuaded to do this with us unless you're completely willing throughout the day. You don't have to use the word unless you want to stop. For any reason, okay? You say the word. We back off."

She nodded solemnly, her eyes narrowed, and she asked, "Like what kind of word?"

Zack smiled with a patience she'd never experienced with another man in her lifetime. "Like one you'd never say in the throes of passion."

Daphne tried to think up the most ridiculous word imaginable. "Like maybe…pomegranate?"

Jeff laughed. "Perfect. I've never heard a woman scream pomegranate when she came, not even once."

Zack placed his hands on her shoulders, garnering her complete attention. "If anything happens here that you are uncomfortable with, then say that word, and the both of us will stop what we're doing."

Jeff's hands pressed against the center of her back suddenly and then slid down to rest casually at her hips. Merely having four manly hands resting lightly on her body all at once sent a potent spiral of arousal through her body.

And Daphne wanted more.

"Okay, but I'm not feeling anywhere close to uncomfortable." The tone of her voice had lowered of its own accord.

Zack's simmering, half-lidded appraisal made her heart pound a thunderous beat in her chest.

Jeff reached around her waist, and he undid a button on the shirt she wore. One by one, he released each of the rest of the buttons from their holes until the oversized shirt she wore revealed her nakedness.

Zack leaned in and kissed her, his tongue dancing with hers in sublime rhythm against the backdrop of Jeff pulling the garment over her shoulders, ever so slowly trapping her arms. She wasn't even wearing any panties. Zack cupped her face in his large hands. He twisted his mouth across hers to deepen the kiss to a more scorching level as Jeff stroked his fingertips along her outer thighs on a path upward.

Zack broke the kiss. "You're beautiful," he whispered and took her mouth again. His compliment distracted her from Jeff's actions. Zack stroked his tongue in her mouth one last time and pulled away to help Jeff remove her shirt as effortlessly as if they'd choreographed it in advance. Her body made the futile effort to relax as Zack's discarded shirt from the night before slipped off her body with the help of four masculine hands.

The muscles in her legs melted like warm maple syrup when Jeff bent to place a kiss at the base of her spine. He trailed a soft, stimulating path up toward her neck, stopping only long enough to slide his fingers along each side of her unbound breasts. He didn't touch her nipples, but caressed just about every other available inch of her breast. Zack leaned back as if to watch Jeff caress her.

"Gorgeous," he whispered and bent over, latching his lips around one perky nipple.

Jeff's hands slid away. He plunged them into her hair, brushed the long strands to one side, and kissed a sensitive spot on her neck repeatedly, licking and nibbling the area until her head fell back onto his shoulder. Zack alternated kissing and licking each of her nipples until a warm trickle escaped her pussy.

"You are so sexy," Jeff whispered in her ear before resuming his tactile massage of her neck with awe-inspiring kisses.

Zack released one very happy nipple. "Let's get in the shower."

"Shower?"

"Yes." He pulled her away from Jeff's stimulation for another soul-searching kiss. When Zack released her, Daphne realized that Jeff had stripped down to nothing. Half a head shorter than Zack, Jeff was still taller than she was by several inches. His body was lean yet muscular and completely unlike Zack's heavily developed physique. She found the differences exceptionally arousing.

Jeff grabbed one of her hands, kissed her palm, and led her to the spacious stall, which was already steaming the room with moisture from three decorative showerheads all running full blast. He snagged an accordion of three condoms from next to the sink and followed her inside the warm space.

On the left of the opening was a quarter round shaped seat facing the right-hand side of the luxurious granite-tiled shower with three heads all shooting out streams of hot water. Leading her beneath one of the spray heads, he kissed her cheek and backed away a step. "Allow me to get dressed for the party," he said with a grin. Daphne watched as he opened and secured a condom onto his fully erect and very impressive cock.

Zack entered the shower quietly, and the large space suddenly seemed a little more intimate. He closed the door to the shower behind him and seated himself on the quarter round bench opposite of where she stood with Jeff. Daphne noticed that Zack had also undressed completely. His cock jutted out from his body from the nest of dark hair between his legs, fully erect as if ready for pleasure.

Daphne half turned beneath the showerhead and faced Zack. Steamy moisture wafted past in waves of mist between them. Behind her, Jeff pressed his chest into her back, slipping his arms around her waist for a quick hug before moving his fingers to her breasts to stroke her sensitive nipples. Water cascaded down her body in rivulets. Zack watched her with a simmering gaze as Jeff caressed her body with a tender touch.

"I think you should soap her up, Jeff. Do it slowly. I want to see your sudsy hands gliding across her body."

"Great idea." Jeff leaned away a moment. Before she caught her breath, his hands slid around and touched her everywhere with the slick, jellied feel of liquid soap across and below her belly button.

"Don't forget to wash her breasts. Pay special attention to her nipples," Zack murmured.

Jeff's hands promptly cupped her breasts before sliding across her mounded flesh in a circular, scintillating fashion. Daphne's eyes closed for a second as Jeff's slick fingers danced across her flesh, stopping to tease and pinch her nipples through the slick, soapy film.

"Now between her legs," Zack uttered in a low, sexy tone.

With the soapy layer helping, one of Jeff's hands took an express elevator straight over her tummy and dove directly between her thighs to her clit. He nipped at the back of her neck, sending a spiral of electricity vibrating beneath her skin.

Every kiss, every lick, every stroke sent a riot of sensations through her body. Zack's gaze was so intense, she almost felt it like a caress.

Jeff touched her everywhere with the slick, soapy foam.

"Now rinse her off," Zack directed, and Jeff complied. Reaching overhead, he adjusted one of the showerheads to her shoulder and foamy soap rushed down her body in waves. Jeff ran his hands across every single inch of her flesh, ensuring the soap was completely gone.

His hand went between her legs again. Fingertips brushed back and forth several times as if to make sure no soap still clung to her flesh and then his cock dropped down to join his fingers to probe her pussy lips briefly. She was breathless from his tender caresses.

"I'm going to spend some time getting you ready for me, darlin'," he whispered and pinched her peaked nipples even has his cock shifted and dug into one of her butt cheeks. "Once I'm certain you're wet enough, I'll stick my cock into your pussy from behind so Zack can watch me fuck you slowly until you climax…hopefully screaming. That will be optional on your part, but keep in mind that we both love verbal responses."

Daphne sucked in a slow, aroused breath, keeping her eyes on Zack as Jeff whispered his naughty intentions.

One of Jeff's hands dipped between her legs and dove inside her lower lips to ascertain her readiness level. Truth be told, she was very wet. Dripping even.

His low chuckle the moment he realized she was likely very ready for him to fuck her earned her a kiss on the neck beneath one ear.

"You're already hot, wet, and ready, aren't you, darlin'?"

She nodded, and a low, sultry smile came her way from Zack. She watched his eyes flick from her face to below her waist and Jeff, who had started stroking her clit, obviously realizing that her level of readiness was set for go-right-now.

Daphne placed a hand on the tile to steady herself as Jeff penetrated her pussy with his fingers and alternately rubbed her clit and repeated the process as he pinched her nipple to a rhythm only he could hear. All the while, Zack watched as Jeff aroused her to a fever pitch. His wide, impressive cock stood erect and proud as he gazed at her tactile seduction by another's hands.

Jeff kissed the back of her neck and got her attention with a little nibble. "Turn and put your back against the tile, darlin'. I'm really hungry for you."

Daphne broke the eye contact with Zack to comply, never

expecting Jeff was about to kneel and lick her clit. His "hunger" was apparently fierce. The stiff lapping of his tongue across her pussy lips ensued.

Her knees buckled, and her hands landed on his shoulders the second his tongue glanced across her clit.

"Look at me, Daphne," Zack commanded as she tried to steady herself from Jeff's surprise oral assault.

She turned her head to one side, shifting her wide-eyed gaze to Zack's half-lidded appraisal, and her body fairly vibrated with piercing arousal. Her knees trembled, and her limbs shook with powerful need as Jeff licked her, but she kept her eyes on Zack.

Once her gaze was firmly fixed on him, Zack started stroking his cock one-handed. The sight of him with his own hand on his wide, hard shaft nearly undid her. Jeff's clever tongue danced across and between her pussy lips and stroked her clit, sending her eyes half closed. She popped them back open and bit back a moan when a fresh stroke crossed her clit and was accompanied by two of Jeff's fingers thrusting deep inside her body.

In and out, out and in, his fingers mimicked the motion of Zack's hand on his cock, and right before she was about to lose it and climax, he stopped. She groaned as Jeff rose from his knees to his feet and crouched in front of her. He promptly sucked one happy nipple into his mouth. He cupped her other breast with his free hand and rubbed his palm across the hardened tip. Daphne inhaled and exhaled slowly and deeply, trying to find her balance. She was on fire from the whole voyeuristic nature of this sultry sexual episode.

Jeff stood, releasing her nipple with a smack, and pulled her from the tile and into his arms for a very tight embrace. She rested one cheek on his shoulder, squeezed him in return, and stared at Zack, who was still methodically stroking his immense cock. Jeff's hand went to her ass, and he pushed her hip into his cock, which was already digging deeply into her belly.

"It's time to show Zack what we're in here for, darlin'. Are you ready?" Jeff whispered his question.

Daphne nodded, and without further words, he turned her in his arms, placed her forearm against the tile, and came behind her, slipping his cock between her legs. Now she fully faced Zack, hand still stroking his cock. A quiver ran through her at the sight, and she turned her attention down.

With Jeff's cock sliding back and forth across her slit, and his finger rubbing her clit, Daphne had just about hit her level of arousal before climax. She swallowed hard. Her gaze fixed on the shower tile at her feet.

"Look at me, Daphne," Zack murmured for a second time since she entered the steamy shower.

Whispering again, Jeff added, "Say whatever you want, darlin'. If you want to tell him what I'm doing to you or for you, go ahead. It just makes all of this even sexier. Or if you'd rather not speak, then maybe I will."

"I'll try," she said in a low tone.

"Good girl." Hands firmly positioned on each of her hips, Jeff pulled her against his groin, and the tip of his shaft glanced across her drenched slit.

Daphne stared at Zack as Jeff rubbed his cock back and forth across her pussy without entering.

"She's really wet, Zack. I think she likes having you watch me *almost* fuck her."

Zack smiled and stroked his cock harder. "Then I bet she'll really enjoy it when you actually *do* fuck her."

"I think you're right." Jeff jabbed his cock into her ass cheek again lightly, but she was mute and unable to respond. Heat infused her from head to toes, and she suspected her entire body was one big red blush.

Jeff kissed her jaw and nodded against her shoulder. "It's time. Don't you think so?"

"Time?" she asked weakly, wanting to come so desperately she couldn't think straight.

"Yes. It is definitely time," Zack murmured. His hand stroked from the base of his cock to the tip slowly and down again. The motion and sight of such an erotic picture filtered into Daphne's mind. Watching him touch himself was very sexy.

Jeff's cock slid across her pussy lips, and with help from the fingers rubbing her clit, he entered her slick passage. Daphne sucked in a shocked, deep breath and said, "He's inside me."

"Is he?" Zack grinned. "Does it feel good?"

She nodded, not trusting her voice.

Jeff pushed deeper, and a quiet groan escaped. "Jesus, your pussy is so fucking tight," came his ardent whisper.

"Oh, God, he's inside me…deeper." Daphne maintained her excited gaze on Zack's face. His half-lidded appraisal and obvious arousal over Jeff fucking her made her even more excited. She'd never experienced anything so wickedly hot in all her life.

The hand squeezing her breast dropped to her hip. Jeff pushed his cock all the way inside her body and then pulled out halfway. His next thrust was harder and even more arousing than the first. She adjusted her stance to allow him easier access, and all the while she stared a hole into Zack's delicious eyes.

Jeff found a steady rhythm to stroking his cock inside her quivering pussy walls. Each stroke to her clitoris sent her closer to the vivid edge of what she knew would be a powerful orgasm.

Zack watched them for several strokes before he stood up suddenly and took a step closer. Daphne straightened her body to keep her eyes on him. The shift made Jeff's cock hit her in a different place and lit her world on fire even more. "Ohmigod."

"Touch me, babe," Zack whispered. "Put your hand on my cock and squeeze me like your pussy is gripping Jeff's lucky cock."

She reached out with her free hand and grasped his wide, thick shaft in her fist. She could only reach the top few inches, but he grunted his approval as she gripped him. Zack reached up and pinched her nipples, and all the while Jeff kept up his steady cock strokes, bringing her closer and closer to the orgasm she sought.

Jeff's hand slid off of her hip, and his finger went straight to her sensitive clit. A low sound came from her throat without warning. A few more strokes across her clit like that and she would come unglued.

"Tell me when you come. I want to watch you the second you fall over the edge." Zack's whisper accompanied his continued rubbing of her nipples.

Jeff pushed his cock extra deep as he stroked her clit. Zack played with her nipples, and his gaze pierced all the way to her soul.

Release was hers.

"I'm coming, Zack. Ohmigod!" A shriek came out of her next as an orgasm of exponential force rocked her body. Her back arched as Jeff's cock pushed its absolute deepest inside her body. She trembled as waves of pleasure rode from her clit to her nipples and shook her to her very soul.

"You're so beautiful." Zack kissed her lips as Jeff sent one final thrust of his wide cock deeply into her body. Jeff stiffened and pressed his hips solidly against her butt as a growl emitted from his throat. Panting, Jeff's chest fell against her back, and he leaned into her hard for several seconds as if resting from his climax. After half a minute, he pushed out a deep breath that brushed her shoulder, and then his cock slid from her. Jeff kissed the center of her back, patted her ass gently, and then left the shower without saying anything else.

"Are you ready for me?" Zack pressed her against the tile as steam swirled around them.

She nodded but then added a quiet, "Yes," to alleviate any doubts.

Without taking his eyes from her, Zack reached out and grabbed a condom. After securing it, he took her face in his hands and kissed her with a tenderness she hadn't expected given this wild sexual encounter.

He lowered one of his hands to her hip. It soon slid to her thigh.

He then lifted her leg and wrapped her thigh around his hip. In one smooth stroke he slid his cock deeply inside her drenched pussy with ease.

Once he was fully seated, he pulled her tight to his large form and walked over to the other side of the shower stall. He pushed her against the glass half wall.

"Now Jeff can watch me fuck you through the glass. He likes to watch, too."

"Oh." Daphne's heart pounded so fast in her chest, it was a wonder it didn't burst from pure arousal.

Zack kissed her again and pushed his cock even deeper than the first stroke. The very idea that another man had been fucking her a few minutes ago and now a second, different man was now doing so sent her already excited libido into the scarlet zone of passionate excitement. "This is so sexy," she murmured when he broke the kiss. Staring even more deeply into her eyes, he stroked his cock inside her pussy very hard and very fast.

"I agree. Watching Jeff push his cock inside your wet pussy is second only to doing it myself."

The shower door opened, and Jeff stepped in and leaned next to the wall where Zack had been sitting as he'd watched the two of them. With arms crossed and a toothy grin on his handsome face, he watched as Zack took her with firm gusto against the glass wall. Her legs migrated one at a time from his thighs to his waist. He helped with the journey. The barrier at her back added to the force of the push and soon her blood pulsed with a staccato beat in her veins.

"Need any help holding her, Zack?"

"Maybe." Zack thrust deeply one more time. "What did you have in mind?"

"Bring her over here. She can rest her back against my chest, and I'll play with her nipples while you fuck her deeper and harder."

"Great idea." Zack slid his hands under her thighs and pulled her from the chill of the shower glass wall. Turning sideways, he pushed her into Jeff's waiting arms.

Jeff grabbed her close and settled her against his warm chest. Hands soon fastened to each of her breasts. He stroked his thumbs over her distended nipples. Daphne had barely adjusted to Jeff's warm chest versus the cold glass of the shower wall when Zack sent his cock deep inside her body again. She gripped Jeff's forearm as he played with her.

Sandwiched in between two hot, muscular men had to be the most erotic feeling ever conceived of, and even in the midst of all this sexual pleasure, she still couldn't believe she was doing this right now.

"This feels so incredible." Daphne pushed her shoulders back into Jeff's chest and her hips forward into Zack's thrusts.

Crossing her ankles to hang on as Zack thrust inside so very deeply might have been one of the single most exciting sexual events she'd ever dreamed of participating in. However, the previously unheard-of idea that a third person would ever hold her in his arms and watch her have sex sent another spiral of excitement into the equation.

Heart pounding violently in her chest, Daphne hoped to survive the onslaught of sexual arousal vibrating through her body long enough to climax before she fainted from the utter intensity of this experience. A soul-wrenching orgasm was imminent as Zack focused his attention between her legs and his cock pumping in and out of her pussy at a rapid pace.

The angle of Zack's cock brushed lightly over her clit and brought her to the ragged edge of yet another seductive pinnacle. Jeff's tanned fingers stroking over her sensitive, peaked nipples sent a stinging thread of pleasure straight to her pussy. She squeezed Jeff's forearm again and reached out her free hand to stroke the center of Zack's chest.

Zack pushed into her again, and an orgasm exploded through her body.

"I'm coming. Ohmigod!" she screamed as her head fell onto Jeff's shoulder. Pleasurable sensation weltered in every direction from her core. Tremors rippled through her body as if aftershocks from a turbulent earthquake shook her body.

A satisfied growl came from deep in Zack's throat. He thrust forward and stiffened, locking his body against hers, as a steady growl emitted from his throat. He leaned closer, and his weight pushed her into Jeff. Securely wedged between the two men was a sensation she hadn't expected, and yet it felt perfect.

After several seconds of panting, Zack pulled his cock from her body slowly. Jeff tightened his grip around her waist as Zack separated from her. First, he leaned in and kissed her mouth tenderly. "That was utterly the best experience I've ever shared. Did you like it?"

Daphne nodded. "I don't think I have the right words to tell you how amazing it was." She couldn't stop the smile shaping her lips.

Zack exited the shower stall, leaving her alone with Jeff. He shifted her in his arms until they faced each other. Daphne slipped her arms around his neck.

He grinned. "I'd like to kiss you."

"Okay."

His mouth came down onto hers, and while his kiss was certainly different than Zack's, it was no less arousing. Jeff's tongue slid between her lips slowly, twisting against hers gently. One hand tangled in her hair, and the other snugly fastened around her waist, Daphne relaxed into his firm body as the engaging kiss continued.

Zack opened the shower door. Daphne stopped the kiss and broke away from Jeff's tight embrace as if she'd been caught red-handed.

"Don't stop on my account."

"It really doesn't make you jealous?"

"Nope. It turns me on." He pointed down to his hardening cock.

Jeff nodded. "We only stop if you say a particular word."

Daphne kissed Jeff again softly and finished by tracing her tongue along his lower lip. "What's next then?"

"Maybe it's time to tie you up," Zack murmured and moved closer. Each of them in turn grinned at her in a completely wicked way.

Daphne sucked in a sharp breath half-filled with desire and half-filled with anxiety. "Bondage?"

Chapter Six

Paul Kelly rarely slept in on the weekends. He didn't get to enjoy much free time due to the time suck his job as director of the Protocol Agency required. He'd been labeled a control freak workaholic, and he couldn't really argue that point. With the group on hiatus for the next couple of days, he'd enjoyed some time off last night and dinner with someone special. It had been an escape a long time in coming. Today was about to be another rare down day for him. He planned to enjoy it.

Saturday nights were often referred to as date night, but he hadn't had a date in ages, at least until last night. And since he considered last night such a success, perhaps he'd make an effort to do it again very soon. It was long-planned rendezvous that had included a great dinner, engaging conversation, and eventually led to lots of sexual satisfaction. Next to him, in bed, his date shifted beneath the sheets and a soft sigh escaped her luscious lips.

He spied the bedside clock of the hotel room he'd rented spontaneously late last night after several rounds of sexual innuendo post dessert. Just after six in the morning on a quiet Sunday, and for the first time in ages, Paul was relaxed and satisfied all the way to the marrow of his bones.

Before he could formulate a plan to seduce his date one more time, his cell phone rang. Odd. Even if he hadn't been off for the day, Sunday early in the morning was an unusual time for a business-related call. He wasn't expecting any calls since his team was on standby status, which meant this call was about to be bad news and his awesome Saturday night date was about to end suddenly.

A glance at the number made his heart rate speed up a notch. The display screen flashed the name Stella Pemberton, his private assistant, and he knew she'd never call and interrupt his off time if it weren't something dire.

He answered the phone with a curt, "What's wrong?" As he asked the quick question, Paul slipped out of bed and made his way to the hotel bathroom for a more private conversation. His date didn't need to hear any confidential information by accident.

"Sir," Stella's low, worried tone in that single word moved his *oh shit* level to the red zone, "one of our Protocol agents is missing."

Shit.

"Who's gone?"

"Francine."

Double shit. Not Frankie. "Did Daphne return safely to her home base this past week?"

"Yes, sir. Daphne arrived back to South Carolina in time for work on Wednesday morning. However, she apparently didn't come home from her part-time job on Friday night. Her handler just called a few minutes ago and informed us she's been missing perhaps as long as late yesterday afternoon."

Paul had to control his spike of fury at being informed so many hours later. *Fuck! Louise was his best handler. Why the fuck didn't she report Daphne's disappearance immediately?*

Tempering his futile anger for his current phone call, he asked in a calm voice, "I'm wondering why it took Louise so long to report in? Is she injured or something?"

"Unknown, sir." Stella's voice became edged with puzzled concern. "However, I get the impression Louise wasn't in the home base residence Friday night and only just now realized her charge is gone. She mentioned that Daphne's bed hasn't been slept in."

What the fuck was Louise doing away from home base?

"Did Louise mention a search anywhere locally?"

"Not to my knowledge, sir. She's waiting at the South Carolina residence for further instructions." Paul wanted his first instructions for "Aunt" Louise to include, "You're fired!" but he needed Louise to do her fucking job just a little longer and ensure a safe return for his agent. Then a disciplinary hearing could be put into place forthwith. He'd do the arduous paperwork himself. Once Frankie was found safe and sound, he'd personally assign a new handler who understood the responsibility of keeping his best agent safe. But his gut clenched because this was very unlike Louise. Her blatant failure indicated that the quiet haven in South Carolina had likely been compromised.

Fuck.

"Get a team together to quietly search the area of her disappearance. Find out the last time we had eyes on Daphne and where she could possibly have gone afterwards. Inform Louise to stay in the home base and alert us if Daphne returns or sends any messages. I'll be in the Protocol office in an hour."

"Yes, sir." Stella disconnected, and Paul tried to calm down. A bad feeling centered in his chest at this development. The possibilities were endless regarding what could have happened, and given the nature of their agents, a disappearance was one of the worst scenarios possible.

He'd gone through the ordeal of losing another Protocol agent, Rachel Miles, due to medical concerns, and the thought of Frankie being gone without a clue made his blood run cold.

His first thought was that his gut feeling regarding a traitor was coming to fruition and he'd been caught with his pants down regarding security within his own organization. Second was a momentary fear that Frankie suffered from the same affliction as Rachel.

But that couldn't be true. Frankie, and the other Protocol agents like her, had gone through every possible medical test after Rachel had left permanently to live a life as her alter ego.

Frankie Belle was born to work as a Protocol spy. She was hands down his best operative. Hopefully, Frankie hadn't been discovered by any nefarious foes. Hopefully, nothing had happened to Daphne in her small hometown. Hopefully, this would all be resolved by the time he got to the Protocol headquarters. Although, *hopefully* wasn't a word he ever counted on.

Whatever relaxation he'd banked from last night was about to be expended on the search for his best agent. Frankie the spy was tucked safely into the deep recesses of Daphne's mind. *Her* safety was imperative to the health of his agent.

Where did you go, Daphne? Are you hurt? Frightened? Kidnapped?

* * * *

"We call it light bondage." Jeff brushed a lock of hair off Daphne's face and tucked it behind her ear. He still held her loosely in his arms. Daphne stared at him, but didn't really see him as she contemplated his words.

Zack came behind her, brushed the hair off of her neck, and kissed a very sensitive spot beneath her ear repeatedly. Jeff leaned in and kissed her lips gently as if to convince her. "You are the sweetest thing I've ever tasted. You know that?"

Daphne allowed the kissing to continue unheeded as her mind raced with the possibilities of what on earth *light* versus *regular* bondage might mean. When Jeff finally broke the kiss, she asked, "Light bondage?"

"We tie you up and take turns making you come. So what do you think? Want to try it?"

"I...I don't know." She didn't mean to sound so frightened, but the unsteady sound of her voice made her sound like a scared little girl.

"We don't have to play the bondage game."

"I don't mean to be a prude."

"You're not even close to being a prude." Zack pulled her out of Jeff's arms and plastered her mouth with a blistering kiss until she couldn't think straight.

Jeff, meanwhile, put his mouth on her breast and pulled her rigid nipple into his mouth. He sucked hard at her breast, and one hand slid down to stroke the outer lips of her pussy. She was overwhelmed with sensation, sandwiched between two sexy, virile men and wondering if she'd withstand another round of sexual inundation.

* * * *

"I received a message from Daphne." Louise Bennett's hesitant voice came over the phone line. She didn't sound too excited about the message.

"When? Just now? Where is she?"

"Well, no. Actually, she left the message Friday night around six thirty or so. I just now noticed the message light was blinking."

Paul, seated at his desk at the Protocol office, pushed his finger into the vein trying to burst open through his forehead. He'd always thought Louise was an exceptional agent. Up until now, she *had* been. His gut churned.

"Where is she?" Paul managed not to shout, but only barely.

"Mr. Benny, her civilian boss here in South Carolina, sent her on a commuter plane to Washington, DC. He wanted her to put something in his safety deposit box."

Paul's calm disintegrated. "She isn't supposed to leave the state. I believe that is what we pay you to enforce!"

"Well, Mr. Benny didn't ask me if she could go, and Daphne didn't call to tell me until she was already there. I can't go to work with her, can I? She didn't show up at the house Friday night as near as I can tell, and Saturday morning I didn't realize she'd left a message on the home phone."

"Disregarding the fact that you weren't at home base when you should have been on Friday night, why didn't you get the message earlier than Sunday morning?"

"I forgot to check when I got home last night. This morning, I assumed she was in her room where she always is. I do have a life, you know."

What the fuck? Had Louise been drugged? Compromised?

"No, you don't. You have the life I gave you. I don't have to remind you of the consequences if she turns up hurt because of your negligence, do I?"

"No, sir."

"Play the message for me."

Paul heard some clicks and beeps as Louise set up the message to play out loud. After a few moments he heard Frankie's voice. *"Aunt Louise, it's me, Daphne. Mr. Benny sent me to Washington, DC to put something in his safety deposit box, but I missed my return flight home. I ran into an old college friend of mine to stay with, so don't worry about me."* There was a beeping sound as if her phone was out of power or about to be. *"My phone is about to die, but don't worry. I'll be back early Monday on the first flight out. Bye."*

Several disturbing things hit Paul at once as he listened to the message. Daphne hadn't gone to college in DC. They'd manufactured her past life, so she couldn't have met any old college friends, which meant she was lying. Daphne, as a rule, wasn't a liar. Not at all. She was the opposite as a matter of fact. What would make her tell a fib? Was someone with her dictating what she said? The stomach acid in his belly shifted, and the bad feeling that had plagued him since Stella's earlier call got worse.

Paul took a deep, cleansing breath and released it slowly before asking the obvious. "Do you know what bank Mr. Benny's safety deposit box is located at?"

"I can try to find out. I haven't talked to Mr. Benny personally, just his wife. Apparently, he's missing, too."

"Great. Her civilian boss is also missing? That would have been good information to have a day and a half ago." The last few words came out in a shout.

"I just found out. Mr. Benny's wife just called looking for him." Louise's surly tone didn't endear her during this crisis.

"What did you tell her?"

"Um...well, I sort of let it slip that I was looking for Daphne, too."

"Damn it." Paul let his head fall into one hand and resisted the urge to scream through the phone again.

"Mr. Benny's wife is pretty upset. She's wondering if they ran off together. I told her I didn't think so..." She trailed off, and Paul was grateful she stopped. He wanted to reach through the phone and strangle her for this continued incompetence.

Taking a deep breath to center himself, he said very quietly, "New instructions, Louise. Absolutely no talking on the phone unless it is to me, Stella, or Daphne. Any other calls come through, just ignore them. They can leave a message. Am I clear?"

"Yes, sir."

"And find out what travel arrangements were made for Daphne."

"Travel arrangements?"

"I want to know what airports she flew into and out of and when, or even if, she's scheduled to come back. Can you do that for me, please?"

"I'll try." Louise didn't sound too hopeful in her success at the task, but Paul ignored her attitude. His stomach burned with the sour feeling that something very bad was transpiring. Until he spoke to either Louise or Frankie in person, he wouldn't know the complete truth.

He hung up the phone and considered whether Daphne had somehow changed into Frankie and was working as a spy this weekend. Unlikely, but not impossible. It certainly wasn't without precedence given the history of her former partner, Rachel.

Stella knocked on the door once and then entered his office. "Ken

Davenport is on the office line. He wants to meet with you pronto."

"Tell him, not today."

"He says it's urgent. He's calling from his car and is currently on his way to the facility."

Both of their covert agencies shared offices in the Protocol building along with several other agencies. "Fine. Tell him he can have ten seconds when he arrives and not a second more."

"Yes, sir." Stella stepped back to the outer office with quiet efficiency. Unlike Louise, Stella was the most dependable person he knew.

Paul didn't relish a visit with Ken, but perhaps he'd enlist his help to find Daphne. Ken's agency was as nameless and as clandestine as his own Protocol group. Perhaps using a few operatives from Ken's pool of resources would help with Paul's possible mole issue.

Was there a traitor ensconced in his organization, or was this threat coming from outside? Paul had sniffed out every possible clue to find something…anything, but thus far had found nothing viable. But the feeling that something wasn't right plagued him night and day. And now, with Frankie missing, perhaps his fears were well founded.

If there was a mole in the organization, he or she was very well hidden. He shouldn't feel so paranoid, but his gut was screaming that his missing agent was only the first step in a more devious plan to thwart the group. This scenario only added to his unease. He'd feel better once he knew that Daphne—and by default, Frankie—was safe and back into the folds of the Protocol Agency headquarters.

* * * *

Valentino called Louise to check on the status of her missing charge, Daphne. The moment she answered, she told him she wasn't supposed to be communicating with him anymore. He asked why as gently as he could, putting as much disinterest into the tone of his voice as possible. He didn't want her to think he cared one way or the other even though the lines of communication needed to remain intact for his amended plan to work.

"But I miss you, Louise. I so wanted to spend more time with you." *Lie. Lie. Lie.* He'd been delighted to finally be away from her clingy, whiney feminine form. However, once she told him that her "niece" was missing and her boss, Paul, was restricting her to her house, Valentino decided it would be very prudent to have trusted men in his employ present at the airport on Monday morning. He knew what flight Daphne had arrived on as he'd made the arrangements himself.

Having her loose for the weekend instead of being back at the bank had changed his plans. She'd fucked up her assignment with the safety deposit box. She hadn't followed his explicit instructions and now he needed to speak with her in person.

A proactive approach on her return flight home would ensure no more mistakes happened to thwart his plans to end her life and bring the Protocol Agency to its knees.

* * * *

Paul paced in his office with a frustration born of being foiled again and again over the location of his missing agent. He'd only learned that Daphne's name was on a boarding pass used to get on a commuter flight out of the Loganville airport headed for a Washington, DC, municipal airport. Ken's imminent arrival with news he refused to share over an open communications line made Paul's blood boil with anticipation.

Stella's voice sounded through the intercom on his desk. "Mr. Davenport is here."

"Send him in."

Ken entered, dressed very casually as if he, too, pretended to have a life outside the office over the recent weekend. They were both obviously mistaken.

"You've got ten seconds," Paul said tartly.

Without preamble, which Paul was extremely grateful for, Ken started talking. "When I went looking for an agent I trusted to help you locate *your* agent in DC, I happened upon an unusual phone call quite by accident."

"How does it pertain to the current situation?"

"A woman by the name of Daphne Kane called the local DC branch of the FBI asking to speak to Zack Mahon."

Paul couldn't believe it. He sank into the chair behind his desk. "What makes you think Daphne Kane is of interest to me?"

Ken rolled his eyes. "Beyond the stunned look on your face right now? I know I'm not supposed to know too much about your agents, but I do recognize her name. Isn't your spy Frankie's alias Daphne?"

"No comment. Why did Daphne call him, and how does Zack fit in with the FBI?"

"The FBI is his cover for undercover ops. I have to admit that when I heard the call, I planned to sanction him for using his FBI cover to pick up women."

Paul stood and fixed a contemptuous gaze on the other man. "He was picking her up?"

"That's my impression, but I'll let you decide. The initial call was recorded along with the conversation once Zack was contacted. Would you like to hear it?" Ken produced a small tape recorder. "I'll go over my ten seconds."

"Fine. Just play it." Paul listened very closely. His mind raced with scenarios, but a part of him was relieved that she was okay and possibly in the company of one of Ken's spies.

Frankie's voice, speaking in a breathy tone suggesting she was Daphne, said, *"Yes. I'd like to speak with an FBI Agent named Zack Mahon, please."*

Then the high-pitched tone of the FBI operator asked, "Your name, please?"

"*Oh, tell him it's Miss Daphne Kane.*"

Zack Mahon's voice then came on the line several long seconds later. "*Agent Mahon.*"

The high-pitched female voice said, "*Sir, this is the FBI central switchboard, I have a call for you from a Miss Daphne Kane.*"

"*Thanks. Put her through.*"

"*Agent Mahon. This is Daphne Kane. I've decided to go ahead and meet with you after all. Are you still available to pick me up?*"

"*Yes. Miss Kane. I'll be there faster than you can say safety deposit box.*"

"*Thank you, Agent Mahon. I'll look forward to the ride.*"

"*As will I, Miss Kane.*"

Ken stopped the tape. "That's it. Subsequent searching came up with the information that the two cell phones used in this conversation were likely very close together in proximity based on cell tower records. In fact, they might have been standing next to each other."

"How did they meet?"

Ken shrugged. "They were within a block of the First Federated Bank of Washington DC."

"Why does that bank sound familiar?"

"Because *that* branch of First Federated was robbed over the weekend. The discovery was made late Saturday night. I understand the thieves got away with quite a bit of private swag from the safety deposit boxes as well as the sizeable cash reserves in the vault."

"Does the robbery have anything to do with our agents?"

"I have no idea." Ken crossed his arms. "So who's in DC? Frankie or Daphne?"

"To the best of my knowledge it's Daphne, but I don't want to rule anything out. So where is your agent, Zack?"

"He's on vacation until Monday morning, and I haven't been able to get a hold of him as of yet."

"Try harder to find him. Once you do, ask him what he did to my agent. Send some people to his house."

"I'm not calling my agents off their well-earned vacation to appease your problems." Ken threw up his hands. "Besides, you don't know that he did anything to Daphne."

"But the call sure sounded like he was about to."

"What do you want me to do? Send in an armed SWAT team to raid his private residence because he got a date?" Ken scowled and crossed his arms defiantly.

Paul shrugged. "Works for me."

Ken shook his head. "No way. You'd stick me with the paperwork. Besides, I can't verify he's at his residence. They could be anywhere, or we're wrong and they aren't even together by now. It's probably a big waste of time."

"Is his cell phone on?"

"No. Soon after the call through the FBI switchboard, it went dead. Could just be a low battery or he switched it off for privacy. Because he earned the vacation."

"If she doesn't come back Monday morning, I'm going to string Zack up by his balls until he tells me everything about her."

"I'm sure that won't be necessary. When he comes back to work, I'll ask him about her. She'll probably be back where she belongs by then anyway."

"You'd better fucking hope so." Paul forced himself to sit in his office chair. He weighed his options. Did he know for certain that she was in trouble? Maybe. Regardless of her possibly innocent antics with Zack over the weekend, she still shouldn't have been allowed to leave her home base. Once she was back with Louise, he'd stop by and reassess the situation.

And perhaps it wouldn't be out of line to have a couple of agents he trusted waiting for Daphne at the DC airport Monday morning to ensure she showed up and boarded the plane back to South Carolina. Or perhaps he'd simply have her brought back to Protocol headquarters. Better idea.

"Zack is one of my very best agents. He'd never hurt her. I'm not inclined to disrupt what might turn out to be a harmless meeting over nothing."

"She isn't where she's supposed to be, but if she's with Zack, I'm less panicked than I was ten seconds ago."

A half smile shaped Ken's mouth. "Maybe we should form a matchmaking service. First it was Colin and Laurie, now Zack and Daphne."

"Shut your dirty, fucking mouth."

Ken exited Paul's office laughing with glee as Paul ground his molars in anger and formulated what he'd say and do to Daphne's inept handler, Louise.

The alarm of traitors harboring Daphne, and torturing her endlessly regarding her life as a spy, abated slightly. He made a call to have a couple of guys bring her in from the airport tomorrow morning.

Chapter Seven

Zack eased his vehicle into the parking lot of the municipal airport bright and early on Monday morning. Fatigue from the rambunctious sexual weekend registered in his satisfied, aching muscles. However, the only subject on his mind was how to broach a topic he usually tried desperately to avoid when saying good-bye to women on the mornings after. Or in this particular case, the morning after a truly stupendous weekend.

When can I see you again?

Daphne released her seat belt and turned to him with a beautiful smile. "Thanks so much, Zack. For the ride and..." she paused to catch his gaze, "for everything."

He twisted in his seat, afraid to speak and more afraid not to tell her how he felt. Taking a deep breath, he managed, "It was my pleasure."

"Next time you see Jeff, tell him..." Her smile faltered as her words trailed off. "I mean. Never mind."

"I can relay a message to him eventually. I just can't depend on seeing him any time soon. His security job sometimes takes him on long trips away from here."

"That's okay. I'm lingering, and I promised Jeff that I wouldn't be clingy when we said good-bye."

"Did you?"

She nodded. "If I swear that I won't grasp on to you and refuse to let go, do you think I could have just one more kiss?"

Zack leaned forward. His lips were inches away from hers. "You aren't allowed out of my vehicle without one." He brushed his knuckles along her face before he cupped his hand around her head. "The truth is I hate to say good-bye to you, Daphne."

A humorless laugh escaped at the same time a tear slid out of one eye. He pressed his lips gently to hers for a chaste kiss. She kissed him back with tenderness at first then slid her tongue into his mouth suddenly, and the kiss progressed to another more carnal level.

Before he realized what was happening, he'd pinned her to the passenger seat and had his hand shoved down her shirt, cupping her breast beneath the fabric of her bra. Her nipple came to pert attention against his palm, and the sound of her moan made his cock throb and ready itself for action.

The sound of an approaching aircraft engaged his brain and made him remember where they were. In public. In his truck. Saying good-bye. But he truly didn't want to. Not this time. Daphne was different. A mystery. A kind soul. And a perfect lover all wrapped into one beautiful, tempting package.

He removed his hand from the intimate touch, gazed deeply into her eyes, and cleared his throat. "I'll miss you."

"You don't have to say that, but thank you. It's very nice."

"I mean it." Another look into her sultry eyes and Zack made an impulsive decision. He had his phony FBI business card which had his real cell number listed. The card he'd put there this morning because deep down he wasn't ready for her to be out of his life permanently. He released his grip on her body long enough to procure the fake card from his shirt pocket.

He offered it to her clamped between the ends of his first two fingers. "Call me when you get back home so I know you made it safe and sound."

"Honestly, Zack. You don't have to do this. I won't be like the other women in your past."

"Take it."

Daphne's eyes zeroed in on the card. She sighed but didn't reach for it.

"It's just a phone call, not a proposal."

A sudden smile encompassed her face, and she finally accepted the card. She then winked at him and tucked it inside her bra.

Zack closed his eyes briefly in reverence to the vision now playing in his head regarding retrieval of his card. "You did that on purpose to make me think about your breast all day."

"I did no such thing." She expelled a giggle which belied her statement.

He plastered his lips on hers again and kissed his way along her jawline. Her bubbly laugh sent a pulse to his cock, and he almost asked her to stay. The words, "Please stay with me," were on the sweet-tasting center spot of his tongue.

Which was foolish. He had to go to work. She had to go back home to South Carolina. And he'd likely never see her again. A truth he wasn't quite ready to accept, it seemed.

"Thanks, Zack. I mean it."

He glanced at the breast caressing his phony FBI business card. "Call me. I mean it."

"Okay."

They each exited their respective doors of his truck, and Zack walked around to the passenger side. The urge to pin her to the passenger door for a good-bye fuck, while completely inappropriate, was the singular vision in his lust-saturated brain. But only to the extent that the action would keep her here in his presence for just a little bit longer.

After the sexcapades of the previous weekend, it occurred to him that he'd love to take her out exploring the city. However, that would take time. And it was time that he didn't even have to spare.

She patted her breast in the general location of where his card rested beneath her shirt and bra. "I should be back well before noon. I'll call you when I land, okay?"

"I'm counting on it."

Daphne smiled, tapped his chest twice with an open hand, and moved an arm's length away.

He grabbed her hand before she got far and stopped her progress. His logical brain warred with his engaged libido. *Let her go* was fast losing the battle with *I want to see her again.*

Zack brought her hand to his lips and kissed her gently. "I'm not ready to never see you again, Daphne." Good lord, *he* was clinging to *her.*

What the hell is wrong with me?

She stepped closer, rested her forehead on his shoulder, and released a long sigh. "I need for you to let me go, Zack. I can't bring you home, and I don't want anyone there to know what I did this weekend. You see, it was only for me. And I loved every single second of our time together, but truthfully, it is way out of my norm. I promise, I'll never forget you, but I need this to end."

Zack nodded. "Then it ends. And I won't ever forget you either."

She tilted her head and gazed into his eyes. He kissed her lips one last quick time, and they both turned away. He rounded the front of his truck and slid into the driver's seat. He started his vehicle and backed out of the parking spot without watching her progress to the small terminal. By the time he looked over in the direction of the path she'd taken, she was gone. The door to the small terminal building snapped shut. It was over. Done. Ended. *Damn.*

He drove forward to the end of the row of parking spaces and stopped. On his left was the road leading to the parking lot exit lane. On the right, the road led to the front drive of a small terminal building. He stared at the short road and shorter drive as two men in business suits entered where Daphne must have already gone.

Zack watched the building, harboring an achy feeling in his chest like he'd forgotten to take something important along with him.

Hand resting on the outer jacket pocket where he felt his cell phone through two layers of clothing, Zack knew he'd have her in the forefront of his brain until she called. *If she called.* He pushed out a frustrated breath and glanced at the double doors to the terminal again.

What he needed to do was get the hell out of here. What was he waiting for?

Zack revved the engine and put on his left blinker to gun his truck into the exit lane. The faster he left the area, the faster he'd be back into his regular routine. He pushed out a sigh and put his hands on the wheel, trying to leave. If he reparked his truck and went in after her, he could watch her plane fly away. A car had pulled up behind him and honked for him to get his ass going. Watching her plane would only delay the inevitable.

He waved into the rearview mirror to acknowledge the other driver and pulled forward a couple of feet to leave. Out of the corner of his eye, he saw the terminal door open, and three people stepped into view with the morning sun pouring over them.

Two well-dressed men on either side of a familiar woman. The men flanked her and had both hands clamped down on the arms of a struggling and visually disturbed Daphne.

Chapter Eight

Daphne never looked back after she turned away from Zack in the small parking lot and walked toward the door to the airport. She had achieved an outward composure that didn't mirror her insides as she crossed through the automatic doors and made a beeline for the small commuter jet ticket counter desk to arrange for a return flight home.

Her mind was filled with visions of Zack, but agonizing over him was useless. It was best to leave Zack and the entire perfect weekend in the back of her mind. She could visit her memories later on. She'd done wicked, wonderful things with both Zack and Jeff, but no one where she was going needed to know about her experimental walk on the wild side. No one.

The terminal was small, but it was busier than she would have expected. Instead of only a handful, there were nearly thirty people milling about or standing in line at the ticket counter.

A few steps into the terminal, she passed a pair of businessmen dressed in suits, and one of them called out to her. "Francine?"

Daphne was not Francine, so she kept walking and didn't even acknowledge him with a look. Three steps later, the man and his friend came up on either side of her and fastened their hands on her arms. She did her best to get them to release her to no avail. She started to resist in earnest when they kept their pressurized grip on her upper arms.

"Frankie. Stop struggling. You're coming with us."

"I'm not Francine or Frankie. Let go of me." They ignored her.

The two of them moved swiftly and had her out the door before anyone else seemingly noticed she was being abducted. She thrashed about and tried to dislodge their hands, but they were too strong. She opened her mouth to scream, but one of them clamped his free hand over her face to muffle any sound.

Daphne screamed anyway, but there was absolutely no one in the parking lot to hear her. She swung her head around wildly, wishing for a miracle and condemning herself for not allowing Zack to escort her into the terminal.

"Stop thrashing around, Frankie. We aren't here to hurt you. Your boss sent us. Relax. We just need to know why you're here."

"None of your damn business." Daphne certainly wasn't about to spill her life story or the lurid details of her amazing weekend to two strange men attempting to kidnap her.

"You'll find out soon enough that it is our business. Cooperate now and it will be easier later on. Just tell us why you're here."

"I don't know what you're talking about. First of all, my boss is the one who sent me here, and second of all, I'm not Frankie! You've obviously got the wrong woman."

They exchanged pointed and seemingly meaningful glances, but Daphne didn't know what they were even doing with her.

"Please, I need to get on that plane to South Carolina."

"There's been a change of plans. You're staying in DC for now."

"No. Please." She struggled and tried to break their firm grip, but it was no use, and they promptly ignored her as they marched her along the sidewalk.

They led her to a car she hadn't noticed parked illegally in a fire lane in front of the terminal. Unceremoniously, they shoved her headfirst into the backseat. She felt a hand on her ass push her in further and then the door slammed shut. Daphne screeched at the top of her lungs and righted herself in the backseat.

She reached for the door handle only to realize there wasn't one. Not on either side of the backseat.

There was a thick plexiglass barrier between the front and back seats so as to keep her confined. Smacking her hands on the clear surface until her fingertips stung was pointless, but she did it anyway. It seemed more insane to sit quietly. The two men entered the front part of the vehicle and promptly ignored her as if she wasn't there.

The driver procured his cell phone from an inner jacket pocket and made a call as she screamed and cried from the backseat.

"Yes, sir. We have her secured."

"Whoever is at the end of the phone. I've been kidnapped! Please help me," Daphne called through one of the quarter-inch holes in the clear barrier.

"No, sir, she doesn't answer to Francine or Frankie."

She pounded on the plastic again. "Help me!" It was probably foolish to expect assistance from the person at the other end of the phone, but she was panicked, and her options were limited.

The man with the phone turned his head and asked, "Are you Daphne?"

Daphne stopped screaming and stared first at the driver and then the other man in the front passenger seat. She studied their faces for a hint of recognition and found none.

So how do they know your name?

* * * *

Zack wasn't sure exactly what he'd seen as he turned out of the parking lot. Had he been mistaken? Who would be stupid enough to haul a struggling female out of an airport in broad daylight? Someone stupid, or worse, someone desperate.

He was committed to exiting the parking lot unless he wanted to crash, but he took the earliest possible U-turn and headed back to the airport entrance.

It took several precious minutes to find an opening in the barrier of the highway as his gut wrenched with self-condemnation for not seeing Daphne all the way inside the terminal.

The route he took was only for law enforcement vehicles, but he decided if anyone stopped him, he'd whip out his FBI badge. The fake fed identification had certainly come in handy this past weekend.

Given his current state of intense concentration, he didn't believe anyone would be able to stop him. Instead of parking, Zack headed to the front entrance, where a lone vehicle was parked.

The front doors of the beige sedan hung wide open, and upon closer inspection, Zack noticed a leg sticking out of the door and resting on the pavement. A bad feeling socked him in the gut. He wished he hadn't had to take so long to return to the airport.

The squeal of tires to his left caught his attention, and on base instinct only, Zack sped past the sedan and followed it to where he'd seen the corner of a van disappear behind the airport terminal on a tree-lined road leading to the outbuildings on the airport property. He followed a trail of dust left in the wake of the other speeding vehicle along the winding road, wishing the forest around him didn't obscure the road.

Zack hoped he followed Daphne's kidnappers and not some crazy maintenance crew headed to a remote hangar for their duty day.

* * * *

Paul gunned the gas on the way out of his apartment building's parking lot, relishing the sound of squealing tires on this early Monday morning. He didn't need to hurry to work exactly, but wanted to be there well before Daphne was brought in from the municipal airport. He'd speak with the medical staff and give them a heads up about the previous weekend.

He dialed Ken's number one-handed without looking. His sleepy answer, "Hello?" didn't keep Paul from snapping, "Meet me at work."

"Why?"

"We need to talk about our agents."

"Screw that. They're adults. I only agreed to help when I thought your agent was truly missing. But she's not."

"Tell me this, Ken, how do our agents keep running into each other?"

Ken remained silent on the line for a long time before saying, "Coincidence?"

"I don't believe in coincidences."

"Then it's a conspiracy. Forces larger than we can comprehend are scheming to keep us working together. What's going on?"

Paul explained concisely what was going on and where he was headed. "I'm having Daphne picked up from the airport and brought in. Zack will eventually be at work, too, right?"

"Yeah, so?"

"So get your ass in gear and meet me there so we can work this out. I want it to stop."

"Shit. I'm a minimum of half an hour from work."

"Your place is only ten minutes away."

Ken huffed. "Maybe I'm not at home."

"Well, get your ass in a vehicle and get here. And try calling your agent. Or have you gotten ahold of him already?"

"Not exactly. He turned his cell phone on to make a call to his partner's phone line about being late this morning and then shut it off again. His cell phone is going straight to messages."

"Any idea if our agents spent the weekend together or what they did?"

"Don't care."

"Well, I do. I'm not running a matchmaking business."

"Zack doesn't make a secret out of the fact he likes being a bachelor. I don't think you have to worry about a permanent relationship."

Paul's earpiece beeped. "Hold on, I've got another call coming in." He steered one-handed to retrieve his cell and see who was calling. It was the agents he'd sent to the airport. Without any greeting, he said, "Do you have her?"

The man answered, "Almost, sir. She's just entered the terminal.

We're parking in the fire lane, and we'll have her secured in five minutes."

"Good. I'm on the way to the Protocol Agency facility. Call me back once she's in your vehicle and find out if she answers to either Francine or Frankie."

"Yes, sir."

Paul clicked the phone over to Ken. "Meet me at work," he repeated. "Hurry up." He hung up without waiting for a response.

Ten minutes later, his agent called again.

"Do you have her?" He could hear her screaming in the background.

"Yes, sir. She's not answering to Francine or Frankie."

"Ask her if her name is Daphne?"

He heard the question relayed and the screaming stopped, but she didn't answer.

Paul heard the distinct roar of a gunshot. And then another accompanied by the sound of glass shattering. More shots from other weapons in a short volley.

Then the sound of a vehicle squealing away Paul's hands tightened on the steering wheel as his heart pounded. "Hello?"

No answer. Not good. *Fuck.*

"Agent, are you there?"

He thought he heard labored breathing and then what sounded like another vehicle speeding by.

Paul called Ken again. "Where are you?"

"On the road. I'm twenty-five minutes away."

"Shit. Step on it. I think my agents are down. Come to the airport."

In the background over the line, Paul heard Ken turn his sirens on. "I'm weaving and dodging through traffic. I'll be there as fast as I can."

Paul flipped back to the other line. No further response was forthcoming from his agent, but he heard Frankie's voice. Or was she

Daphne? Beyond the distant sounds of another vehicle and Daphne's shrieking protests in the distance, which faded with each second.

The sound of silence liquefied his insides. His speedometer read eighty-one miles per hour. He mashed his foot down on the gas pedal and willed his car to go faster as a useless feeling lodged around his heart. *I'm going to lose my best agent.*

He was way too far away from the airport to help his agents or Frankie. Ken was further away. Or was it Daphne? He didn't know which persona would greet him.

If they even found her alive. *Fuck.*

Five minutes more at his currently dangerous speed.

Paul's gut roiled with dread that he was already too late to save her.

* * * *

Zack was glad he'd called in late so no one would be looking for him right about now, but he reached for his phone to call for backup. He didn't know what was going on with Daphne, but didn't want to face the unknown alone.

He dialed his partner, Colin Riley, but got his message about being gone. *Damn.* Remembering Colin was out for the next week after the birth of his kid, Zack pondered the wisdom of calling his boss Ken Davenport. He pocketed his phone after deciding against it.

Not quite yet.

First, he'd see what was going on. His instincts, already on high alert, told him bad things were going on, but he wanted to be completely sure before calling in the troops.

Daphne was his weekend bed partner, and while she was important to him, she wasn't exactly the best reason to use up any further resources if he'd misinterpreted what he'd seen. Especially reasons that would become public knowledge once all this came to light. And he always had to consider that anything he did might come to light. The words *plausible deniability* rang in his head with a sturdy bong. He still had to explain the Friday night FBI call. Ken would be pissed.

For now, he'd see what he could do on his own without contacting anyone in his chain of command. He turned his phone off and pocketed it.

He slowed his vehicle, noticing that the trees ahead were about to open into a field. Dirty air still filled the space in front of his truck as he crept along the lonely road. His heart pounded with the need to know what was going on and if Daphne was okay.

The dust began to settle the closer he got to the edge of the woods. At the rim of the forest and before he could be spotted by anyone in the other vehicle, Zack slowed his vehicle to a stop, leaned over to open his glove box, and extracted a set of binoculars. He looked through them as the fog of dirt in the air dissipated, watching for any sign that Daphne was with them.

There were two trucks parked in front of a large, corrugated metal outer hangar. A large door, big enough for a plane, was open, and he finally saw two men, different from before, dragging a still violently struggling Daphne inside. The two men at the airport had been in business suits. These guys were dressed in casual clothes. He couldn't hear her, but it looked like she was screaming.

Zack considered his immediate options. Given his skills as an agent, he figured he was already the man they'd send to rescue the hostage in a situation like this. Only this hostage was very important to him personally. There wasn't much he wouldn't do to ensure she was safe. And his time was running out.

Once she was ensconced behind closed hangar doors, too many unpleasant things could happen to her. On a bright note, Zack had already known where this road led and what building he'd see because he'd been here before. To the best of his knowledge, no one knew it. He liked to keep secrets of his own. Ones no one knew about and this was a perfect reason why.

This remote building had two ways in and out. The road he was on was the well-known, airport-maintained road, but Zack knew there was another exit on the opposite side of the hangar. He'd found it by accident once and, in fact, used this very hangar for an effective hideout.

Best of all, he remembered clearly the layout and structure details, including all the building's entrances and exits. He pulled his truck off the road and hid it in the woods. He then circled the edge of the trees on foot, staying hidden from any eyes searching the airport access road. He climbed up the outside fire escape of the hangar's far corner and busted into the office he remembered was used as storage a year ago.

Once inside, he realized nothing had changed. In the corner of the room was a door that led to the utility catwalk, roof access, and, best of all, the large skylight in the center of the largest part of the interior structure. It looked down on the main structure below. He hoped Daphne wasn't tucked away in any of the four offices on the ground floor.

He quietly made his way along the catwalk to the skylight. Wiping away an inch of dirt, Zack peered inside.

Fuck.

Daphne was in the very center of the large space tied down to a chair with her mouth taped shut. Even from up here he could see she was crying. There was no way for him to physically get to her without exposing himself to whoever waited inside.

What were they doing? It almost looked like she was bait for someone.

Who could she possibly be bait for?

Zack wished he'd gotten more information about her life in South Carolina. He wasn't even sure what town she resided in.

After pondering his rock-or-a-hard-place choices, Zack decided to head inside the main part of the building. He could skirt around the edge of the large space, stay to the shadows, and disable any of the three people he knew must be here. Unfortunately, there could be more than three. Two in the vehicle with Daphne and a minimum of one who'd driven the other vehicle parked out front. And any number between one and one thousand more already inside waiting for him to come in, gun blazing, for her rescue.

His only shot was if they weren't expecting him. He made his way down to the ground floor by way of a set of stairs. The exit was in the front corner of the building by the open hangar door. He cracked the heavy fire door open and listened. The first thing he heard was Daphne sobbing, and the sound damn near broke his heart. He wished he could comfort her and promised to do just that as soon as he rescued her from these thugs.

"Stop crying, you stupid bitch." The disembodied voice echoed across the space as Zack quietly sidled through the exit door and on to the main floor of the hangar. He closed it with the utmost care.

The ground floor was mostly dark, which worked in his favor. The skylight above turned out to be the only shaft of light in an otherwise gloomy space beyond the open hangar doors. Zack edged along the side wall away from the hangar doors and his entry point.

Daphne had quieted to a few sniffs and snuffles instead of outright crying.

He followed the sound of her misery. Soon he stood behind several large crates adjacent from where she sat.

Who the *fuck* were they expecting?

"How long before he gets here? Wasn't he following directly behind us on the road?" the voice from before asked. "I expected a gun battle before we even got her inside."

"Shut up. He's a spook. He's probably out doing a quick surveillance of the area for the best way in to rescue his girlfriend. If he isn't already scaling the wall outside to enter quietly through the roof. Mr. V said not to underestimate him."

Zack stopped in mid step. If he didn't know better, he thought they might be talking about him.

"Girlfriend? I thought he was only fucking her for the weekend."

Shit. How did they know he and Daphne spent the weekend together? Zack paused and listened to their conversation. Was Daphne playing a part? Had she told them? If she was in on this scheme, she was the best actress in the world. His gut told him she was innocent. His track record with women notwithstanding, Zack planned to do whatever he could to save her. Regardless of what happened to him.

"Probably, but be prepared for anything. Mr. Valentino said he's trained, but not a planner. Just a grunt. Maybe he'll do us a favor and come on a direct frontal attack. We can just drop him where he stands."

"Can we fuck the girl before we discard her?"

Zack bit back a growl. *Over my dead body.*

That question solidified his speculation of her innocence.

"Maybe. Don't get your hopes up. We likely won't have time after we get rid of the body. Well just dump the two of them together and be done with it like Mr. V wants."

"Mr. V won't care if we sample her."

A door opened slowly to Zack's left at the back of the hangar. The two standing next to Daphne turned and walked away from her.

"Hey," one said, "what are you doing here?"

Zack strained his vision trying to see in the dark.

"I've come to take you in." The familiar sound of the man's voice made Zack relax a notch. He had a friend in the room. Finally, a piece of good news.

The echo of two shots being fired and the subsequent sound of two bodies hitting the cement made Zack decide his bad luck had finally changed.

Gun in hand, Zack dashed into the open, keeping his gun aimed at the approaching figure. He made it to where Daphne was in seconds. He watched the approaching figure and dropped the aim of his gun. An ally was always appreciated.

Zack whipped a small knife out of his pocket and started cutting through Daphne's bonds. She screamed behind her gag and thrashed about.

"It's okay, Daphne. The guys who grabbed you are dead."

She shook her head violently from side to side in the negative, her eyes wild with fear.

He cut through the bonds at her feet and then her hands. She stood and pushed against him as if trying to get him to run. She looked over one shoulder and a little muffled yelp came from behind her gag.

Zack saw his comrade approaching. He carefully removed the duct tape from Daphne's mouth and brushed the tears from her cheek. He kissed her forehead, grateful she hadn't been raped or killed.

Against his throat, she whispered frantically, "Zack, don't trust him. He's not your friend. He's here to kill you. They used me as bait to get you here."

First confusion set in, followed quickly by shock. Zack turned to see a new expression on the face of the man he'd trusted.

"Out of the way, Mahon. She's the one I want, not you." His new nemesis pulled out a wicked-looking needle from his pocket. "I need information. And I will kill you if you try and stop me."

Unsure why the needle particularly bothered him, Zack pushed Daphne behind him even as she squirmed to one side. "Don't, Zack! He'll kill you. He already killed his own men."

Zack looked up into the cold, angry eyes of someone he'd trusted. The barrel of the gun his newly discovered enemy held was leveled directly at the center of Daphne's forehead. His finger moved to the trigger. Zack shoved Daphne away. The muzzle flashed in the next second and everything in Zack's world went black.

* * * *

Daphne watched helplessly as Zack's body crumpled in front of her. Copious amounts of blood poured out of the head wound at his hairline. She fell to the ground and threw herself over his body.

Zack was dead because of her. He'd come to rescue her and someone he trusted had killed him. Because of her.

She couldn't come to terms with the senseless loss. The weekend they'd just shared had been amazing. She loved him. He was perfect. She should have agreed to meet him again instead of walking away.

Daphne suddenly heard screaming and realized it was her own voice. "Zack!" She shrieked his name over and over.

The murderer behind her didn't say a word. She wasn't even sure he was still back there. When a gun barrel nudged the back of her head, Daphne decided quickly that she relished the idea of being dead. She didn't deserve to keep living after causing her lover's death. And she did love him.

The sound of a siren close by registered along with the sound of gravel flying. Someone was coming to rescue them. But it was too late.

She heard the man behind her curse beneath his breath, and the gun was removed from her scalp.

Daphne scooted next to Zack's body, cradled his head in her lap, and alternately screamed and cursed the world for causing her to lose Zack.

Sometime later, several men entered the large space, but she tuned them out and hugged Zack tighter. When someone tried to part her from him, she reacted violently, thrashing and trying to strike out at those who'd arrived too late to help.

She registered a needle being thrust into her arm, and soon everything went fuzzy around the edges. She retreated into a safe part of her mind where she couldn't be hurt. Where Zack still lived in her memories. It wasn't the first time she'd hid out here. She'd spent a considerable amount of time in this place in her childhood as bad things around her happened.

Zack was dead, and she didn't care about living anymore. The drug finally kicked in, and the black curtain of unconsciousness descended. She sank to her knees.

Two concerned-looking men she didn't recognize held her and kept her from hitting the cement floor. The last vision she registered was Zack's lifeless body being loaded onto the stretcher.

She closed her eyes and prayed for her own death.

* * * *

Paul looked out on the roof of the building and did something he hadn't done in over ten years. He lit a cigarette. The acrid burn of smoke stinging his lungs only made him feel worse. After the single drag to light it, he dropped the butt on the roof and pressed the orange glowing end with the toe of his shoe. Lapsing into bad habits wasn't going to solve his current problems. He pocketed his old lighter and waited for news.

Behind him, the door to the roof squealed open. Paul looked as Ken appeared in the doorway, then turned away. The somber expression on his face wasn't reassuring. Apparently, the news was bad.

Paul spoke first. "How is Zack?"

Ken strolled over to where Paul waited next to the edge of the roof line barrier. "They removed the bullet without causing further damage but had to put him in a coma until the trajectory trauma to his brain heals. The doctors say his odds are about fifty-fifty for now."

"Sorry about your agent."

"Me, too. What about yours? When will Frankie wake up?"

Paul released a long, frustrated sigh. "Don't know. They can't get her alter ego, Daphne, to stop screaming long enough to change her over to Frankie. We had to sedate her at the airport to keep her from screaming the airplanes out of the sky as she clung to Zack. We couldn't even get her to let go of him until she was unconscious. Now she's awake but completely catatonic. Like the lights are on but nobody's home. We still have no idea what happened or why they were together."

"I'm sorry."

"Me, too." Paul turned to Ken. "I'd like to find out what happened to sideline two of our best agents. Off duty, no less. "

"Agreed. It's left to us to sort this disaster out sans witnesses."

"Apparently."

"Whatever it takes, you have my cooperation and resources." Ken didn't often take second place in any competition, so Paul was touched that he acquiesced power in this matter.

"Thanks. We should combine forces."

"Fine. Let's get to work. What do we know?"

"We found Benny, Daphne's civilian boss, stuffed in the trunk of his own car, dead. We have no idea why he sent Daphne out of state to DC."

Ken nodded. "I have a friend at the bank. He sent me some interesting video. Our agents met at the bank. No sound on the feed, but it looks like they are friendly. They left the bank together. Given the phone conversation the FBI recorded a few minutes later, I wonder if they simply went on a date. Perhaps Zack is the old college friend she told her aunt about to alleviate her worry."

Paul shook his head. "That would be out of character for Daphne, but then again, leaving the state is also out of character. And the actions of the agent posing as her "aunt" are suspect, as well. She was left behind with signs that someone drugged her. She has limited memory of the past week and no clue why Daphne left the state. I don't know who did it or why. Something isn't right, but I can't prove anything more nefarious than simple trip to put something in Benny's out of state safety deposit box."

Ken rubbed a hand across his eyes. "Unfortunately, we may have to wait until one of them wakes up to find out what really happened."

"Not my first choice."

"Me, either. Any ideas on where to get more information?"

Paul turned to Ken. He looked as tired as Paul felt. "One of the bad guys that got shot, and left behind in the airplane hangar, isn't dead."

"Can we question him or, better yet, beat a confession out of him?"

Paul smiled, agreeing with the sentiment. "He's in a coma. No wallet. No identification whatsoever. His prints do not come up on any database we've put it through. There is a large square scar on his left forearm. We're guessing he had a tattoo removed. I sent a tech to scan it and see if he can find out what used to be there. It's a miniscule lead at best, but pretty much all we have now. The other dead body also had no identification or any way to trace who he is."

Ken crossed his arms. "And the vehicle you saw drive away?"
"Stolen the night before from a used car lot a block from the bank. Dumped three miles away from the municipal airport at the side of a road fifty feet from the interstate. No traffic cameras in place at that feeder lane to the highway, so that's a fucking dead end, too."

"Anyone caught in the bank robbery yet?"

"Nope. They don't even have any suspects to my knowledge. The local cops have deduced the intruders must have had inside help, but they can't find out which of their longtime bonded employees was involved. The bank's assistant manager Edna Hodge was suspected at first, but she came back to work. As a matter of fact, no one failed to show up for work by Monday after the robbery. No one is suddenly spending inordinate amounts of money. And even after a week of intense questioning, no one has broken."

Paul heaved a long sigh. "So basically, we've got two agents down and complete shit for information as to the reason why."

"Precisely."

"I hate this fucking case."

"Me, too."

Chapter Nine

Three months later

The strident ringing, which brought Paul out of a rare deep sleep, had him fumbling for his phone in the dark. The fuzzy red numbers on his clock signaling the wee hours of the morning gave him a quick pounding headache.

Usually, a phone call between the hours of midnight and five in the morning meant the caller likely wouldn't have good news. Paul took a deep breath, closed his eyes again to temper the ache in his head, and pushed the button on his phone to speak.

"Yes."

"Sir. It's Dr. Denton. I have bad news." Of course it was bad news. As only an early morning call can possibly deliver.

"What is it?"

"There's been an explosion in the medical wing."

Paul sat up in bed, ignoring the sharp pain between his temples. "What happened? Accidental or deliberate?"

"The firefighters on scene haven't determined the cause. They are still trying to get all the patients out of the place."

"Any casualties?"

"Not so far, but still we're pulling people out of the rubble of the blast area."

"And Frankie?" Paul held his breath.

"She's already been pulled from the debris of her room. She was closest to the explosion, but she's alive."

"How bad are her injuries?"

"She has a head wound and is unconscious. It's possible she has a concussion. We'll know more after she's assessed. I called to tell you that we've already sent her by ambulance to the alternate off-site facility for treatment."

"Which one?"

He didn't really need to ask. Fatigue must still be a major player in his movements. As expected, Denton reported that Frankie was at Saint Margaret's. It was the only other hospital with a classified wing for government agents and routinely used for backup in overflow events like this one. It was the only other place Frankie *could* go for emergency medical treatment.

"I'm on my way."

The more disturbing question had to do with what caused the explosion. Was Frankie the target? Perhaps he needed to step up his efforts on that front.

Paul dialed Ken Davenport's private cellular phone number as he exited his home heading for the hospital.

"Where are you?" he asked the moment Ken answered.

There was a short pause. "Why?"

"Something's happened at the hospital."

There was another pause before Ken responded. "Really? What happened?"

"An explosion. Someone may have tried to take out my agent, but they failed. Meet me at Saint Margaret's."

"All right. I'll get there as soon as I can."

Ken's tone sounded odd, but Paul didn't take the time to figure it out.

* * * *

Frankie's eyes opened slowly to see Paul Kelly hovering over her bed like some dark, displaced, avenging archangel ready to exact retribution for she knew not what crime. Shifting in bed and testing her muscles was an exercise in pain awareness. She felt like crap. Every part of her body ached as if she'd fallen off a cliff or perhaps climbed one and then taken a header down it.

"Where am I?" she croaked, only didn't expect to sound so horrible.

"Hospital."

Squinting against the brightness of the florescent lights above Paul's head, she brought up her fingers for a shield and asked, "Accident?"

"No. You're hurt. And it was on purpose."

"From what?"

He paused as if considering whether to tell her. Finally a two-word answer came from him. "Bomb blast."

"Bomb blast?" Her eyes narrowed again. "I don't remember anything."

"Unfortunate. What's the last thing you *do* remember?"

"Heading for the medical lab and my two weeks off for hand-to-hand combat training."

Paul looked surprised. "You don't remember leaving the building?"

She searched her memory, but came up blank. She shook her head and tried without success not to be alarmed at the devastated expression on his face. "No. How long have I been out?"

"For several weeks that we know of, and you've been in a coma. Before that you were AWOL."

"What! Where was I?" Frankie sat up in bed, but her stomach lurched at the effort. She swallowed bile. She clamped a hand over her mouth, closed her eyes, and tried to settle her stomach.

"It's unclear." With hands on her shoulders, Paul pushed her gently back down on the bed. "Relax. We can talk about all of this when you've recovered."

She inhaled and exhaled a few times, calmed down considerably, and said, "I'm ready."

"You need at least another month minimum to recuperate before we can put you in a wheelchair, let alone back in the field. The doctors say it's a miracle you're even alive. Settle down. Take advantage of some quiet time and rest up. You're going to need it. I believe the bomb was set to kill you since it was so close to your room. It's a goddamned miracle you're alive, Frankie."

"Who set the bomb?"

He shrugged. "Don't know."

"Where was I found before that?"

"Someone found you off-site."

"Where?"

"A small municipal airport just outside of Washington, DC."

"Why was I there?"

"Good question. Do you remember the last conversation we had before you left the Protocol Agency building?"

Frankie closed her eyes against the piercing light, hoping shutting it out would help her think better. Through the thick bog of her memories, the word "traitor" surfaced. Her eyes snapped open to bore a gaze through Paul's arctic blue one. "Yes. I do. You wanted me to look for someone. A possible traitor."

Paul looked relieved, but just as quickly his eyebrows narrowed sternly. "Did you start looking for that *bad* someone before I authorized you to do so?"

It sounded exactly like something she'd do, but Frankie couldn't remember for certain what she'd done. "I don't think so. But my memory is like a large, churning fog bank, and it won't dissipate right now."

"Once you're back to normal, I'm pairing you with a new special partner. You haven't had a formal one since Rachel over a year ago, but I think it's wise right now."

"I don't need a new partner, special or otherwise."

"Apparently, you do." His eyebrows rose alarmingly high.

"You know it's hard for me to trust anyone. Rachel was unique."

"Yes. I know. And yet I insist. You need a dedicated backup."

"Who's going to back me up? I don't need to be training a new Protocol agent while I tackle some faceless evil entity." The faces of a few other Protocol agents flashed in her mind. They were all good agents, but she liked working alone. No one to let you down that way.

Frankie's former partner, Rachel, had been a good egg, but medical problems sidelined her career in the Protocol Agency. It wasn't common knowledge, but Rachel was Paul's niece. She and Rachel had shared a great working relationship once upon a time. Frankie hadn't wanted anyone else as a partner after Rachel had retired from the Protocol program.

"You need some muscle for this particular mission. I've selected someone outside our group for your escort."

"A thug to trail along behind me? No thanks."

Paul rolled his eyes. "Not a thug, just another agent in a different group. I don't know that I trust pairing you with anyone in *our* group just now given how my gut is churning. While I still don't have any evidence, I believe there is someone out to bring the Protocol Agency down. Or perhaps they'll be satisfied with simply killing off all my agents. I'd really rather avoid that. So you get someone to back you up, and that's final."

Frankie nodded. "Fine. Who is it?"

"Don't worry about it. You have a ways to go before any field assignment is handed out."

She slowly sat up in bed, taking care not to rock her unsteady stomach. "Tell me, or I get up and start on my own without an official one."

Paul's eyes narrowed. "Jesus, you're so contrary. I can see some things never change."

She pierced him with an intense stare. "And you like me that way. Name the partner."

"Fine. Do you remember Zack Mahon? He's in Ken Davenport's group. We worked with them in Las Vegas just before Rachel retired."

Zack Mahon. Now there was an unexpected blast from her past.

Fog bank memory or not, what Frankie remembered about Zack Mahon was his voice and that during that Las Vegas assignment he'd been suggestively sexy and intriguing. They'd never met in person, but she'd seen pictures and video of him in action. Beyond the sexual overtones that might crop up between them, he'd be perfect. Likely Paul had already made up his mind anyway.

Averting her gaze, she plucked at the blanket covering her. "I guess he'll do."

Paul lowered his face to hers and fixed his gaze directly on her. The weary look in his expression gave her pause. She hadn't seen him so upset since Rachel had been kidnapped on her final mission before leaving the Protocol Agency. He rubbed his eyes one-handed and pinched the bridge of his nose. After the ritual of his face massage, he spoke, "Don't get up from this bed until the doctors give you the go-ahead."

"Why are you so distraught about this?"

"Besides the fact that before someone tried to blow you to kingdom come, you'd been comatose for over three months, and that delightful experience came after I found you in some strange municipal airport bleeding out? No reason."

Frankie relaxed a notch. Her boss had been worried about her. She wished she had any inkling of memory regarding what he talked about, but she didn't. She opted to soften his anger. "Watch it, Paul. I might get the idea that you care about me or something."

He shook his head and looked away. "I thought you were dead or as good as dead," he murmured.

"Don't cry. I'm fine."

He huffed. "It's not that. Do you know how much time and money has been invested in your training? A lot. I'd hate to waste it." His expression relaxed for the first time since he entered her room.

"Ah. That's so sweet. Admit it. Secretly, you like me, don't you?"

He shook his head and rolled his eyes, but she could tell he had been seriously worried about her impaired condition and was relieved she was almost back in business.

"We'll speak soon, but in the meantime, rest up and get ready to work."

"The second the medicos release me, I want you to bring me up to date."

Paul nodded. "I'll also have your muscle brought up to speed on what little we know."

"Swell. Just make sure he understands that during the coming mission, he works for me, not the other way around."

Paul rolled his eyes again. "You two will have to hash that out. He's your security detail. Someone wanted you dead. They've made more than one attempt. I want to know why. There may be times when you have to listen to him because his job is to keep you alive." He clapped his hands together like a kindergarten teacher about to announce recess. "I know! Why don't you two work together? Do you think you could manage that without coming to blows?"

"Your sarcasm is annoying, Paul."

"Regardless, stay safe. Let him do his job and keep you alive as you *both* investigate this issue." There was something in his eyes that gave her the impression he hadn't told her everything, but what he'd given was plenty. She put her mind on trying to remember the lost time he spoke of. An airport warehouse? A bombing at the hospital she lay comatose in? Why couldn't she summon even the least minor detail about either place?

"I want to hear you say you agree to let him protect you as the two of you work together to solve the mystery of who's out to get you."

"Fine. He can be my protection detail and backup," Frankie said. The problem wasn't going to be sharing an investigation. Likely shielding her inappropriate feelings and keeping her hands off of him would be the more difficult aspect of their assignment.

* * * *

In the conference room where she'd once met and ultimately worked with Colin Riley, Zack's regular covert partner, she now came face to face with the man himself, Zack Mahon. Until now, they'd never formally met. She'd only spoken to him over a microphone connection in Las Vegas.

The distinctive tone still echoed in her mind all these months later. Zack's voice was a deep, rich baritone, slightly guttural and laced with lots of attitude.

Zack was a man she'd thought about once or twice since they'd worked together back then. She'd seen pictures of him, and she'd watched him on various monitors during that field operation from long ago.

After the Las Vegas op, she read his redacted file, but seeing him up close and in the flesh made her heart pound wildly in her chest. She resisted the urge to put a hand over her heart to keep from exiting her body through her rib cage.

This was not the way she wanted to start this mission with him. She also had a new private mission, keep her emotions bottled up and buried deeply.

The photos she'd studied carefully from all angles didn't come close to doing him justice. He was well over six feet. His file said by four inches, but in boots he was likely six and a half feet of pure masculinity poured into jungle fatigues.

Close-cropped military style hair only added to his badass posture and stance, which was currently filled with even more attitude. Not to mention that he smelled like sex and sin and someone she should avoid close contact with before he and anyone within five feet realized how attracted to him she was.

The curve of his mouth, the I-want-to-fuck-you-long-and-hard gaze of his bedroom brown eyes and his overall well-developed, body made for a mouthwatering package. Frankie hadn't even been formally introduced, and she was already glad to make his acquaintance.

Paul's introduction was short and sweet. "Zack, meet Frankie. Frankie, meet Zack. Now, let's get to work."

The wicked smile playing around his lips made her recall what he'd told Colin in Las Vegas when he thought she wasn't listening. *"I like her voice. Makes my dick get hard."*

He didn't repeat that inappropriate statement, but she felt the seductive pulse of it in the tone he used when he said, "Good to *finally* meet you, Frankie."

Instead of sticking her hand out, she answered with a single curt nod, not trusting her voice. She certainly didn't need to squeak out a greeting in an utterly weak, feminine way. More than that, she knew she shouldn't touch him. She was close enough to smell his male scent, and it was driving her libido into the red zone.

Reading between the lines in his limited file, he likely wouldn't appreciate any girly, love-tainted overtures anyway. It seemed that Zack didn't like working with female partners. Not difficult to understand, as his past was littered with incidents where several fellow female operatives hadn't been able to resist his charms after the liaison was over. Or understand his attention span was short when it came to permanent relationships.

But Frankie understood. If she got the chance, she'd certainly take advantage, but she'd never chuck her career for a love life, even if a certain man was yummy beyond all words. Perhaps she'd show Zack that she was a woman he could trust not to cling on like a leech after a little fun in the sack. Perhaps he'd be so enthralled that he'd beg *her* for a permanent relationship. That unlikely event made her smile.

Back in Las Vegas she'd teased him. Today, she hoped he'd forgotten their little sexually charged conversation.

One glance at his eyes said he hadn't. The fact that Zack kept looking at her as if memorizing every detail of her body made her wonder if working with him was a good idea. She hadn't been with a man in a long while. Even before the recent hospitalization. The initiating incident of which she didn't remember.

Zack had recently recovered from an injury, as well. She noted the one-inch scar at his hairline, and a sliver of appreciation slid into her mind. He was a survivor. So was she. Maybe they *would* work well together.

Having a man protect her was something that would be difficult to get used to under normal circumstances. However, these were not normal circumstances, and she didn't kid herself about the idea that someone wanted her dead. Not to mention that having Zack close during this mission would have other benefits.

Not that in the field she would act on any sexual urges that might endanger her mission. She was a professional. She'd wait until a quiet time to act on her inappropriate feelings. Zack's file indicated he was also a "get down to business and no screwing around" kind of warrior. It was a code of conduct she appreciated.

The true test would be in not going all girly when he looked at her. A glance in his direction and her mouth went dry.

God help her, she was getting wet from Zack's intense gaze. Paul sat down and motioned that they each do the same. Ken Davenport seated himself next to Zack.

"Let's get started. Here is what we know." Paul rattled on, presenting the information they'd gathered while she'd been hospitalized. She already had it memorized. She knew where she wanted to start.

Frankie's mouth had opened because she assumed her boss would naturally ask for her opinion initially. That was her first mistake.

"Any thoughts on how you'd like to proceed, Mr. Mahon." Her second mistake was shifting her gaze to Zack as he spoke. "I've studied the available information, which is slim to practically nonexistent. The tattoo removed from the arm of the man who survived the shoot-out in DC was identified as Blood Wrath, a gang of thugs currently located in Brazil. I believe we need to go undercover together in Brazil.

"The purported leader of Blood Wrath is a man affiliated with the owner of the Brazil's Best hotel chain. A hotel there would be a good place to put our base of operations. From there we can search the city for other members of the gang or anyone with critical information." His smile for Frankie was slow and seductive. "Since Brazil's Best is exclusively a honeymoon retreat and anniversary hideaway for wedded couples who are also ultra wealthy, I guess you and I are about to get married and pose as a filthy rich couple."

"What do you think, Frankie?"

She was focused so intently on Zack's mouth as he spoke that she almost faltered when Paul finally called on her. She was grateful that her voice didn't quiver when she said, "I'm fine with starting there. We also need to consider spending some quality time with the remaining members of Blood Wrath's group in our overall plans. Also, will we have a local contact in the city?"

"Yes. But only for general information and not as backup. You'll be mostly on your own. Fitting for a newly married couple, I guess."

Whew. Was it getting hot in here? Her traitorous eyes slid to Zack when Paul mentioned them being on their own. The slight curve of his lips signaled that he either saw her staring or was amused by the thought of the two of them holed up in a honeymoon suite for the duration of their stay in Brazil.

Either way, she had made her own plans. She wasn't above getting a little action as long as the assignment wasn't compromised. Her only caution was not wanting him to follow her afterward demanding anything more permanent than whatever time they could carve out in the quiet spaces of their imminent mission.

Frankie was a realist, and she mostly liked a singular existence. She was a loner by nature and had been all of her life. While Zack did wild and erotic things to her libido, she wasn't ever going to want to settle down.

But a temporary situation might be in order. A quickie to take the edge off of her lust. While it was often difficult to determine any man's skills in bed beforehand, Frankie had a strong feeling that Zack was well-versed in the subject.

After this job, she planned to ask him if he wanted to roll around in the sheets with her for a weekend or two. In the meantime, she'd do her best to maintain a strict hands-off policy. Unless, of course, it wouldn't jeopardize the mission. Her libido was about to go to war with her professional ethics. She didn't need the distraction during this crucial task of finding the traitor in the Protocol agency, but if the opportunity came up, pun intended, Frankie planned to take advantage of it.

* * * *

Zack Mahon did his best not to stare openly at his new partner, Frankie, temporary though she may be. His regular partner Colin was on family medical leave because his wife, Laurie, had just had twins.

Frankie was beautiful, in a no-nonsense way. Usually Zack avoided work relationships like the proverbial plague and didn't expect anything to happen, but she was nice on the eyes.

A tingle at his hairline from his newest scar distracted his thoughts from Frankie's lush figure and back on the case at hand.

A month ago, Frankie had been in a coma, until a bomb blast at the long-term facility where she was staying woke her up. Zack wasn't supposed to have this classified information, but his boss, Ken Davenport, felt it was necessary, given that he and Frankie were about to embark on a mission to find out who set the bomb, along with the identity of the man who'd shot him in the head three months before that.

How the two agencies, his and Frankie's, knew the incidents were connected was unclear. Perhaps Paul and Ken suspected but weren't sharing the information without corroboration.

The thing was, Frankie had been in the abandoned aircraft hangar when Zack was shot. He didn't remember her from that weekend. Didn't remember being in a gun battle the hangar. What was also unclear was why she'd been in a coma. No gunshot wounds had been mentioned in the report he read, and it was insinuated that she'd had some sort of mental break, but Zack wasn't supposed to know anything about that either.

Zack wished he could remember how he ended up crumpled in the deserted hangar of a small municipal airport bleeding out from a head wound, but even after all the physical and psychological therapy, there was no memory. Nothing at all, not even a glimmer.

It was assumed by Frankie's boss, Paul Kelly, that the culprit was after her and Zack somehow got in the way. Perhaps he'd heard her voice and tried to intervene.

The miracle of her survival from the bomb blast apparently gave her the impetus and the verve to search out whomever had tried to do her in. Paul expected him to be her muscle during their time together. He suspected Frankie didn't want him for anything more than a driver. She was in for a surprise. He wasn't trained as a chauffeur. He was trained as a spy. She'd learn soon enough not to treat him like the hired help.

Chapter Ten

"Did you have anything to do with assignments?" Frankie practically yelled over her shoulder once they were all alone. They'd retreated to a quiet out-of-the-way place in their building after being dismissed to go on their mission.

Zack kept his voice controlled and answered, "No. Did you?"

She whirled around and pegged him with an angry gaze. "If I'd had my way, I'd be alone right now."

"Ditto, sweetheart. I hate breaking in new partners."

Her eyebrows rose in obvious surprise. "Trust me, I don't need breaking in. Especially not by you."

Zack grinned, but remained quiet. He'd love to break her in all right. But not in the way she might imagine. Undercover work, like what they both did for different agencies, was risky, and it was usually a bad idea to mix business with pleasure.

But with her, he might make an exception. Scoffing at the idea of sleeping with his partner, Zack tried to get his head back in the game. "Seeing as how we'd both rather be on our own for this assignment, why don't we initiate a truce right up front."

Her expression softened. "A truce, huh?"

"Yeah, you know, we both promise to play nice until the end of the mission, get the job done, put the bad guy in jail or into the ground, ladies' choice, and then part ways with no bloodshed between the two of us."

"Intriguing idea. I'll think about it." She allowed the barest of smiles to shape her lush lips. "In the meantime, when we get to the hotel, try not to slobber all over me."

"Ditto, sweetheart."

She rolled her eyes.

They headed for the airport and the next available flight to Brazil. Talking tactics and strategies on the way had led to a rocky start. The first disagreement had been over who would drive to their "fake" honeymoon hotel once they got to Brazil. Zack had insisted that as her new "lord and master," he was driving and she could learn to be happy about it.

She disagreed. Vehemently. He'd only been half kidding, but didn't like women bossing him around as a rule. Frankie interested him quite a bit, although he was loathe to admit it. It was something about her voice that turned him inside out and had from the first time he'd ever heard it back in Las Vegas.

She released a long sigh and mumbled something about, "Arrogance in the male species."

After a short, tense discussion, Frankie came up with an agreeable alternative solution, and they warily reinstated their truce.

As honeymooners, they both agreed on first class tickets. Seated in the private lounge awaiting their flight, they continued their discussion.

"Once we're in the room, we can contact our respective agencies and make our next move."

Frankie pushed out a sigh. "Unless the room is bugged. I have information which suggests this hotel isn't exactly a spy's best friend. We'll have to do a discreet search once we're inside."

"And in the meantime we have to pretend to be on our honeymoon. We should start now. Think you can resurrect a smile to direct my way when others are watching? I'd hate to be found out as a covert operative on our first day in Brazil because you keep shooting daggers at my head when I'm not looking."

"I'll be fine. Every spy goes through liar's training. Don't you worry about me." She winked at him. They stood by a bank of windows facing the tarmac as their plane fueled. They were early for their flight, and no one else was in the lounge with them.

"We need to practice being a couple. Let's kiss."

"What?" Frankie's eyebrows went straight to her hairline.

He leaned closer and cupped his hands to her face gently. Her whole body went rigid the moment he touched her. "Let's practice once, shall we? I need to know you're ready for this mission. And loosen up for Christ's sake. We need to be okay with touching each other in the public eye, don't you think?"

She nodded, and her whole body visibly relaxed. "Yes. You're absolutely right."

Zack moved his mouth forward to capture hers in a kiss. He started out very chaste and moved quickly to devour mode. He pushed his tongue inside her warm mouth and curled it around her tongue. She tasted like cinnamon gum.

Frankie didn't stop him from french kissing her or tighten her body up and act like he was violating her. In fact, she practically climbed up his chest the moment he ramped up the level of their intimate embrace.

His cock woke up thirty seconds into the riotous kiss, and if he didn't stop it soon, she'd know he was impacted by this dare. Her hand curled around his neck and pulled him even tighter against her body as the kiss went volcanic with heat.

Frankie's hips pushed forward so far he knew she felt his hard cock digging into her belly. He didn't care. He was a guy. She had to know that's what guys did. A guy's cock was going to get hard when an attractive woman shoved her tongue between his lips and ground her crotch against his growing erection. If she was upset about his physical response to their kiss, she didn't show it. Instead, she moaned into his mouth, shifted her hips against his groin. His cock went to full staff in a heartbeat.

Zack finally broke the kiss and realized he was panting. So was she. "Did you want something else?"

She grinned. "Like what?"

He grabbed her hand, placed it on his lap and wrapped it around his fully erect cock. "Something like this."

Frankie laughed and squeezed his cock through his trouser pants. "Well, it's very impressive. I'm so glad I married a man with a big cock."

Zack's dick throbbed in her hand as she spoke. "You are playing with fire, woman."

She leaned forward and licked his bottom lip. "And you started this. If you want to finish it, I'm not opposed, but not until the job is done. And don't get any permanent ideas regarding us. Once we fulfill our mission, and whatever else happens between us, I don't want you chasing me."

"Ditto, sweetheart. I haven't had much luck with women walking away from me after we've been intimate. Maybe it's because my cock's so big."

She smiled and kissed him again. "Probably true. Once they've tasted you they become ruined for anyone else. They say size doesn't matter, but it's a big fat lie. So have you ruined lots of women, Zack?"

He laughed out loud. She was playing with him. And more shocking than that, he liked it. "I like you, Frankie. I think this mission is going to go a lot better than I initially thought."

"Because both of us are all about the job and not about settling down to play house and raise babies?"

"Exactly." Zack thought about his partner, who'd recently gone the way of the family life. Colin seemed pretty happy about it, though. Now that he had kids, his immersion into the American dream was complete.

Zack, however, had never wanted that life. It wasn't that he didn't like kids or was against marriage, it was just that he didn't want any of his own or to be tied down. Best-case scenario, he'd find a woman in his same occupation who didn't want any children and they'd spend the rest of their lives fighting bad guys. Frankie was the first contender he'd ever considered seriously.

His gaze centered on her promptly when she squeezed his cock again. "One other question."

He nodded, wondering if his eyes were glazed over in pleasure.

"Do you know what else women like in bed besides a big cock between their thighs?"

He shrugged. "I'm assuming you want me to say orgasms. And yes, I know all about how to bring you off. No worries there, princess. I won't let you leave my bed unsatisfied."

This time her eyes glazed over. She pressed her lips to his once more and dipped her tongue inside for a small taste. Before extracting her luscious body from his, she murmured, "And I wouldn't ever think of letting you leave my bed unsatisfied, in case you wondered."

"I have not a doubt." He grinned as he watched her decidedly gorgeous ass walk across the private lounge to a loveseat. She motioned for him to join her there.

Zack grinned again and followed her. This promised to be a mission to remember.

* * * *

Truce firmly in place, Zack and Frankie departed the Brazilian airport with a hired driver to quell the argument of who drove. Well-documented and rehearsed cover stories securely in place, their plan was fairly simple. Register at the hotel as a newly married couple, entrench themselves in the large honeymoon suite they'd secured, and sneak out at night to rendezvous with their respective contacts and hunt down any and all information about the man associated with the Blood Wrath tattoo and any of his criminal affiliations.

They each had a contact here. Hers, she wouldn't share, and his was likely not to be too much help in their quest regardless of if he shared the name.

Local drug dealers didn't traffic in espionage, but perhaps they had extraneous information that would be helpful. He didn't hold his breath, though.

Zack hadn't been here in quite awhile, so along with trying to keep his hands off of Frankie, he needed to acclimate to the environment. The weather, first and foremost, was hotter and wetter, and didn't help take his mind off Frankie at all.

This time, instead of being a grungy gringo drug runner, he was a yuppie newlywed. Same dangers, better accessories. The first better accessory was the plush hotel, the second better clothing, the third...

"Will you get my satchel, darling?"

...was a more attractive partner.

Frankie's sultry voice intruded on his trip down memory lane. The limo had stopped in front of the luxury hotel amidst palm trees and lush tropical vegetation. The scent of loamy earth and exotic flowers hung in the air like an invisible fragrant haze.

"Yep." She opened the door and exited before he even unbuckled his seat belt. Time to rock and roll on this adventure.

Zack exited the limo slowly and took the time to carefully stare at his new *bride*. She was like sex on a stick. Her clothing a wispy confection of see-through fabric over a skimpy bikini and high-heeled sandals giving her enough height to reach his shoulder. He liked that she wasn't too short.

Deciding to set the mood and get this honeymoon started off right, Zack hooked his hand around her hip and pulled her in tight to his body. To her credit, she didn't resist in the least. Instead, he was gifted with her lyrical laughter. Zack slipped his other arm around her neck, anchoring her to his body securely.

The trace of what looked like a genuine grin on her lips, Frankie stared deeply into his eyes. He lowered his mouth and kissed her. He only planned on a peck, but she had other ideas. Her arms circled his neck. She leaned heavily into him, slanted her mouth across his, and slipped her soft tongue into his mouth. Surprised not only by her overture, but by the way their lips seemed to know exactly what to do,

Zack tightened his grip and ramped the kiss up a notch by licking his way aggressively into the soft warmth of her mouth. They'd only kissed that one other time, but it was as if he'd tasted her before. Odd.

Frankie's soft moan caught him off guard, and the intoxicating taste of her lips sent a frantic pulse straight to his cock. And he'd just gotten the unruly beast to calm down before leaving the vehicle from snuggling next to her there. Damn.

Beside the open door of the limo, the driver started stacking up their luggage, discreetly ignoring their passionate embrace.

Zack hugged Frankie as the kiss continued and wondered why this felt so achingly familiar. A stray thought drifted across his conscience. *Shower sex.* And just as quickly, he snapped out of his lustful reverie. Abruptly, he broke the kiss, unwilling to admit that Frankie touched him on some level he thought long dead. Desire with the intent to pursue.

Why would he ever pursue a fellow agent? He wouldn't. He'd learned that abhorrent lesson long ago. But there was something elusive about his "bride" that touched him on a visceral level. Something he couldn't explain or deny.

He wanted her.

And for much more than just this mission.

The more time he spent with her, the more devastating his need became. He stopped the urge to bet with himself about how long they'd be here before he could seduce her.

* * * *

By the time they got checked into their Brazil's Best hotel suite, the sun was already setting. Frankie knew they'd likely stay in the room all night. They were pretending to be newlyweds, after all.

The door to the lavish honeymoon suite closed behind them after the porter deposited their luggage in the beautiful foyer.

Marble floors beneath their feet in the entryway led down a long hall and into the living area. The elegantly furnished room opened to cathedral ceilings. Two steps into the room, Frankie's feet sunk almost to her ankles in the lush carpet.

No expense had been spared. Every fabric and piece of furniture in the room was of the highest quality in an understated blue and tan tropical design.

"I love this room," Frankie proclaimed in an overloud voice.

Zack laughed boisterously as he silently retrieved something from his luggage. He walked around the perimeter of the large space, presumably checking for listening devices, as Frankie followed behind and commented on each and every detail in the suite.

After a full circle of the room, he held up three fingers and pointed to a picture frame and two light fixtures.

"I'm really only interested in the bedroom," Zack said in a low sexy tone. He winked at her. "Why don't we go check *that* out?"

"Of course, darling." Frankie led the way this time.

Not surprisingly, the bed was the focal point in the adjoining room. What looked like a hundred yards of sheer, white, diaphanous fabric was generously draped over all four sides of a dark wood four poster sleigh bed.

The tropical design carried into this room as well, but didn't overwhelm. A ribbon of different sized hearts was carved into both the head and foot boards of the massive bed. Satiny bedding the color of pale peaches graced the mattress.

Frankie wasn't lying when she said, "Wow. This is really beautiful."

"I agree," Zack added. But when Frankie turned to look at him, he was looking at her and not the bed. The man had a sultry gaze that could start a blazing fire in a deep freezer. They held the stare for several long seconds before he broke it and continued looking for any more intrusion devices.

He circled the room with his detector and found a single audio bug in the lamp on the nightstand.

The bathroom was next. After a thorough search, Zack didn't find any bugs in there. Thankfully, they'd have one refuge for whispering their mission plans.

"I'm going to go freshen up, darling," Frankie said.

"I'll help you." Zack shut them into the bathroom and turned both the shower and sink faucets on.

"We should be okay even if water isn't running," he whispered. "But after we leave this bathroom, we have to take care with what we say."

"Got it. And we should probably to pretend to have sex tonight, right? I mean we are on our honeymoon."

Zack's eyes slid shut, but he nodded once. Frankie decided that the torture of pretending to have sex with him might kill her. Maybe if they hurried through a sexual performance, it wouldn't be so bad. "How do you feel about a couple rounds of 'slam-bam-thank you-ma'am' tonight?"

"Not really my style, but for the purposes of our cover, that will likely work better."

"Let's go get it over with then." Frankie, resigned to her fate of no satisfaction for this evening, promptly turned away and headed to the door.

Zack grabbed her shoulder. "Don't be so bad-tempered about it."

Frankie turned to him. "I'm not. I'm being professional. There will be no distracting sexual engagements for us until our mission is complete, agreed?"

Zack pushed out a long sigh, but then nodded. "Agreed."

Frankie got flat on her back in the center of the bed. Zack pressed his muscular hot body over hers. For the next thirty minutes, they bounced on the bed springs and gave any listeners a winning performance of their pretend sex life. Frankie was about to explode with unrelenting lust after the first five minutes.

A granite hard body complete with Zack's stiff cock pressing into her belly repeatedly made Frankie glad they planned a tryst after this mission. She hoped she could last.

After two rounds of loud screamer sex, Zack and Frankie said their good nights and shut the light off.

They waited a few minutes together. Then Frankie grabbed her cell phone and headed into the bathroom wishing for things she didn't have time for right now.

Zack followed her in and closed the door. He checked the space with the bug sweeper once more, as she held her breath to keep quiet.

He shrugged and whispered, "Maybe they don't put them in here because of the moisture."

"Lucky break for us."

"Yeah. Lucky." But he didn't sound happy about it.

Frankie reached out and stroked his face. "We deserve at least a good night kiss. I'm game if you are."

She barely got those few words out before he closed the short distance between them and plastered his sexy lips across hers. The sensuous slide of his mouth sent her heart rate skyward. Her wobbly knees almost caused her to collapse when his tongue breached her lips.

The kiss seemed to go on forever. Zack's hand slid to cover one breast. Her nipple pebbled in his hand as if he'd commanded it. Losing herself in this sultry embrace was far too easy.

She moaned into his mouth, and the intensity of the kiss ratcheted up another notch. She wanted to have sex with Zack with every fiber of her being. Embraced in his arms and having his lips caressing hers felt like coming home after a long absence. She felt warm, secure and protected in his arms. Odd considering they were veritable strangers.

Frankie didn't know how long they spent so decadently engaged, but loved every moment. When the cell phone in her pocket vibrated, the interruption didn't stop their kiss. In fact, it took several vibrations for her to come back to reality.

Pulling away from Zack was very difficult. Panting as if she'd run a mile uphill, Frankie turned on her phone and the message waiting.

Zack backed out of her personal space and leaned his hips on the sink. "Who is that?"

"My in-country contact sent me a coded text."

"And?"

"It says he knows who we're looking for and we're in luck. We have a chance to get the information we need maybe as early as tomorrow."

* * * *

After several hours of playacting as a newlywed couple, Frankie and Zack were gifted with the possibility of information on the group where the tattooed man came from. But things were never as easy as she wanted them to be.

The hotel supplied all honeymoon guests with a lavish in-room breakfast and both she and Zack indulged in the meal with gusto. The added conversation containing a bit of sexual innuendo for anyone listening in completed their breakfast.

Secreted in the bathroom of their ultra swanky honeymoon suite the morning after their faked wedding night and catered morning after breakfast, Frankie slumped her butt onto the edge of the whirlpool tub and resisted the urge to bang her head against the marble half wall next to the shower door.

The perfect opportunity had cropped up for them to get inside the place they desperately needed to search. Tonight, a grand party was planned in the very place they wanted to access. However, as with every mission, there were huge unforeseen challenges. The last party she'd attended in this fashion years before in this area had taken weeks of planning.

Getting a last minute invitation would be difficult, but forgery would suffice if they couldn't acquire entrance any another way. The seemingly insurmountable problem they currently faced was the culture of unescorted females being a glaring no-no in this arena.

Frankie wanted to go to the party alone, but unless she was the infant daughter of the host, Miguel Santos, she needed an escort for this evening.

Someone familiar with the culture, and who spoke the language would be essential. It would also be helpful if that someone were presentable as a member of the criminal element. Did this part of the country have access to any dial-a-thug services?

"How are we going to be able to get into that fortress without having someone who's been there before tagging along with us? And in less than..." Zack held up his wrist and checked his watch. "Eleven hours."

His question was valid. Frankie was about to get a raging headache from the lack of any answer presenting itself.

Every lead. Every possible way into the place they needed to go was thwarted by the fact that they were either strangers here in this area or hampered by their previous undercover roles down here. Her contacts were tenuous at best. While she could go on her own from a skill level, no one down here would let her in unless she had a male escort.

Unfortunately, Zack had worked undercover in this area for a completely different criminal. In fact, he'd been entrenched with a bitter rival. He'd be unable to go in at all, even in disguise. Due to his size, there was a good chance he'd be recognized. The powers that directed their actions didn't want his extensively tended undercover identity compromised. He'd worked too long to attain it.

The upshot was Frankie and Zack needed to find someone else to aid them in their mission. Someone who would be above suspicion among a vast array of local criminals. Someone they could trust on a short-term basis.

Her gaze went to Zack and a thought occurred. Where was Zack's partner, Colin? When she'd worked on that mission with Zack in Las Vegas, he'd had a regular partner when he wasn't undercover.

"Any way to get your partner down here pronto?"

"Colin?" Zack frowned in thought then shook his head. "Even if he caught an international flight in the next hour, he'd never make it in time for tonight's party. Besides, he's otherwise occupied with his personal life right now."

"Then we need to find a guide. Someone involved with a group that is not a bitter rival of the host. A special guide that wouldn't be questioned or recognized at the door of this party. A western someone would be best. Someone familiar with the area, but also bilingual. Know anyone down here like that?"

Zack shrugged. "Not anyone willing to be paraded around in this venue. I only know spooks. They do their best to stay *out* of the limelight."

Frankie thought furiously of a way to find someone. Then she turned on her cell phone with the built-in encryption device and called Paul.

If anyone existed in this country who could help them out, Paul would either have a name at the ready, or he'd produce one quickly. With his endless contacts, he'd surely come up with someone to participate in this unique opportunity.

Unfortunately, Paul was less than helpful. "No fucking way! I'm not sending you inside a security nightmare crawling with criminal filth all alone. Not even if I had months to plan for it."

"I wouldn't be alone if you'd pony up someone to go with me."

She heard his exasperated growl over the phone. "The only guys I'd trust to help you are undercover. They won't risk blowing their cover on a search that might, or more likely might not, yield us what we need, and I'd never ask them to anyway. If you're going to dream, why don't we conjure up someone who's already been in the place and can lead you right to the evidence you seek, for Christ's sake?"

"That's a great idea. Find someone local who's worked for the host in the last six months and see if we can convince that person to help us."

"You are out of your mind. There isn't anyone like that who

exists."

"But you haven't even tried. Can't you call up one of the thousand contacts you have and at least try?"

"Fuck. I should have never sent you down there."

"Well, I'm not leaving. All roads lead to that place. We need in. And one way or another, so help me God, I'm going in, with or without your help. So get off your ass and help me get in there."

There was a long pause. "Fine. I may have a contact with some people in the area. No promises. But I'll call you in an hour. Don't do anything until I call you back, do you hear me, Frankie?"

"Loud and clear. But don't make me wait too long or I'll dream up something on my own."

"Of that, I have no doubt at all."

Frankie hung up with a sense of self-satisfaction. Paul would pull something out of the air. He always did.

Zack smiled at her. "So is he going to help us?"

"He's working on it. Said he'd call me back in an hour."

"And if he doesn't?"

"Then I have an outrageous plan of my own."

"Do tell."

"Not yet. I'll give Paul an hour, but if he can't or won't help, I've got the stirrings of an idea. I need to make a few calls." She shuffled him out of the bathroom under the guise of wanting privacy to make her secret calls, but mostly he distracted her into a dangerous place.

She didn't need it. Spending copious amounts of time with Zack was having an impact on her libido. The crazy thing was, the more time she spent with him, the more relaxed she became. Usually, working with someone new put her on edge and made her senses hyperalert until the end of the mission. On this mission, her clit became hyperalert in his presence.

Several times she caught herself about to move into his personal space as if her body recognized him. And he smelled so amazing. Every time he came within a yard of her, even if he just walked past, his scent floated across the space and lured her thoughts in a more primitive direction. She didn't know what cologne he wore, but suspected the ingredient list contained some sort of crack-like sexual additive created especially for her. A fragranced formula that made other aphrodisiacs pale in comparison. She needed to quit thinking about how amazing Zack smelled.

As if from a distance, she heard Zack speak. He'd come back into the bathroom. Something about a quick trip out of the suite.

He then put a hand on her shoulder. The sudden connection, given where her thoughts were currently directed, made her clit pulse in longing. "Hey, did you hear me?"

"Yes. I heard you. You're leaving. Don't expect me to be waiting for you, Valentino." Frankie backed up a step, and he released her shoulder. Calling him Valentino made her uncomfortable for some inexplicable reason. He wasn't her knight in shining armor or her current lover. At least not yet.

One of his eyebrows went up nearly to his hairline. "Don't leave this hotel without me, princess. I'm your muscle. That's what I was sent here for."

She glanced at the scar on his upper forehead and that wound made her just as antsy. What was wrong with her? "I can take care of myself." The words came out of her mouth, but the tone behind them didn't live up to the meaning of the terms. She wanted to take care of herself, but a strange sensation gripped her insides. An alien feeling of wanting him to comfort her.

After a few seconds, the uneasy commotion in her lower gut receded, but didn't dissipate completely. She was almost afraid for him to leave. What on earth was that about? The day she needed a man to complete her for any aspect of her life was the day she hung up her spy toys forever.

Zack pushed out a long-suffering sigh. "Undoubtedly, you can single-handedly balance the world on your shoulders, but all the same, I like to be in the loop. I won't be gone long. Just a quick errand for *my* boss. Wait for me before you head out this door."

"I'm not making any promises. But you have my cell phone number."

He rolled his eyes. "Yeah and I know you only turn it on occasionally."

She shrugged. "Hey, it's for *my* convenience, not everyone else's whims. Leave me a message and I'll get back to you."

He suddenly moved so close that his chest made contact with hers. Her traitorous nipples tightened. She looked up into his simmering bedroom eyes. "Don't be foolish," he growled. "I don't want to have to hunt you down, but I will. And make no mistake, I do have the skills necessary to do so."

Frankie was so turned on, it took every bit of willpower not to knock him to the ground and fuck him raw. She laughed. "And what will you do when you find me?"

Her gaze zeroed in on his mouth.

"I'll let your imagination work on that one, sweetheart. But I'm not above tying you down before I leave the next time if you disobey me this time."

She shivered pleasurably at the thought. "You don't scare me, Zack." *Liar, liar, pants on fire.*

A half smile appeared on his luscious mouth. "Oh, yes I do. And if I don't, then maybe you want to be punished." He pulled away and exited the hotel room seconds later.

Good Lord Almighty, that man was sexy. Frankie needed a cold shower, but didn't have time to take one.

While she waited, for Zack to return, she called the hotel's information desk to ask about caterers in the area able to handle the business for a large party. If this grand party tonight was as big as she suspected, then nothing had been left to chance. The best of everything would be ordered and purchased and ready or already delivered for the festivities. All she needed were the names of the service people. She included escort services on her list as well. If nothing else came available in the way of a connected escort, she'd follow the food, the wine, or the women into tonight's gala event as her creative last resort.

It certainly wouldn't be the first time she'd crashed a party as a fake hooker.

Seconds before the hour was up, Paul called with the name of a group that had provided security services less than a month ago for the scumbag host of tonight's gala event. One of the men in this group was a deeply embedded spy.

Paul's contact would never release his name, but if she could find the group in the next few hours, she might get lucky. Paul told her to look for someone who could pass for an American and further to listen for a southern accent.

"Use the words *bastard* and *abyss* in your pitch and the spy will know it's a code for assistance. He'll respond and use the word *gentleman* in whatever he says, so you'll know it's him."

"Clever."

"Whatever. I still don't like this."

"You never like anything."

She heard him push out a long breath like he was counting to ten to temper his displeasure. "The guy won't break his deep cover and reveal, but he knows the layout of the place you want to search. He can at least get you in and out of the place with a minimum of contact with anyone inside. Just don't blow his current jungle cover."

"Good." The operative's information would be valuable regardless of the part she played to gain access. But the best option was to dress up the spy and take him out for the evening. Hopefully a deeply embedded spy would clean up well enough to play escort, but not break his cover. And if not, she could always pick his brain regarding the home she wanted to crash.

"Thanks, Paul."

"Don't thank me. This is a foolish plan. What if you don't find the right guy? Don't even think of taking just anyone into that party."

"Well, they all know the layout of the house since they provided security for the host."

"That's not the point. You find the American spy or change the mission parameters. I'd rather Zack went in there with you than some thug we don't know."

"He's too big and distinct not to be remembered."

"Oh, he's a pretty good operative. I'm sure he'd be able to change his appearance."

"But he doesn't know the property. We'd have to stumble around to find our way. No. I'll get the right guy. Don't worry so much."

"But you won't even know if you have the guy you can trust until you get him alone."

"Not true. I'll get them to talk for me and listen for his dialect."

"Jesus, Frankie, this isn't a Boy Scout troop out camping, these are South American criminals living in the woods and selling their services to the highest bidder. You know, mercenaries. This particular group also sidelines their criminal activities with occasional gunrunning."

"As you well know, I can spot an American dialect every time and twice on Sunday or you wouldn't have given me this tidbit in the first place." Dialects was a subject she'd excelled in during her initial training to be a Protocol spy.

She had an ear for those with particular western accents. She'd be able to pick out her spy with no problem. She'd probably be able to name the southern town he originally hailed from in his youth given enough time to study his voice rhythms.

The ace up her sleeve with mention of this particular group of mercenaries was that it was one she was already familiar with. She'd made friends with the leader when she was here a few years ago. With any luck and some well-spent cash, she'd have the exact man she wanted with time to spare for tonight's shindig.

For the first time since this mission started, Frankie had a good feeling about its success.

The traitor threatening the Protocol group was about to lose his anonymous status. The name *The Scorpion* had been used in conjunction with Miguel Santos. It had also been bandied about regarding this elusive entity she sought and the criminal element connected to the group with the Blood Wrath tattoos. It was said, according to her in-country contact. The information she sought was in the computer of tonight's party host, Miguel Santos. In no time at all she expected to reveal the entity responsible for their troubles. It couldn't come fast enough for Frankie. She wanted to identify the person who wanted her dead and eliminate him by whatever means necessary. Very simple.

Harder was leaving Zack at home while she traipsed into the criminal party with a stranger she hoped she could trust.

Chapter Eleven

Jeff Coleman adjusted the rifle's webbed strap on his shoulder so it wouldn't slip off and entered the filthy cement room behind four other equally armed mercenaries. They were extraordinary scumbags, every single one of them. The building they sought refuge in was partly underground but only slightly cooler than the hot assed jungle they'd been tramping around in this morning. He was glad to leave the steamy forest behind and get under a roof, if even only for a few minutes.

This long-assed mission was just about over, and he for one was grateful. He'd spent several months with these moronic assholes and feared any longer might turn him into one corrupt son-of-a-bitch. Or perhaps a soulless homicidal maniac.

Getting so deeply lost in an undercover assignment was one of the pitfalls of spy work. He knew he'd never stray far from the golden rule, but after so much time underground with the wrong element, criminal pursuits became part of the daily routine and dangerous to his psyche. He needed a break from this saturating asshole mercenary practice.

Soon.

He'd be back in the states before too much longer, and first on his list was a trip to Zack's hideaway house and a long weekend there to reacquaint himself with the American way of life. Fifty to a hundred hours of cable television, watching everything from *Girls Gone Wild* to reruns of *Gilligan's Island*, ought to do it.

Also, he'd find some delightful feminine company to help him change the channels. But until then, he was stuck here in the jungle with men he'd just as soon kill as listen to ever again.

Ultimately, Jeff was not a homicidal murderer, so he endeavored and endured to maintain his balance. Just a little bit longer. He was not a criminal. He put the bad guys away. But it always took so goddamned long to accomplish the simplest of tasks, it was a wonder he didn't explode before doing so.

Luckily, the end result was worth it in satisfaction from the assholes gracing prison cells for all their atrocious crimes. This bunch set a new record for nasty. He couldn't wait until these monsters were out of circulation.

The rush of fulfillment that came with long sought after criminals finally meeting their end was almost as powerful as an orgasm. A blessed mind fuck of blissful contentment. The operation in the coming week would finally get these jerk-offs into prison where they belonged and might register a singular gratification only measurable on an earthquake Richter scale.

The maze of dark, damp, and dingy rooms they traversed with their tightly centered group in search of the score got more dismal and shitty with each room they passed in this underground bunker. The smell alone was enough to make him vomit.

"Over here," their obnoxious leader finally called out, and they all watched him approach a table in the next dingy, shitty room. This one had an overhead light hanging down low and shining down on a sturdy table. The deluxe suite, obviously.

Jeff entered the room last and gathered with the others around the singled out table. He didn't notice anyone else in the room until she spoke.

"Are these all of your men, Carlos?" The sultry female voice of the questioner echoed in the desolate room. A feminine voice was so egregiously out of place here, Jeff turned his head to locate her.

Carlos responded, "*Sí*. Did you want more?"

"Are they all as dirty and nasty as you are, *conocido amistoso*?" she asked. Carlos and the sultry sounding babe were friendly acquaintances? Interesting.

Jeff could certainly answer for Carlos. "Yes. They were all more dirty and nasty than their idiot leader." However, he remained silent and mulled over the fact that the contact's siren voice sounded vaguely familiar.

Where did he know her voice from? His gut, or maybe it was his dick, told him he'd had sex with the woman attached to that voice. Either way, it was unlikely, right? The smoky female tone coming out of the darkness made his blood fire with need, and now wasn't really the best time for that sort of reaction.

He heard her walk closer, each step punctuated by the sound of her solid heels striking the cement floor. Slowly she came into view, boots first, creased, battle dressed uniform fatigues surrounding sexy legs, nice hips, narrow waist, great tits he could see even through the roomy shirt and...no fucking way. Jeff almost swallowed his tongue as he saw her face. It was shadowed, and her hair was pulled back, but she looked, and more importantly, she sounded like...no fucking way!

Daphne?

No fucking way it was Zack's Daphne, but if Jeff didn't believe in doppelgängers before, he most certainly did right now. Goddamn, it had to be her identical twin or something. Her gaze swung around the room to the face of each man hired and brought to do her bidding on a special job tonight.

This was a job Jeff hoped would result in lots of arrests or deaths of the group he worked with. It coincided with the end of his miserable time in this hellhole country. Never in his wildest dreams did he expect Daphne to show up. Or her twin.

Daphne's twin studied Jeff's face for a moment and seemingly didn't recognize him, although she could be really good at her undercover job or the criminal activity she was participating in.

Either way, he looked quite a bit grungier and unshaven than the last time they were together. If it even *was* her, and Jeff tried to think of every possible scenario where it wasn't her.

Her face was sternly bracketed in a haughty frown. Her hard eyes said she was a longtime world-weary professional in this underground arena. She had spy's eyes.

Daphne had been so girly and innocent. Well, innocent at first, anyway. Until he and Zack had their wicked way with her. In the shower. In his playroom. In his oversized king-sized bed, tied up, going down on his cock…no, it couldn't be Daphne. Her hair was styled differently. Her posture was different. The aura of her physical presence was different.

Besides, Zack didn't date women in the company. Then again, maybe Zack didn't know about her being a spook.

No. Zack had a sixth sense about women sharing the same career path, and he didn't dip into the company pool anymore. The first and only time taught him a lifelong lesson.

"Of course. *Mi amiga*, they will do you proud or die trying."

Her sultry laugh sent a pulse of lust along Jeff's spine as a snatch of misty shower time memory crossed his frontal lobe. "Good. Tonight is so very important to me."

"I know this," Carlos glanced over one shoulder and said. "Hector, take the men into the next room while she and I negotiate."

"*Sí, el jefe.*" Hector led the way.

Jeff remained wary about this new and unusual development.

* * * *

Frankie looked at each and every one of the disgusting men in her contact's pool of criminals. She couldn't think of a reason to get each of them to speak. It would come across as an odd request since supposedly she was only looking for a guide and not a specific man.

Each man, save one, turned her stomach on more than one level, but she knew she needed one of them to complete her mission. She wanted the person responsible for trying to kill her, and that end required a guide. The path to her would-be killer was aided by the host of tonight's party. His destruction lay in the familiarity with this group of men to tonight's mission. They had worked for the in-country host briefly. Mercenary work mostly, and all provided for the filthy rich patrons in this country.

The one she wanted was the slim, wiry built man on the end. Even through the dirty smudges on his skin she could tell he was the most "western" looking of all the men lined up. Not as dark and swarthy as the others here.

Not only were his eyes a heart-melting baby blue color, his hair seemed lighter than all the other men assembled. And for some reason she got a good feeling as she passed by him. Perhaps he was the one she sought and exuded his "good guy" undercover spy vibes her way, unlike all the other thugs who merely leered at her as she walked past them and made her want to punch them in the nuts for being too forward.

Paul provided information on this group that the company had been unable to prosecute. But now they'd be used in a different capacity. She needed someone who could lead them into the Scorpion's South American habitat.

Carlos leaned forward. "What do you need one of my men to do?" His breath nearly curled her eyebrows in its ferocity. His suggestive leer caressed her. He wouldn't step over the line, but she could tell he wanted to, and any encouragement from her might sway him from good sense.

"I need a guide. One that speaks English. One that could escort me about town and not embarrass me in front of my friends. He'll need to clean up well and have a western look. And by that I mean me must have either pale skin, light eyes, or blondish hair. Do you have a man you could spare to fulfill my requirements?"

"Sí. I have such a man."

Frankie leaned forward half an inch. "My boss will be so very grateful."

"And how about you, *mi amiga*, will you be grateful, as well?" He crowded even closer, his offensive scent circling around her clothing.

She forced a coy smile to form on her lips. "Of course, Carlos, however, you know what my boss requires."

His eyes narrowed, but nothing else moved.

"He demands my unfailing loyalty and chastity. Or else *my* life ends."

He released a sigh. "You do him proud, *mi amiga*."

"Thank you. Now if you'd be so kind as to send in your man. I'll be on my way."

He moved back a step and she stopped breathing through her mouth. "Hector," he called in a loud voice, "bring Diego."

The tall second-in-command soon entered with another of his filth-encrusted men following close behind. The one she wanted from the beginning.

Carlos pointed to him and said, "You will go with my special American friend and help her with whatever she needs for as long as she needs you. Return when she commands it."

Frankie turned to the man recommended. Diego. Beneath all the dirt and jungle muck, he was very attractive. She cast a glance from head to boots before asking, "Do you speak English well enough to be understood by American ears?"

"Sí."

She rolled her eyes and inhaled deeply. If this was her "good guy" spy, he was trying her patience. Staring at him as she exhaled, she said tartly, "I need to hear you say something in English to ensure you'll fulfill my needs."

Diego's eyes widened, and a cocky grin appeared surrounded by smudges of grime. "What are your needs, bella?"

He called her beautiful, and his command of the language, with a slight American southern accent, was perfect. This was her man. He was likely from Texas, based on the few words he'd spoken, but she would need to speak to him a little longer to determine his exact origin.

She needed to mention the code words Paul had given her. As she pondered the right phrasing, she studied Diego. He looked like he'd clean up very nicely.

None of the others had come close to a western appearance beneath all their dirt and grime. Once she'd gotten Diego away from this dilapidated camp, she'd quiz him on upscale mansions and recent American activity in his past jobs. She did truly need a guide, and instead someone who could identify her only lead would also be helpful.

She turned to the leader. "He'll do. *Gracias*."

Carlos bowed once and gave her a particularly leering gaze as she departed. She did her best not to race from the encampment as she longed to do. She pondered the question of whether to just *ask* Diego if he were the undercover man she sought and decided against it. He wouldn't tell her anyway. From his dialect, she knew he'd been raised in Texas, and that was good enough for her.

"You aren't going to be a bastard about helping me, are you?" Frankie asked. "I need a man who won't send me into an abyss of trouble."

His eyes widened slightly. "No. I'll be a perfect gentleman."

"Excellent."

With her new guide in tow, Frankie headed back to the Jeep she'd appropriated. No one would miss it until tomorrow morning. Surprisingly, she had finished this goal with a long time to spare. She'd left Zack a text message on his cell phone a few minutes before speaking to the group and asked him to meet her at an unoccupied cabin on the hotel property in two hours. Then she turned her phone back off so that he wouldn't call and yell at her for leaving the hotel when he'd told her not to. She smiled and wondered if he would punish her in some diabolical sexual way later on.

Regardless, the short time used in finding Diego in the group left her plenty of time to question him before Zack showed up, brief him on the mission for tonight, and get him cleaned up.

She waved at the leader in farewell, motioned Diego to follow, and took off in the direction of the Jeep she'd stashed a couple of hundred yards away in some covered brush. Halfway to their destination, he coughed. "Excuse me, Bella. How long will I be assigned to you?"

Frankie looked over one shoulder at the man selected to be her guide. "A day or two. Why?"

He grinned. A grin which disarmed her a little. She stopped and turned to face him. He also stopped an arm's length away. Diego's overall build was slim and athletic. Probably an expat military guy who enjoyed living like a caveman in the jungles of South America so he could shoot his gun off whenever he wanted without facing charges.

He shrugged and smiled. "My pet iguana only has enough food for a week. I did not want him to suffer if we were off for a monthlong adventure."

"Not to worry, you'll be back in plenty of time to tend to your lizard." The moment she said it, she wondered if it sounded a little naughty. He grinned again at her comment, but didn't respond.

"And if I might ask. Where are we headed now?"

"To a little place I know tucked away off the beaten path a couple miles from here. I believe the house is called *Oasis*."

There were a few properties in the local area that had house names instead of actual addresses.

His smile actually seemed familiar for some reason. Beneath all the dirt, he was very good-looking. Even as attracted as she was to Zack, this charming guide also pulled at her long-neglected sexual needs. This alarmed her to a certain degree as she rarely found men engaging enough to warrant looking at twice. She should get laid and get it over with. Zack would cooperate for a night, but not until their mission was over. Perhaps her new guide wouldn't be opposed to a quickie in the jungle to take the edge off of her lust.

Frankie mentally laughed at the train of thought her mind took.

She didn't need to sleep with anyone this trip. She needed to find a traitor, but then again, if it didn't hurt her mission, why not tend to her desires?

Spending the night before with Zack and not acting on the potent need to pounce on him had only served to heighten her libido today. That's all it was. Hormones. If they hadn't been interrupted by room service this morning, she might have been late to today's meeting. And likely the reason she now panted for a complete stranger. Unsatisfied and built-up sexual longing made her foolish enough to waste time drooling over inappropriate stranger sex. Stupid hormones.

She glanced over her shoulder at Diego once more. Still, he *was* very nice-looking. Her pulse pounded through her veins from the inappropriate visions of Diego running though her mind. He gifted her with another sexy grin.

Could he read her mind? Was he picturing them together in a shower? Her pressed against the cold tile, him pounding his cock deeply inside her pussy from behind as Zack watched them.

She shouldered her bag and turned away before the rush of heat claimed her cheeks.

What on earth was wrong with her? Where did that astounding vision come from?

She really needed to get laid.

"Can I carry that for you, Bella?" Her guide had slid into her personal space from behind, startling her out of her sexual shower fantasy starring Zack and this stranger who intrigued her beyond reason.

"What was your name again?" She knew his name but needed a distraction.

"Diego," he whispered. His breath caressed her ear. Good Lord, she practically pulsed in sexual need with him so close.

"Right. Diego." Frankie shook her head to clear the sexual fog before she ended up giving her guide the wrong impression about the services she required from him.

"I can carry my own bag. Step away from me, *por favor*."

"Sí, senorita." He grinned, but only backed off a half-step.

Frankie walked toward the bank of thick brush hiding her Jeep and waved for him to follow. "We don't have much time. I need to get you cleaned up before we embark on our journey. And we need to get you some new clothing to wear."

"*Gracias*." His tone was so filled with gratitude, she cast a glance over her shoulder again as they walked. His ever-present charming grin sent another pulse of sexual longing spinning through her body. Turning forward with a sigh of disgust at her own lack of control, she pushed through a thicket of bushes with a height well above her own and found her semi-hidden Jeep now surrounded by four men sporting big guns and bigger smiles.

Frankie cursed a blue streak internally for her carelessness. She shouldn't have barged into this space until checking for unwanted animals in the area.

"We heard a *gringa* was in our jungle searching for a guide," the closest man said. "For a price, we'll help guide you." His leering perusal of her body from head to toes turned her stomach.

"No, thank you. I decided I don't need a guide after all." Standing her ground, Frankie wondered if Diego had run in the opposite direction at the sound of four men encroaching on her Jeep. He hadn't followed her through the thicket, and she didn't hear him at all behind her anymore. Likely she was alone in this uneven fight. So be it. She took note of the position of the four, ticking off the best way to rid herself of them quickly.

The only man who'd spoken advanced on her. He pointed his rifle at her belly.

He took another step closer. "Take your clothes off, *gringa*. We always enjoy sharing a little American pussy when the opportunity arises."

* * * *

Zack spent a frustrating day learning absolutely nothing that would help them with their quest. Frankie had looked good enough to eat whole this morning. And he'd wanted a big bite.

As they were supposedly on their honeymoon, the hotel provided in-room meals each and every morning to those here celebrating wedded bliss. He'd forgotten since he'd been too busy trying not to drool overtly at his *pretend* wife as the sun rose in their still-too-small palatial suite.

For the first time ever in his life, Zack wished he were blissfully wedded. But only to Frankie. Given that she didn't cling to him behind closed doors, perhaps she'd be a good candidate for a future relationship. He shook his head. He'd sworn after Heidi that he'd never dip his wick into the company pool ever again. Perhaps fifteen years was enough time to berate himself for that long ago mistake. Zack simply knew that Frankie was special and sexy and a woman he didn't mind hanging out with in the least.

Frankie had sent him a text message regarding her special recruiting activities and then promptly turned her phone back off. He couldn't call back and scold her for leaving the room when he'd asked her not to. He smiled and wondered if he should threaten to spank her for her audacity. And would it excite her if he did? The very idea certainly excited him. He couldn't wait to get her alone again.

Good God, how had he let her so far into his psyche? He *never* chased company women. *Never*.

Why Frankie made him feel so on edge and horny was a complete mystery. Sure, he remembered the first time he'd ever heard her voice. The sultry tone still made his blood fire up and sing.

With the memory of her voice dancing in his head, Zack headed to the secret safe house. While he hadn't learned any news of significance on his own, Ken had imparted more bad news during their short conversation. It was news she needed to hear sooner rather than later.

Someone else knew they were here pretending to be married. Someone bad.

They'd been followed here by a man referred to only as Valentino in a long-ago message they weren't supposed to know about. Valentino was the mystery entity once suspected of being a traitor to the Protocol Agency and someone who'd threatened Frankie's life a while back.

Zack found he was also eager to stop this man from harming a woman fast becoming very important to him.

* * * *

Jeff Coleman crouched down before she parted the branches to step through into the clearing. His sixth sense had been on red alert for the last several steps. Watching her ass didn't help his ability to sense danger, but he did it anyway.

He needed to remember where he was and that he had a cover he couldn't blow. This would be an opportune time to get in with a rival of his current boss, Carlos, or better yet, show Carlos what a good little bad-assed soldier he was by taking out a few rival members.

Besides, choice two also allowed him to save the girl.

He flanked her position, careful not to make a sound, and pulled his favorite weapon from an outer expanded pocket of his camouflaged pants. Rifle fire would only bring more rival combatants to the party. That was no good. He and the girl didn't need any more combative assholes added in.

Time to survey the odds.

Jeff peeked through a bare patch of the thicket to view the scene playing out. Four against one wasn't too bad, if she had any hand-to-hand skills. Bad if she didn't and expected any mercy from the assembled animals. He knew they didn't possess any mercy.

The rivals obviously didn't recognize her as any sort of threat. Nor did they seem to know who she was. They just wanted to gang-rape some *gringa* stupid enough to be out here all alone. He had to admit to a certain curiosity regarding her agenda of being out here in the jungles and request for his services as guide as well, but he wouldn't let her suffer at the hands of these idiots.

He peered through the bushes again and sized up his best plan. Keeping his wits about him and carefully selecting a target, he rose, putting weight on one leg, aimed, pulled back the cup of the sling, and fired a rock at the head of the closest man threatening the lady he'd promised to serve. His shot struck above the brigand's eyebrow and the leader went down. Another man went to grab her, but she dropped him with a boot kick to the groin. The other two should have run, but instead they advanced on her. *Damn it.*

Jeff loaded his slingshot and hit one guy in the back. He slowed and spun around as if shocked at a surprise attack.

The remaining goon grabbed for the woman as if unwilling to let the prize go. She balled up a fist and then bashed him in the jaw with her opposite elbow. Jeff, still a few yards away, loaded another stone, the last one he had, in his slingshot. He took out the guy he'd hit in the back with a shot to his forehead.

The man she'd kicked in the groin shot out a hand and grabbed her ankle. With a short scream, she fell against the Jeep, trying to keep her balance as she valiantly kicked her foot from his grasp. Jeff heard her hit her head with a thud and go down. He pulled his pistol and chanced a single head shot. He took out the guy still clutching his nuts in one hand with his other gripped around her ankle.

Once the threats were gone, he ran over to tend to his beautiful patron. A circular red mark promising to turn into a bruise was already forming high on her forehead. He moved closer and smoothed away a strand of hair from her face.

A while back, he'd had the occasion to study Daphne while she and Zack slept. This girl was her exact duplicate even more so in slumber. He'd give her a chance to revive on her own before taking drastic action.

He glanced around at the fallen scum littering the forest floor and for the first time got a good look at one of the unconscious faces. One troubling aspect of this ambush, Jeff recognized one of the men as someone he'd worked with before.

She moaned and grabbed her head one-handed.

"Are you okay?" he whispered. He squatted next to her and leaned in close. She smelled just like Daphne. Looked exactly like her. Jesus. Focus.

Her eyes opened. A dreamy expression encompassed her face. She hooked an arm around his neck and pulled him closer. He let her. Then she kissed him, and he let her do that, too. No sense in turning down gratitude in any form. After a few seconds she broke the connection. The kiss almost stopped his heart. The look of love on her face also tugged at long-neglected heart strings.

"Jeff?" she whispered. "Is that you?"

"What?" *What the fuck!* He automatically looked over his shoulder to ensure no one was around to hear her questions. Absolutely *no one* knew his real name here. Not even his in-country contact. When he swiveled his head back around to look at her again, she caught him off guard and pushed her lips against his once more. Her chaste kiss almost burned this time. Jeff relaxed a bit and kissed her back.

She pulled away suddenly. Her face shifted to one of sadness in an instant. "Zack is dead." She sobbed quietly. "I got him killed. It's all my fault he's dead. I couldn't warn him in time."

Jeff wasn't sure what surprised him more. Finding Daphne in a place like this or her revelation that Zack might be dead. He hadn't seen either of them since that amazing weekend several months ago.

Her eyes drifted shut. She stopped moving.

"Senorita?" *Shit.* He leaned in to see if she still breathed. "Daphne," he barely whispered her name. She didn't wake, but her breath caressed his cheek. He put his hand above her breast, and the reassuring feel of her beating heart galvanized his next action. She'd mentioned the safe house they were going to, but if the place wasn't secure for any reason, he'd have to take her to *his* secret in-country domain.

Usually, he only went there under the cover of darkness, but he'd make an exception this time. He needed to know how and why Daphne was here and why she hadn't acknowledged his identity before now.

Another disturbing tidbit of information crossed his mind. Was Zack really dead? He looked down at Daphne again. Gorgeous. His and Zack's recent history with Daphne was the most important and powerful in his life. Some days the memory of that final weekend before this shit-hole assignment was the only thing that helped get him through the day-to-day insanity of being here.

He glanced at her once more. A gust of wind stirred a lock of hair that had come loose from her bun in the melee. She was so beautiful. The memories of their time together still moved him.

Jeff hoped she wasn't marked for death by his own people. Given the alternatives, he obviously didn't want any harm to come to Daphne. While he owed his allegiance to his country not his personal feelings, at some point he'd have to make a choice as to which was more important. Keep her safe or rat her out.

Chapter Twelve

Zack checked a safe house Ken had told him about that supposedly didn't have any bugs, but someone was there. He waited around for an hour to see if they might leave, but the place deep in the woods off the main road was definitely occupied.

As a precaution, Zack hadn't driven all the way to the structure in case any unfriendly folks were about, but parked just out of sight on the long, winding dirt road leading onto the clearing of the property. He was glad not to have barged into a situation.

He'd only wanted to find a quiet place without pervasive surveillance, but it wasn't this place. He pulled out his binoculars and spied at least three different people inside the small cabin. The place looked desolate on the outside, but the occupants didn't look like they'd be leaving anytime soon.

After Ken had told him about Valentino possibly being in Brazil, Zack had wanted to find Frankie. He wished she hadn't gone off on her own.

Starting to worry a little that he hadn't heard from her, Zack tried to think of where she might go.

He got back in his vehicle, but before he could think of heading in any particular direction, his cell buzzed. He didn't recognize the number, but he did know the area code.

"Yes."

"Where are you?" His suspicions as to the identity of the caller were confirmed when Paul Kelly's surly tone came through the line.

Zack snorted into the phone. "Joyriding. Why?"

"Very funny. Put Frankie on." The underlying tone of his voice shifted to one of concern. Or was it fear?

He slowed his vehicle in traffic as the light several yards ahead turned yellow and then red. "We aren't together."

"Trouble in your honeymoon paradise already? Where is she?"

"She's making contact with your people to get a guide. One that supposedly will have knowledge of the criminal we seek and the house he lives in for tonight's mission."

"I know that, but she should have checked in already. Even with the shitty service down there, she should have gotten word out. And why didn't you go with her?"

"I had my own contacts to get in touch with."

"Any luck finding information for this mission?"

"Nope. I got squat."

"Figures."

"Tell me where her hidey-hole is and I'll go check up on your girl."

Zack heard Paul sigh heavily over the phone. "Normally, I'd tell you to go to hell. Frankie can usually handle herself." He paused, and Zack wondered if he'd talk.

"But?"

Paul pushed out a long breath. "But to tell you the truth, I'm a little bit concerned. Normally, she would have contacted me by now." With grudgingly cryptic directions, Paul gave Zack the coordinates.

Luckily, Zack knew that area from his time here before. And it wasn't far away from another place he knew of from an old friend. "I'm on my way."

"Call me the minute you get there."

"Yes, mother."

"Screw you. And don't say anything in there that you don't want others to hear. This particular hidey-hole isn't exclusive or likely secure. Never know who's listening in these days."

"Great. Thanks." Another confirmed place he'd have to pretend to be married to Frankie. Although, perhaps if he was able to kiss her again, he could just come in his pants like a randy teenager with his first girl and allow the throbbing to subside for a short while.

Whacking off in the shower this morning had done nothing to quell his raging attraction to a woman he should leave alone. Unfortunately, the more time he spent away from her intoxicating presence, the more he longed for her nearness. What was that old adage? Absence makes the heart grow fonder. It also made his cock grow faster each time he thought about her. Was he really about to break his cardinal rule and sleep with another agent? Maybe. Probably.

Shit. The answer likely came down to a matter of when and not if. His past issues with female agents faded into the back of his mind. He didn't care if she clung to him afterwards. He wasn't even sure once in the sack with her would be enough to quell his formidable urges.

He shouldn't attempt a sexual encounter, but the distant reasons for that long-followed rule faded with each mile he got closer to his mission *wife*. If the opportunity presented itself, he planned to kick his persuasive skills into high gear.

Frankie didn't seem like the clingy femme fatale type. Quite the opposite. It might be worth the risk. Without conscious effort, his hand drifted to the scar at his hairline. The lack of memory surrounding that recent incident was never far from his mind.

What had he been doing? Had Frankie been involved? Sometimes, in his infrequent dreams, he heard a sultry laugh, not unlike Frankie's, and a warm, loving sensation encompassed him. He always woke in the night with a raging hard-on and the almost memory of the musky taste on his lips of an elusive dream woman. He was currently imprinting that vision with Frankie's features. A secret report Ken let him scan showed that she'd been somehow involved at the hangar, but to what degree had never been fully explained.

He'd long suspected that Ken hadn't told him everything about the time he'd lost. He assumed there was more to that incident than had been fully explained. Even though Ken had assured him early on he'd divulged everything, some sixth sense in his gut kept his misgivings high. The visit to the bank his last memory, his absence from the poker game he'd planned to attend, and being found shot in the head at an abandoned airplane hangar at a municipal airport were his only clues.

One of these days he'd park himself in Ken's office and refuse to leave until his boss shared all knowledge about the days missing from his memory. Or the lack thereof. A week completely gone. Seven days, four of which he'd spent unconscious in a hospital recovering from a bullet grazing his head.

The ricochet likely caused his memory loss, or perhaps, as the doctors had repeatedly suggested, the trauma of the situation had made him forget. He couldn't fathom any trauma or actually anything at all that would make him fail to remember key events. But three days were gone possibly forever. That was the most troublesome aspect of all. For a man who prided himself on ultimate control, losing time, any time, even forgotten time, was a nightmare.

With a new agenda to locate Frankie on his mind, Zack shoved his troubles out of the forefront of his mind. Time to work.

He called her cellular phone, but she didn't answer. A slight worry nagged him. He probably *should* have gone with her. If Ken hadn't sent him on a secret side mission, he'd be with her now.

Ken wasn't going to like what Zack had learned on his sojourn either. Bad news could wait though. He wheeled the car back to the place he'd come from and headed in the direction of where he'd been with the idea he'd beat down the door if necessary.

And from now on, he wouldn't allow a separation on this mission, no matter what she did to him or what Ken threatened to do.

* * * *

Jeff sent one arm across Daphne's limp body to block her into her seat and steered the car one-handed around the final curve in the main road on the way to the hidey-hole she'd mentioned before they'd been ambushed. *Oasis*. Thank god he knew the place she was talking about and the undirected way there.

Not that he'd stop and ask for directions anyway.

If she hadn't told him where they were going, he would have gone to his own private place located close by. Perhaps that's why all these houses were tucked away in the forests. A massive number of hidden safe houses littered throughout the extensive forested region with one faction or another hiding out in every one of them. The image amused him, but he discarded it. It wasn't time for fun.

She remained unconscious, and her lack of response in all this time worried him. He pulled into a rutted dirt road and drove several hundred yards shielded by a canopy of shadowed forest before the small house appeared in a sun-filled clearing around the final bend in the driveway. The sun was only a few hours from setting, and for tonight at least, they'd hopefully be safe here.

He parked and got out of the vehicle quickly. With only one short glance over his shoulder at his sleeping beauty, Jeff did a perimeter search to ensure they were alone. It was still possible there were electronic bugs inside, so he'd play his part as guide until he knew for sure, but at first blush, this place was deserted.

A quick stop at the front door to unlock it, an even quicker check inside to get the lay of the land, and in less than five minutes, he was back at the car to check on his gorgeous girl. He opened the car door, unbuckled her seat belt, and carried her into the house.

The house was simple in its layout. Living area combined with dining and kitchen formed a lazy L shape and took up the bulk of the space. In the far left corner a room protruded into the space with the door opposite the kitchen, and a second door he'd discovered earlier was the only bathroom here.

Jeff placed Daphne carefully on the threadbare sofa, took off his jacket, and made a cushion for her head. Seated next to her, bracketing her against the cushioned back, he snuggled in close. He wanted to kiss her again.

She looked so serene he almost didn't want to disturb her, but was compelled to lock his lips to hers once more. The taste of her lip gloss flavored his tongue with a strawberry tang. His cock stirred with long-ignored impatience as to his sexual appetite of late. He'd been busy working and collecting information on the group of degenerate gun-running jungle criminals for months. So focused on his job, he hadn't answered his libido's call in too long a time. Staring down at the perfection that was her face, an interesting thought occurred to him. Had his last sexual liaison been since Daphne? Perhaps.

Glancing around the room, he didn't see any overt places where a listening device might be housed, but he knew they were here somewhere. A contact had used this place within the last year and he'd heard the tape of the goings-on.

He'd best stay in his assigned role as recently acquired guide and play by ear whatever she had in mind.

Time to try in earnest to wake his sleeping beauty. He lowered his face to hers and planted his lips across her. Sweeping his tongue into her mouth, Jeff suddenly felt her respond. Her tongue curled around his, and she kissed him back. One arm, formerly lax at her side, came up to encircle his neck.

He broke the kiss long enough to whisper, "Senorita, you honor me with your attention." She pressed her lips to his once more before he could finish with, "I'll do anything to make you happy." It was the truth. He'd do anything for her.

After another consuming kiss where she became bolder and more ardent, Jeff pulled back slightly. He wanted to ensure she knew who he was.

Her eyes opened slowly and recognition lit her eyes with passion. But it didn't last very long. Her eyes narrowed and her facial muscles tightened as if in fear, or perhaps anger. The shift in her expression to suspicion surprised him very much. But not as much as the gun now securely positioned beneath his chin.

Jesus, where had *that* weapon come from?

"What the hell do you think you are doing?" Her breath caressed his chin along with the cold hard steel of a gun barrel. How had she reached her gun? Or did she acquire his without him feeling it. He surreptitiously felt for his weapon and realized it was gone. Damn, she was good.

"You were hurt. I brought you to safety."

"And putting your mouth on mine then licking your tongue between my lips was a safety measure?" She pushed the gun up and the rim of the barrel bit further into the soft tissue at his throat.

"Not exactly, senorita. But since you kissed me right after the four men attacked. I thought...well, obviously I was wrong. I'm terribly sorry to have overstepped the boundary of your earlier simple gratitude."

She didn't move. He couldn't see her expression as his head was tilted all the way back due to the weapon she wielded. The ceiling he now concentrated on was planked wood and filled with cobwebs.

"*I* kissed *you*? Dream on, mister." But her slow tone of voice sounded like she wasn't completely convinced of her own statement. "I don't remember that at all. What I remember is being alone when I came through the bushes and then..." She stopped abruptly as if the search of her memory for more information had failed her.

Her previously riled up tone suggested he was about to get his head blown off, but after a second or two the gun lowered and eased away from his chin. He sent his puzzled gaze down to stare at her again. Suspicion clouded her expression. Maybe she couldn't remember what happened.

He relaxed a notch. Maybe she was still hurt. She *had* been unconscious for quite a long time. "What *do* you remember?"

She sent her gaze across the room, and he figured she was trying to remember the recent scuffle.

"I remember the four men waiting at the vehicle. I remember deciding to take them all out by myself. But one of them grabbed my leg when I turned my back and then…nothing."

"Senorita—"

"Stop calling me that," she snapped at him. "My name is Frankie."

"Frankie? I thought your name was…" Luckily, he caught himself and didn't finish the sentence because the domain in which they spoke was not secure. *Pay attention to where you are?* He was grateful to have remembered his ultimate role before speaking out of turn. Even though her declaration truly shocked him.

"You thought my name was what?" she asked, and the first smile since she'd awoken appeared. Her whole body relaxed. She looked good enough to eat. Her beauty was unparalleled in this seedy world.

She twisted his gun around and offered it to him handle first. Stunned into disbelief that he hadn't felt her take it, Jeff took it gently from her fingers. He really did need to focus.

Zack was right about one thing. Women in this business could be very dangerous. As hard as he tried to keep that tidbit of good advice in his mind, one look at Frankie and her overall vulnerability in this world and he softened again.

He returned the smile and relaxed his body just slightly. "I thought it was something else, but Frankie suits you perfectly."

"Do we know each other from somewhere?" she asked suddenly. Her faint whisper as if she were coming out of a dream made him want to check over his shoulder to ensure they were completely alone.

Jeff widened his eyes as he forcefully shook his head in the negative. "Just from when we all lined up and you selected me because I spoke English so well."

Her eyes drifted closed as if contemplating his answer. With each passing moment, she became softer, more desirable. Jeff should back away, but knew he didn't have the capacity to do so. Even after only knowing her for a short time long ago, he still cared about this woman. And he wanted her with a desperation he'd never experienced before.

She shifted and sat up. Her gaze caressed his face, his mouth, and then back to his eyes. "You seem so familiar to me. Or rather, the taste of your kiss seems…" She stopped speaking. Her expression became more seductive, and Jeff leaned forward as if pulled by the magnetic force of her will. Frankie met him halfway, and they kissed again. This time she led the level of passion. Her tongue slowly entered his mouth as if tentatively testing her memory of their shared past.

Was this merely a show for whatever listening devices were activated in this building? Jeff didn't care. He'd be willing to test all sorts of things regarding her memory if she wanted. His cock swelled with each stroke of her tongue in his mouth. Her hand traced a quick path from his collar to his cock. He couldn't help groaning when she stroked the bulge still growing in his pants.

He slid his hand down her shirt, palmed one breast, and thumbed her nipple. She moaned into his mouth, and his cock went to full staff. He had her uniform shirt unbuttoned and one breast exposed in no time. She unzipped his pants and had his shaft in her bare hand before he realized his fly was undone. She wiggled her hips against him so he stretched out on top of her.

The sofa squeaked with his weight, but he didn't care. He ground his hips against her and realized she still had her camouflage pants on. He lifted up and straddled her body until he could get her pants undone and down to her ankles. Feet bound by her clothes, she widened her knees and opened her legs. Jeff lowered his trousers to his thighs and practically fell on her. His cock grazed her pussy, and if he died in this moment, he'd die a happy man.

He took the time to open her uniform shirt all the way and push up her T-shirt to reveal both perfect breasts. Just as he'd remembered. This was Daphne. It had to be. He didn't care what she called herself now. He didn't care if this was a crazy spontaneous activity. He wanted her. She obviously wanted him. Daphne definitely had a body he remembered. Intimately.

She moaned again. Jeff kissed her mouth and trailed more kisses to her breast. He sucked a nipple into one mouth as his cock rested at the apex of her hot pussy, ready to push into nirvana.

The sound of an approaching vehicle didn't register until he heard the car door slam shut. He only had time to leap from the sagging sofa and pull his pants up before the front door banged open. Daphne, or rather Frankie, was completely displayed as if for feasting.

Pants twisted around her ankles, body exposed from breasts to ankles and uniform in disarray, it took everything to pull away. But safety first.

Jeff pulled his gun up to chest level as a figure stepped inside the room. He aimed center mass and put his finger on the trigger.

The good news was, he'd been caught about to fuck a beautiful old flame. The bad news, he hadn't finished the interlude to either of their satisfaction. But the best news, and the one he currently focused on, was the fact that his old friend, Zack, wasn't dead after all.

Chapter Thirteen

Whatever Zack expected to see once he foolishly burst into the safe house front door with his gun drawn was not the vision that greeted him.

Assault, attempted murder, or, at the very least, torture of his charge were the three most worrisome acts he expected. The sight of his old friend, Jeff Coleman, standing gun in hand after very obviously having been sprawled over Frankie as they'd begun to have sex just seconds before didn't even make it into the top ten of his imagination.

Most surprising of all was his jealousy over not being in Jeff's place and not the shock of seeing his old friend about to fuck the woman he'd become fascinated with. The mere thought of seeing Jeff having sex with Frankie only enflamed his already aroused libido. He wanted to watch Jeff finish pleasuring her and then take a turn himself.

Eyes narrowing for only a moment was the only sign Jeff gave of recognition. This location was not safe for conversation about their friendship or their sexual past. Or whatever future might reveal itself.

This should be an interesting conversation.

"Who are you?" Jeff asked, narrowing his eyes again briefly.

"I'm her husband. Who the fuck are you?"

He thought he saw Jeff's eyes widen for a second. "I'm Diego. She hired me."

"For what?"

Jeff's eyelids twitched again, but he didn't break eye contact. Zack trained his focus on Jeff and waited for Frankie to intervene. But she didn't.

The two of them waited, locked in a staring contest, until the count of three passed before turning to check on her. Her eyes now shut, his errant *wife* looked to be out cold.

"What did you do to her?" Zack advanced towards his Frankie serenely posed on the ratty, threadbare sofa.

"I did nothing." Jeff gave Zack a signal with his hand that said "attacked" and then added four fingers. Zack took this to mean they were attacked by four men.

"Was she hurt?"

Jeff nodded, but said, "She told me she wasn't feeling well. I brought her here to rest. I guess she hasn't recovered from her fainting spell." Jeff turned towards Frankie. He reached her first since he was closer, but Zack came around to access her injury.

The second they each touched her, she opened her eyes and sat up with a start. Her gaze traveled first to Zack and then to Jeff. Next she looked down at her loosened clothing and her near-naked body. She pushed out a long sigh.

"I guess I have some explaining to do."

Zack sent a puzzled gaze to Jeff. "I guess you do. Are you feeling better?"

Frankie looked up at the ceiling and back at Zack. She tapped her ear, and he nodded that the place was likely bugged. "I feel fine. Nothing to worry about."

Jeff put a hand on her shoulder and squeezed, which put a frown on her face at first. Zack thought she was going to bite a few fingers off for a second, but then just as suddenly she gifted their guide with a sincere smile. Zack felt the first pangs of what was likely jealousy, but that notion was so foreign, he almost didn't recognize it. Not to mention the fact he'd never been jealous of Jeff. They had an understanding. They'd shared women. Often. Just not since over a year and a half ago. A sudden memory creased his mind from the day he'd gotten shot four months ago.

Jeff had called him the day he'd gone to the bank, which turned out to be his final memory before waking up much later in a hospital suffering a gunshot wound to the head. On the way to the bank, he listened to a message that Jeff had left about being in town and crashing at his place after inviting not one but two beautiful women over. He left an open invitation to share.

Zack had returned the call and told Jeff he was welcome to entertain any number of the fairer sex, but he was on his own as Zack planned to be out playing poker. When Zack woke up in the hospital a week later, he'd forgotten that exchange until right now. Once they weren't in a bugged building, he'd have to ask Jeff if they'd spoken again that weekend.

Given that he'd introduced himself as "Diego," Zack surmised Jeff was down here in this country deeply undercover. Since Zack knew who he worked for and that man also knew Frankie's boss, Paul, it wasn't a stretch to assume that's how he'd been brought into their little mission.

Suddenly, Zack was glad he'd found the two of them together. Jeff was one of the best black ops agents he knew. Someone he considered a rare and true friend. Not only was he very skilled in this business, he was also very skilled with women in the bedroom.

Zack suddenly pictured sharing Frankie with Jeff, and a bolt of lust hit his groin so hard he almost moaned. He cleared his throat to cover and signaled that he wanted to leave the room.

"So tell me about you and Diego."

"You see, darling, I went to find a guide to lead us around the local area." As she spoke, she stood and put her clothes back right. "Not only has he agreed to show us all the best places to see and eat, Diego here has also agreed to help us find a vacation hideaway to purchase. And best of all, going through him means we won't have to pay any exorbitant real estate fees. Then, whenever we travel here in the future, we won't have to always stay in a hotel."

Jeff closed his eyes and pointed to the ceiling again. "But we shouldn't let anyone find out we've circumvented the rules."

Zack tried not to laugh. As if whomever listening cared a shit about errant real estate fees. They likely waited for government officials to wave their weak little wangs at the wrong sexual partner so as to record it for future extortion schemes. With all the available technology, it was a wonder anyone in politics still had the balls to attempt a secret affair. But they did. Looking at Frankie again, Zack knew exactly why. At this moment in time, he might consider an affair with Frankie over his career.

"So you hired Diego here to find us a vacation home, huh? Are there any nearby we could look at? I'd love to sightsee today." The sarcastic tone of his voice didn't change anything.

"Sure. Why not?" Frankie finished straightening her clothes. "Let's go."

* * * *

Frankie wondered if she suffered from a concussion after the recent attack. Losing time before waking up into Diego's arms had been disconcerting. Plus, she'd almost been caught bare-assed by her fake husband after hiring a guy who was likely an undercover mercenary to get her into a local drug dealer's party, but first they had to pretend to go look for a vacation home.

She understood immediately that Zack and Diego knew each other. The fact that they didn't come to blows was evidence enough of that. Or maybe Zack didn't care if she slept with other men. It was definitely an intriguing discussion for another time.

Once outside, Zack suggested that he and Diego ride together and she could follow in her vehicle, but Diego insisted that she shouldn't drive after being unconscious for so long.

"Unconscious?" Zack's immediate concern touched her. "How long was she out?"

"Over thirty minutes."

"Traitor," she muttered. Diego's only response was a quick grin.

Zack forced her into his own vehicle and told Diego to drive hers ahead of them to the safe house only he knew.

The second they were on the road Zack began his lecture. "I told you to wait. Why did you go off on your own? I'm your fucking bodyguard. Next time wait for me."

"I didn't want to *wait* for you. Besides, I didn't have time. I only had a short window of opportunity to grab Diego before his group left on another assignment."

"So why him?"

"Although he'll never admit it, he's undercover for one of our clandestine groups. And he was in a unique position to have worked as a temporary security for our target a month or two ago. He knows the layout of the house we want to break into tonight, and he speaks the language."

"How do you know?"

"Because I got the information from Paul. My impression is that Diego's in a long-term undercover operation and his handler doesn't necessarily know we've appropriated him."

Zack sighed. *Shit*. Jeff hated to be pulled away from one assignment to help with another. He knew that because not only had they discussed it at length in their past, Zack also loathed being forced to do the same thing. It was like being an undercover pawn in games you didn't have the full rules on. He could get killed or hurt or, worse, be revealed as a spy. And this might negate the mission he was currently on. Given the way Jeff looked, Zack figured he'd been under for a while. Not the clothes, but the haggard expression etching his face.

He'd do what he could to help Jeff and not destroy his current cover, but he wasn't the lead on this mission, Frankie was. "I hope you take into consideration the fact you're putting *Diego* at a huge fucking risk to his primary mission here."

She shot him a quick surprised look. "Yes. I get it, but it isn't as though I haven't done the same thing a hundred times before either. That's how this secret government community works. Lots of back scratching goes on all in the name of what's good for the overall mission and assignment hierarchy you happen to be in the middle of. Sometimes one mission exceeds another in the pecking order. I have someone trying to kill me. He's likely on a gun run."

"Regardless. Don't do anything to compromise his cover if you don't have to."

"I won't. I understand how the whole back-scratching agenda works."

"Speaking of scratching backs, are we ever going to scratch any sexual itches while we're here? I mean, we are on our honeymoon. Given how I just found you with Diego, maybe I should have made my move this morning." Zack was only half serious. He wanted her, but not if she wasn't interested. He decided to simply ask if she wanted to have sex so he could stop torturing himself.

Best to know her feelings on the matter and act accordingly. He'd abide by whatever she said. Unless he thought some light urging might be a positive influence. He wasn't above using his vast understanding of persuasion.

Frankie laughed. "I hit my head. I wasn't myself. Perhaps, if the right set of circumstances comes available, like we amazingly have some uninterrupted time, then I'd likely assault you. But we'd also need an undisturbed place to do whatever our hearts desire, and that hasn't presented itself yet. Plus, I don't want any permanent obligations."

"Oh, all that goes without saying. And will Diego be invited to this once-in-a-lifetime party?"

"What!" Her cheeks flamed with color.

"It didn't take a genius to figure out what you two were about to do before I showed up. I wanted to put it on the table that I don't mind. My sexual appetites and tastes are vast and varied." He sent what he considered to be his best sexual gaze her way before focusing back on the road.

"So…you want to watch me have sex with Diego?" Her sudden husky tone suggested she was intrigued or possibly had already considered the idea.

"Yes. And then I want to have sex with you while *he* watches us."

She swallowed hard and nodded. "Okay. I'd be open to the idea."

"Excellent." Zack figured that after they took care of this mission tonight and before they left tomorrow, he'd ensure that they found the time and a place to act on this scorching passion they'd discovered.

And since he and Jeff already had a signal for such activities with special women, Zack felt confident the best part of this trip would happen later tonight.

* * * *

"We got interrupted earlier," Diego whispered. He slid his arm around her waist and pulled her into his solid frame as they disembarked from the limo in front of the brightly lit hacienda.

He likely referred to the interlude they'd "almost" shared on the sofa of the not-so-safe house before Zack burst in unexpectedly. He was right about the interruption, and wrong if he thought she was going to do anything about it now.

"So what?" She smiled and stared up into his beautiful eyes, with a lusty passion not at all faked, as if she'd just said, *then let's just fuck right here on the porch.*

"You owe me." He stroked her torso from one hip to the outer curve of her breast as he kissed her cheek. His fingers lingered below her breast, which was easy to feel in this thin, almost-there dress. A few of his fingers rested on her bare flesh, and she was embarrassed to note that her nipples pebbled lightly as a result of his familiarity. Likely his touch had nothing to do with the sexual lust she felt. It had been building up for days. Now with two men turning her on repeatedly, it was a wonder she hadn't imploded with sexual need.

"I owe you nothing." The grin was harder to maintain through clenched teeth. Besides, she already had enough images of what Zack had suggested in her mind distracting her. She didn't know if Zack had told Diego what they planned for later on, but she figured he'd be amenable to it. He was of the male species, after all. Men didn't often turn down sex, even if they had to share. Her panties were already soaked as flashes of the possibilities of tonight traipsed into her mind when she least expected it.

He leaned close as if to whisper something in her ear, but instead licked her neck in a very sensitive place. Her nipples hardened completely, and she heard his chuckle. "Your body disagrees, senorita."

"Regardless, stop it for now." *We'll have plenty of time afterward. I'll make sure of it.*

"I see, a challenge for later then." He abruptly removed his body to a manageable distance. This helped to keep her nipples and libido in check. They strolled to the door and entered the party behind another several guests pretending they'd all arrived together. Hopefully, they wouldn't even encounter any others. They were only here to steal some information, and then they'd be out.

Cleaned up and dressed in new clothes, Diego looked completely different and cut quite a handsome figure. Frankie hoped no lonely women sought him out to dance as they made their way through the throng of guests. Luckily, it was a big bash, and they'd arrived fashionably late in order to blend better.

Entering with a group made for a less noticeable entrance, but no one seemed to care if they were supposed to be there or not. The party was loud and crowded. They each grabbed champagne from a passing server and skirted the edge of the room where the bulk of the guests had assembled.

Diego led her with expert ease into a darkened corner where a short, deserted hallway led to a narrow set of stairs likely used only by servants to access the upper rooms. They deposited their glasses on the first side table in the lower hallway.

"Take your shoes off," he whispered.

Frankie nodded and slipped the stiletto slings off her feet quickly and with great relish. It would be agony to put them back on later. These shoes, while the height of haute couture, were only good for at best ten short steps before pinching and mangling her toes with relentless intent.

Fashion, she found, often had a higher price of regular pain than spy work.

They made their way up the staircase, Diego on her heels. Due to his knowledge of the house and a lengthy planning session in the hotel, she knew exactly where she was headed. The dark, narrow staircase had a landing and a right turn halfway up. Once they made it to the turn, they stopped as if in unison to listen and ensure no one had seen them or followed.

If discovered, the plan was to pretend they searched for a quiet place to have sex. Frankie knew she wouldn't even have to fake any feelings should they get caught. Diego was even more attractive all cleaned up. She wondered again if he knew about their plans for later on. Having him think about sex with her while they worked was as arousing as thinking about surprising him. But now it was time to work. Frankie set her libido in a dark, quiet place for the time being.

"Let me check before you open the door," Diego whispered. He passed by her with a full frontal sweep of his body pressed against hers to gain access to the top stairwell door. She closed her eyes and tried to keep focus. A nagging headache was trying to assert itself, and she fought it. No time for pain right now.

He cracked the door, stuck his head through quickly, and promptly motioned with one hand that it was clear.

This time she followed him to the study door they sought. Having seen the host for the party downstairs in the center of the room, Frankie felt they should be okay in here for now.

Unless there were any invisible alarms. To that end, she pulled out a bug detector that also subbed as a radar finder out of her small purse. Any security would be detected with the small device. She lifted the antenna from one side, which doubled as a probe, and slipped the tip beneath the door. She turned the portable machine on and watched the meter. No security devices were detected inside the room. That was a surprise.

The door was unlocked, and they both entered quickly. The room was an upstairs office or perhaps a den and home office combination.

She hurried to the desk. He followed at a slower pace. She bent over and began searching desk drawers. As he approached, Diego loosened his tie and the first couple buttons of his shirt to make it look like they were getting busy. Then he slid behind her and pushed his groin into her backside. She sucked in a tight breath.

His hands slid to her breasts and stroked her peaked nipples. "Looks like we won't have to fake this at all."

"Stop it," she whispered, but her tone didn't even convince her own ears that he should stop touching her.

He laughed and sat down in the office chair. In the bottom drawer of the left side, she discovered what she sought. The thumb drive to their host's computer.

She held up the drive like a prize. Just as quickly, her heart stilled in her chest as the muffled sound of someone outside the door registered. Her heart then skipped a beat when the snap of a latch echoed into the room and the door swung open.

Chapter Fourteen

Jeff acted the moment he heard others just outside the entry of this closed-in room. They didn't have time to make it to the closet, so he shoved the device into Frankie's already open purse, grabbed her ass and pulled her backwards against his groin. He yanked one strap of her gown down to reveal one succulent breast and covered it with his hand so that whoever entered the room didn't get an eyeful.

Her breast was warm, and her nipple hardened against his palm in seconds. He pressed his lips against the space beneath one earlobe. She moaned. Whether it was from his hand squeezing her breast or his mouth against her neck, he didn't know. But the sultry sound made a profound impact on his neglected cock. His shaft swelled as her ass shifted and pressed harder into his groin.

Damn, he wanted her.

The interruption from earlier had gone unrelieved. He planned to ask Zack later if they were a couple and would he be willing to share for a night.

The door swung open slowly and revealed two other partygoers deeply engaged in slobbering all over each other with obviously the same intent. The location of a private place to fuck.

He pulled his mouth from Frankie's neck, voiced a low curse, and put his glare on the couple who'd already entered three steps inside. The female had her hand strategically located on the man's crotch and the gentleman had his hands on her tits. At his voiced curse, they both stopped kissing, fixed their drunken gaze on the two of them in the chair, and then giggled, murmured a few apologies, and retreated the way they'd come.

Frankie stood and turned away from him. She replaced her strap and covered her nipple. A damn shame. The blush staining her cheeks was unexpected, but perhaps he would have felt the same way if one of his testicles had been exposed to strangers. Then again, he was a guy. Accidentally showing off his balls to anyone wanting to cop a look didn't usually bother him.

She pulled her purse open and removed another small device along with the thumb drive. She inserted the flash drive into her cellular phone and accessed the information. "This is what we want."

"Great. Make a copy."

She nodded and pushed several buttons on her phone then pulled the thumb drive out, wiped it off, and put it back in the bottom drawer.

Frankie grabbed her purse and snapped it shut with her phone inside. "Let's go."

"No quickie on the desk first?"

She rolled her eyes at first, but then focused her gaze on his face. "We're leaving, but perhaps later you'd be interested in a threesome with me and Zack if the opportune place presents itself."

He couldn't help it. His mouth fell open. "Are you kidding?"

A slow smile spread across her sensuous lips. "I'd never kid about something like that. Didn't Zack mention it?"

"No. But I accept your offer." Jeff did an internal happy dance at the possibilities. The last time the three of them slept together not much sleeping had taken place. "I can't wait. I've dreamed about it all day long. Perhaps we'll rival our last adventure."

Puzzlement crept into her expression, and her head tilted to one side. He would have explained further, but another noise from the hallway interrupted him. Jeff raced across the room to secure the door. Locking it would give them a little more time if anyone entered.

He listened at the door, but the loud voices continued down the hall and finally disappeared. He motioned her to join him, and they scrambled to the back staircase and descended the way they'd come in record time.

Once at the doorway into the ballroom, Jeff grabbed Frankie into his arms and pushed her against the wall. His mouth swooped down on hers with careful precision. Tongue sliding between her lips, she didn't resist him. If fact, she clung to him until someone grabbed his shoulder and pulled with enough force to separate them.

He broke the kiss and turned an angry glare to the intruder. The one he'd heard rounding the corner to the staircase which prompted the surprise kiss in the first place.

Jeff's next surprise was profound. He certainly didn't expect to see his undercover black ops boss here at this party. He felt certain given the look Matt Timberton drilled into his eyes, he hadn't expected his deeply planted covert ops agent to be playing suck face with another agent at this party tonight either.

Shit. Probably the threesome he practically salivated in anticipation of was about to be cancelled.

Matt's face was uncharacteristically crimson, and his demeanor signaled he barely kept his sizable anger in check. "Get rid of her," he said between gritted teeth. "Meet me outside in the garage."

Jeff shook his head and knew Matt would be really pissed, but the less he called attention to himself and the faster he got out of this house, the better his cover would be protected. "I'll call you later and explain everything. This is a sanctioned mission."

Matt's lips pressed together in a line. "Not by me it wasn't."

Frankie tensed up beneath him. He still had her flattened against the wall with her face turned away. She swung her head around and pierced Matt with a sharp look. "Ever heard of Paul Kelley?" she asked in a whisper. "Talk to him."

Matt's face tightened at first then he looked at Frankie more carefully. The look disappeared, and Matt's face hardened. Jeff understood it to mean that he *did* know Paul Kelly and disliked him intensely.

Frankie leaned closer to Jeff and fixed her hard gaze on Matt.

"Please don't ruin this op over a pissing contest you can win later against my boss. We're almost out of here. Let us go. I'll have Paul explain everything to you after we've gone."

Jeff watched as Matt transformed from pissed off boss to suspicious, puzzled boss in two seconds flat. He turned his gaze to Frankie. Once he focused in on her, Jeff noticed he did seem to recognize her.

She ignored his stare and scanned the immediate area, turning her head quickly in all directions. Jeff did, too, ensuring no one had entered the hallway and listened to their conversation. Although, again, there could be bugs. Matt must be insane to stop them here. He could very well compromise them at any second.

"Tell Paul Kelly to expect a call from me very soon." He turned to Jeff with an expression that could have melted steel. "I'll deal with you later. If your cover is blown with the goons in the jungle, you're done in my organization. We clear?"

"Crystal." Jeff didn't know what Matt was so bent out of shape about. It wasn't unheard of for black ops groups to share intelligence and resources. Especially ones sent into foreign countries.

Matt used other resources from fellow organizations all the time. In point of fact, Zack had helped him once several years ago. The ferocious look Matt had shown after hearing Paul Kelly's name was something Jeff tucked away for later. Hopefully, it wouldn't interfere with their plans for later tonight.

Matt did a fast one-eighty and left them in the hall. No one else had entered or exited, but Jeff was worried about any security that might be in the room. He didn't want to ask Frankie to check. He didn't want to take the time. He just wanted to leave as quickly as possible.

"What a prick," Frankie muttered.

"Yeah, he's not usually so bold as to try and ruin me when I'm out in the field. I'm not sure what his problem is, but then again, he always *has* been a power hungry control freak. And I guess I can add, doesn't like to share assets' to his long list of faults."

"He could have fucked us big time if anyone heard what he said." She glanced around the elegantly detailed, tall ceiling of the room, moved in close, and put her mouth at his ear. "We still might be screwed if anyone's listening right now. And not in the good way." Her words barely registered.

"Unless someone has added more security in the last month, there isn't any here. I remember from when I was here before," he whispered back. "The host thinks extra guards are enough protection and doesn't believe anyone would dare steal from him anyway. He's arrogant and foolish."

"Good. Let's get going. Maybe we should find another way out of here besides the front door."

Jeff reluctantly pulled away from her warmth. "I never intended to leave the way we came in." He grinned at her. She was so lovely. He couldn't wait until the three of them were alone. "Let's go out the back door by the garage. Signal our ride to pick us up at the side of the house instead of the front, okay?"

She nodded, made a quick phone call, and they took their planned egress carefully to the outside. "Sorry, he caught us. I didn't mean for you to get in trouble," she whispered as they skirted the edge of the host's property. Jeff knew a way through the security. A minor hole in the sensors he'd never mentioned when working here before. As he suspected at the time, it came in handy for tonight's mission.

"I volunteered when my undercover criminal boss asked a favor. I did it to help boost my credibility and as a suck-up gesture." Jeff shrugged. "I don't care if Matt is mad about his resources being tapped. He does it all the time. He acted worse than he should have, and it sounds like your boss is about to take the brunt of his wrath, more than us anyway. I wouldn't want to be in Paul Kelly's shoes right now."

She shrugged, and a grin lit her face. "That's why he gets paid the big bucks."

The limo driver pulled up in a Lincoln town car with a very roomy backseat. "Are you ready?" Jeff held the door open for her.

"Yep."

"Let's get back to where Zack is waiting."

"He's likely wondering why we're taking so long."

"No. He's wondering what we're doing and if you've screamed in climax yet."

She paused in mid-step and shot a smirk over one shoulder before climbing into the limo. The privacy shield was up because the driver already knew where they were going. "That's why we're all going to get it out of our system tonight."

This time Jeff stuttered in his step. "Are we? I mean it might take me several times to get you out of my system."

She laughed, and Jeff's cock resumed its state of hardening as quickly as possible.

"Don't be greedy, now. Time will dictate our experience. I think we'll be okay in the hotel, but likely there are people listening in so no spy talk."

"Great. Nothing like voyeurism in a sexual experience. I'm in. Should heighten things, don't you think?"

"Perhaps. So you're okay with a threesome?"

He made a face. "Why wouldn't I be? This isn't my first time at the rodeo. I'm still quite a bad boy, you know."

She nodded, but her expression was unreadable. "I see. Well, I want you to understand a few things—"

"Oh, but I want to make sure you understand completely all the luscious things I plan to do to you with Zack's help tonight."

She grinned. "Good. But I need to know that you can you keep your mouth shut. No telling tales about our sexual adventures to others, right?"

He rolled his eyes and pointed at himself. "This is me we're talking about. I'm the very definition of discreet."

"Because if anyone ever hears any sexual tales—"

"They won't hear anything from me, darlin'." He spoke in a low tone, but she didn't stop.

"—I'll deny even knowing you."

"You have my word. I've never divulged any sexual information from my past, and I won't be inclined to share going forward." Jeff now understood all he needed to know. She didn't want her boss to know she was partaking in sexual pleasures while on a mission. Fine with him.

Dim lights flashed by the tinted windows of the limo, and the closer they got to the city, the more lights there were. Jeff scooted closer. Frankie leaned her head on his shoulder and released a small sigh. He stroked her bare shoulder until she raised her head and moved in for a kiss.

He let her kiss him the way she wanted. At first her lips were tentative, but soon became more aggressive.

The only thing that truly puzzled him was her lack of mentioning their affair from before. Perhaps she didn't want it to slip out. She had obviously been undercover as someone named Daphne and probably wasn't supposed to be engaging in sexual antics back then either. He would make it his personal goal to pretend everything was brand new tonight between the three of them. Hopefully, Zack understood her rules.

The kiss ended when she pulled away with a sigh and put her head on his shoulder. He brushed her temple with his lips and looked forward to the coming night.

Jeff wondered if Zack had known she was a spy last year. He'd play along with the charade and pretend they hadn't tripped the sexual light fantastic a year ago. It wouldn't be easy, but he wanted her so much he was willing to do pretty much anything.

Perhaps she'd used an alias, the shy, sexy Daphne, to get away for a weekend of sexual indulgence. And his memories were filled with all sorts of fabulous and rarely experienced pleasure.

Tonight would be another night to remember, or forget if Frankie had her way. But he wanted this evening more than anything. He wondered if it was okay to chat with Zack about the previous weekend they'd shared.

He'd not spoken to Zack since. And he'd noticed an ugly new battle scar on Zack's head that hadn't been there the last time they were together.

They could catch up after tonight's sexual decadence. After they'd made Frankie climax several times and put her to sleep with satisfaction, they could drink expensive booze and chat in cryptic dialogue regarding what had transpired after last year. It was always fun to talk around any listening devices. Or he could simply use his personally obtained signal jamming device.

Jeff wondered if Frankie and Zack had been a couple since way back then. It didn't seem like it from their earlier conversation. Perhaps they'd only recently connected. Which made this time together even more special. Serendipitous even. He couldn't wait.

With tonight's plans firmed up, Jeff moved on to the earlier battle with his boss. He contemplated Matt's unusual actions tonight. He knew his black ops boss well enough to know he hadn't been faking his anger tonight. However, there had been no reason for his attitude. Now that he analyzed the scene, Matt had given Frankie the hairy eyeball several times, too. Matt had been surprised when he finally noticed her. And that had only been when she spoke.

Her voice was very distinctive. Throaty. Smoky. Sexy.

Or was it that Matt hadn't wanted to be seen attending the party of a third-world drug lord in a country currently at odds with the US? That was the better possibility. If Matt wasn't supposed to be hobnobbing with the criminal clientele at the party, he'd be pissed if someone saw him. Although, Jeff wouldn't have seen him if he hadn't accosted them in the hallway. He'd have to have a heart-to-heart with his boss. Or perhaps there would only be his butt being chewed by Matt. But he was clean. Carlos, his superior in the jungle organization, had ordered him to go with Frankie.

Having one of Matt's deep in-country assets show up at a party with an agent from another clandestine agency made for gossip. If anyone in the know saw them.

Perhaps Matt wasn't being a good boy with regard to his agency affiliation. And this possible information made Jeff reconsider *his* often tenuous position with the agency. Matt could do some damage to his career. Best to tread lightly. Or have a plan of attack if he got pushed out of Matt's organization.

Maybe he'd ask if Frankie's boss was looking for new people.

His only other nagging question was why "Daphne" had told him Zack was dead before she kissed his lips off in the jungle.

Frankie must have gotten hit on the head a lot harder than he thought, or something else was going on that he didn't fully understand.

* * * *

They met Zack at an Internet café. Frankie gave him the stolen files to send over an encrypted laptop for analyzing back at the Protocol Agency Headquarters. There it would be sifted through for the specific info they needed. Diego kept his distance, but remained within visual range. He'd acquired a baseball cap from somewhere and exchanged his formal coat for a casual jacket, managing to look completely different for the third time since she'd met him in the jungle.

Once Zack uploaded the information, their next logical step was to return to DC. She hoped they were wrong about a leak coming from their own secure building. She hadn't been able to get in touch with Paul since escaping from the party. She'd try again in a few hours. The cellular service in this area was notoriously inconsistent.

Unfortunately, or maybe fortunately, there were no more flights out until tomorrow. They had an entire evening to do whatever they wished. And she wished for a lot. Two men. In her bed. For as long as possible.

Zack asked her where she wanted to go as they left the Internet café. Diego followed discretely, and she knew he listened to their conversation. Even though it was possible there were a whole rash of bugs in their room, she opted to return to the hotel.

It was opulent. The bed huge. The shower large enough for three comfortably. One eyebrow rose on his handsome face as if he questioned her sanity, but then a smile emerged.

"Choosing luxury over privacy?"

"Exactly. If anyone wants to listen in, let them. I don't care."

She glanced over her shoulder at Diego, and he grinned and nodded. He then turned and walked in the opposite direction to get his own transportation.

Zack helped her into the car, and once he drove away from the café he added, "You know, Diego may not want to join us given the lack of privacy in that location."

"Then it's his loss." She settled back in the seat as Zack drove. "But I think he'll show up."

"I hope so."

Diego, in fact, beat them to the hotel.

They walked into their room to find him sipping champagne and lounging on the sofa in the main room. Frankie kicked off her uncomfortable shoes the minute the door closed behind her and padded barefoot to where Diego waited.

The spectacular view of the island lights greeted them as they walked further inside.

"Great room. I can see why you chose to come back here for our…discussion."

"Discussion?" Frankie asked with a laugh. "And here I thought we were all going to have sex."

Diego cleared his throat or perhaps choked on his beverage at her outrageous words. She felt a little high at the very thought of what was going to happen. Were they really going to have sex here? The three of them? The thrill of it sent a spiral of desire through her limbs.

"We are." Zack poured himself a glass and one for her as well. He handed it to her and kissed her before she could take a drink. "Don't go too far. I'd hate to have to leave the room before we're all satisfied."

Frankie laughed. "We're adults. Aren't we able to do as we please?"

Zack shrugged. "I suppose so. Where would you like to start? Here or in the bedroom? Or perhaps you'd like to shower off tonight's mission grime."

Diego stood up and moved towards the master bedroom suite. "I vote for the shower first. What do you say, Frankie?" He finished the wine in his glass and sauntered past her towards the bathroom without waiting for her to answer.

She shrugged and followed him into the master bathroom. The shower stall wasn't the biggest she'd ever seen, but the three of them would fit inside with no problem. There were two showerheads, a nice bench that ran the length of the tiled space, and plenty of glass to steam up along one wall.

"Brings back memories," Diego murmured loud enough for her to hear. Was he having memories of other women he'd fucked in the shower? Odd comment to make, but perhaps he simply wanted her to know he was experienced. If they'd shared women before, he had plenty of know-how when it came to pleasuring women.

He peeled off his shirt and dropped it to the floor. He approached her and started undressing her by unzipping her dress all the way from mid-back to ass. Braless, she put her hands over her breasts to keep the dress from falling to her ankles.

Diego pulled the straps off her shoulders just as Zack entered and closed the bathroom doors. He clicked the lock in place, to perhaps further ensure they remained alone, and turned to watch them finish undressing.

"You are *the* most beautiful woman," Diego whispered. He gently placed his lips on the top of one shoulder and eased her dress from her light grasp. The fabric pooled at her feet, leaving her only wearing wet panties.

The dress she'd worn tonight hadn't been much more than a wisp of sheer black fabric and a promise. Diego had mentioned a couple of times earlier his appreciation for her garment. She suspected he preferred her out of it though.

He palmed her breasts and stroked his thumbs across her sensitive nipples. They pebbled the moment he touched them. With each brush of his fingers, a physical reaction occurred. There was more juice flowing between her legs than the hourly volume of water at Niagara Falls.

His dark slacks didn't hide his appreciation for her body. The trouser fabric barely contained what looked like a very impressive erection. Hands at her sides now, she moved her arms and began unfastening his belt. If it was possible, she thought his cock grew even longer as she worked. He bent his head to fasten his mouth to one nipple. Frankie glanced over his shoulder and caught Zack staring at them with palpable lust in his eyes.

Diego moved to suck her other nipple as she unzipped his trousers and slid the fingertips of one hand around his large cock. He hissed in what sounded like pleasure as her bare hand stroked his cock up and down. He kissed a path to her throat and shucked his pants off. She let go of his cock briefly to help, but when he straightened up again, she bent over and took his huge head into her mouth.

"Fuck, that feels amazing."

"Looks amazing," Zack murmured from where he leaned against the bathroom doors. "Let me get the water started warming."

Zack crossed the room behind her as she sucked on Diego's cock. One hand caressed her ass as he walked by to turn the shower nozzles on full blast.

Diego's fingers slipped into the strands of her hair. He pulled out the few pins she had and carelessly scattered them on the tile floor.

She gripped his hips and sucked him as deeply as he would go down her throat.

"Jesus God Almighty. You need to slow down."

Frankie released his cock. "What if I don't want to slow down?" She grinned and sucked him back into her mouth.

"I'm only human. And I'm going to come in your mouth if you continue." He pulled her hair gently as if in an effort to get her to release his cock. She wasn't inclined to do so and in fact, sucked him even harder.

"Oh, God. I can't..." His hands clenched the strands of her hair. He stiffened, and his salty cum shot down her throat seconds later. She swallowed every drop. Diego sighed blissfully.

Zack came up behind her as she released Diego's cock. He looped one arm around her waist, pulled her upright, and slid his other hand between her legs. He zeroed in on her clit and began fingering her. "My, my, you're very wet. Does sucking cock make you horny?"

"I guess so," Frankie said, although the last word ended with a long, pleasurable moan. His fingers slid into her pussy as his thumb continued stroking her clit with perfect pressure. A few more strokes and she was going to come.

Diego seemed to recover after a few minutes. He bent at the waist and put his mouth on one of her breasts. The suction from his lips on her pert nipple sent zings of pleasure to her core. He palmed her other breast and lightly pinched that nipple as well.

Steam drifted across the room from the shower and surrounded them in a swirling mist. Frankie was on the verge of a long-desired climax. She cleared her mind of extraneous information and focused on how fantastic it felt to have two men giving it their all to bring her off. Zack whispered, "Want to come in the shower?"

"No. I want to come right now."

"Oh, too bad. You'll have to follow us into steamy nirvana if you want us to finish." He released her. Diego also backed away with a grin. He'd already gotten rid of his pants and walked into the shower carrying something. A closer look revealed two condoms folded together.

"You're a bad boy, Zack." His only response was low laughter. Behind her she heard the shuffling of clothing. She glanced over Diego's shoulder to see him kicking his pants out of the way as she headed for the shower. Once inside, Diego pressed his chest to her back, brought his hands around to her front, and continued teasing her nipples.

"Does that feel good?"

"It would feel better if you fingered my clit."

"Can't you reach it?"

She laughed. "Jesus, do I have to do everything?" Instead of pleasuring herself, she reached behind her hip and grabbed his cock. "You're already hard again."

Diego pressed a soft kiss to the back of her neck. "You have that effect on me, Bella."

Zack entered the shower and seated himself on the bench halfway between the two showerheads, facing her. "Soap her up, Diego. Make sure she's all clean."

"No. Make her come, she's about to burst," Frankie said with a laugh.

Zack pushed out a long sigh as if miffed, but she could tell he wasn't. He stood up and stepped into her personal space. "I'll tell you what, sweetheart, he can soap you up, and I'll play with you."

"And you'll bring me off, right?" She grinned at her own audacity of begging for pleasure.

"I'll think about it."

Diego had the soap and had begun smoothing it over her wet torso as Zack leaned in to kiss her lightly on the lips. The showerhead shifted and a spray of warm water hit the space between her shoulder blades. Runnels of soapy water fell from her body and pooled between her feet. Zack took pity on her enflamed state and slid his fingers between her legs. All she needed was a few solid strokes across her clit and the long-awaited orgasm she sought would be hers. She'd likely scream like a banshee the moment of her release.

Before he touched her clit, Zack reached behind him and grabbed a condom. He had it smoothed over his large cock in no time and pushed his erection between her legs.

"Mind if I come with you?"

"No. Not at all." Frankie lifted one leg and placed her foot on the bench behind him. Zack stepped even closer and pushed his hard cock into her pussy partway. "Christ, you're tight."

She shook her head. "You're just extra large."

Diego's hands slipped to her breasts, and he pulled her backwards against his chest. This move gave Zack better access. His cock slid deeper into her body, and the sensation of being breached was like heaven itself. He filled her completely with his huge wide cock. The second he touched her clit, she was going to explode in bliss.

Zack grabbed her hips to aid his strokes. He pulled halfway out and then thrust his cock all the way inside again. He felt so incredibly good completely lodged into her pussy. He pulled out and plunged in again, the head of his cock pushing into the end of her core and igniting her already enflamed arousal to a near peak.

"Fuck me, Zack. Do it harder."

Without pausing to question her, he simply complied. She'd never been able to come from vaginal stimulation alone, but with each thrust of his cock, she got closer and closer to nirvana.

Without warning, Diego slipped his hand between her legs and pinched her clit. Frankie let loose a shriek as her climax crashed down on her. Her pussy clamped down on Zack's thrusting cock immediately. The sensation was primal and startling.

She never wanted him to stop. He pushed his cock deeply into her body one more time, before he stiffened and fairly growled his release.

Chapter Fifteen

Zack couldn't even remember the last time he'd been so relaxed. He and Jeff exited the bedroom and left Frankie asleep.

With a care to those listening in the room, Zack referred to Jeff as Diego. Seated on opposite ends of an L-shaped sofa, Zack grinned.

"So, Diego, wherever did my wife find you, and how long can you stay?"

Jeff made a face, held up one finger, and pulled what looked like a swollen pen out of his pocket. He pushed the button on the end and a high-pitched beep emitted.

"Jesus, you want to get me killed? Don't say anything to me, at me, or about me unless this bug diffuser is on."

"What did I do?"

Jeff rolled his eyes. "I'm not supposed to be here at all. We saw Matt at the party on our way out."

Zack stood up. "And you're just mentioning it now?"

"Well, we sort of got preoccupied, didn't we? Just like last time."

He squinted at Jeff. "What last time?"

"You know, like at your house earlier this year."

"What are you talking about?" Zack wondered if Jeff had sustained a head injury in the jungle, too.

Jeff rolled his eyes and nodded at his gadget. "We're safe with this on. And I'm talking about sharing Daphne the last time we were at your house before I left on this assignment. Frankie is Daphne, right?"

Zack stood up. "The last time I remember you being at my house was like seventeen months ago. And we each had our own girl as I recall."

"No. Not then, four months or so ago. I called and left a message that I had two girls ready to go at your place. I got a return one, and it said you were busy. You were supposed to go to a poker game, but instead you came home with Daphne, and the next day we shared her."

Zack sat back down hard. To say he was shocked was an understatement. He rubbed the scar at his hairline. "I have absolutely no memory of that weekend. Tell me everything you know."

Jeff gave him a concise and thorough recounting of the weekend along with the information that Zack was supposed to take Daphne to the municipal airport Monday morning after their salacious weekend.

"Are you sure it was Frankie? Not a look-alike?"

Jeff nodded. "I wasn't at first. I mean, she was so different as Daphne. Seriously, she deserves an Oscar nomination for her performance. Then and now. But when she and I first left my jungle criminals, and she got hit in the head, she called me Jeff, and no one knows that name here. Not even my in-country contact."

"I have a suspicion of what may be going on. Do you know anything about the Protocol Agency?"

"Not really. Just that my boss, Matt, really hates Paul Kelly. Which was reaffirmed tonight when we saw him at the party."

Zack had a sudden recollection of his partner Colin, but more specifically, Colin's wife Laurie, who shared the exact same look as an agent named Rachel. Zack knew she shared personalities with the same body. He also remembered she'd been a part of the Protocol program. He hadn't thought about that in a long time.

Colin had confided some interesting information regarding Laurie's time there with Paul Kelly and his merry band of brain doctors. Likely Frankie and Daphne shared the same peculiarities as Colin's wife, Laurie. He hadn't connected the dots until now. And he hadn't remembered Daphne, her counterpart, at all.

One thing became very clear. He needed to talk to Paul Kelly.

Zack left Jeff alone with Frankie and headed to the place he knew he could make a private call without being overheard.

"What." Even with the belligerent single-worded opening, Paul sounded like he'd been asleep before answering the phone.

Zack didn't mince words. "I need to know what happened between Frankie and me four months ago in DC."

No hesitation from Paul when he said, "I disagree."

"We were together back then. First at the bank and two days later at the airport."

"You remember." A statement not a question.

"No. But someone else does."

There was a long silence at the end of the line. Zack wondered if Paul had hung up on him until he asked, "Who else knows beyond the agents at the scene?" The quiet tone of his voice surprised Zack, but he wasn't in the mood to play nice.

"Not telling. My source won't tell anyone, anyway. I want to know how the Protocol program works."

"Take a number." Paul's argumentative tone came through the line clearly once more.

"Is she Frankie Belle, Daphne Kane, or both? How does she flip back and forth?"

There was silence on the line for a full minute. Zack thought he'd hung up yet again, but he asked quietly, "How do you know the name Daphne Kane?"

"We met at the bank Friday night and I drove her to the municipal airport on the following Monday morning. Right before I got shot in the head. I just don't remember any of it after my injury, but someone I trust just told me what happened for part of that weekend, and I'd like to know more. He says she identified herself as Daphne Kane for that weekend we spent together. I know that Frankie was discovered in the hangar four months ago."

"You aren't supposed to know that."

"Well I do, so what gives?"

Another long silence ensued. Zack was fast losing his limited patience. Not that he'd had an abundance of tolerance to start with.

"When you return to the states, we'll chat. I'm not telling you anything in an open phone call."

"This line *is* secure." Zack didn't mean to sound petulant although it was how he felt.

"No phone line will ever be secure enough for me."

"Fine. We're on the first plane out of here in the morning."

"One more thing. Don't tell Frankie anything about Daphne Kane. Don't even say the name."

"Why not?" Zack seemed to remember Colin mentioning something else about the two different personalities being unable to recognize each other without consequences or something.

Paul's tight tone confirmed it. "Just don't mention it. *Jesus*. It could hurt her."

"Fine. Anything else I need to know?"

"Probably, but I'm not sharing anything else over this line." He was silent for a few seconds then added, "She hasn't had any nosebleeds, has she?"

"No. But during a scuffle earlier in the day, she hit her head and was knocked out for a while."

"Shit." Paul mumbled something else Zack didn't hear. "How long was she out?"

"I wasn't there, but I was told for over thirty minutes."

"You're her bodyguard on this mission for Christ's sake. Why weren't you with her? And why don't you have firsthand knowledge?"

"She's a big girl. Besides, she's fine. The picture of health. You must know she's very capable all alone. And here's a newsflash for you, she prefers being on her own." *Plus, you don't need to know that she ditched me.*

Paul muttered another curse. "Bring her directly to our facility from the airport. Do you understand? Do not pass go. Do not collect anything."

"Got it." Zack clicked his phone off and pocketed it. He rubbed the scar at his temple absently, wishing more than ever that he hadn't lost his memory of that incident.

If he believed what Jeff had told him, and he did, Zack had been with Frankie the weekend before his life changed. No wonder his body remembered hers when they started this mission. No wonder he'd wanted her from the first moment he'd seen her. No wonder he was willing to risk heartache and headache and pretty much anything else to pursue her.

Zack wished that his memories hadn't been decimated by the gunshot to his head. From what Jeff had told him, it had been a decadent and luscious weekend worth remembering.

Interesting that Frankie didn't remember that weekend either. Regardless of what Jeff implied, no one in the world was that good of an actress. Zack wondered what memories her alter ego Daphne had about that time.

Zack couldn't wait to meet her and discover firsthand.

* * * *

Frankie fairly hummed in sexual satisfaction the morning after she'd spent the night with both Diego and Zack. Even though it was the first time in her life to experience such decadent pleasure from not one but two men, Frankie had easily fallen into the rhythm of threesome sex. Like a familiar old dance routine being reenacted, they'd loved each other with enthusiasm and urgency over and over again, melding each act into the next seamlessly as if choreographed in advance. She'd loved every second.

The interlude in the shower ended up being only round one. Rounds two, three, and four took place in the oversized king bed meant to cater to honeymooning couples. She guessed threesomes also needed extra space.

Two sexier men had never existed in her world, and she suspected never would again. The evening before had been a one-time good deal, and while she'd gladly taken advantage of the opportunity, she certainly didn't anticipate a repeat performance. A pity.

The memories of the night would have to sustain her for a good long while. Her only true regret this morning was that it would likely never happen again, but a longing deep inside made her wish that it might be possible. If she continued her relationship with Zack, perhaps they'd try and get away here again. In a perfect world, they'd be able look up Diego, call him to join them, and then recreate the memories of last night.

But she had a long way to go before that would happen. Her time was better spent focused on the job.

Zack had been in his own world since they'd left the hotel. Perhaps he had regrets. Although, she doubted it because when they'd still been in the airport lounge right before takeoff, he'd blistered her mouth with a kiss that belonged in a hall of fame for sensual intensity. If they'd been able, she would have insisted he follow through with sex in the nearest bathroom. But they'd started boarding the first class section of the plane.

She eyed the too-small bathroom as they'd made their way to their assigned seats, but discarded the idea. Everyone in first class would witness them cramming themselves into the space. It wouldn't be a stretch to imagine what was going on. Another whiff of Zack's cologne as he stowed his bag in the overhead compartment and Frankie wasn't even sure she cared if anyone saw them enter together, heard them fucking each other, or even witnessed the act.

Zack crossed his arms and dozed off before the plane left the tarmac. They hadn't slept much last night. She smiled in memory, leaned her head on his shoulder, and dozed off, too. Her dreams centered on the night before and all the wild decadence that sex with two men encompassed. After a kiss goodbye to Diego the night before, Frankie knew she'd carry fond memories of this mission for the rest of her days.

Some light turbulence woke her some time later. She lifted her head in time to notice Zack had been likely watching her sleep. Like her own personal smokin' hot guardian, Frankie wasn't in a hurry to say goodbye to Zack.

The commercial flight they were on was due to land in DC soon. They were supposed to head straight for Protocol headquarters, but Frankie wondered if she could talk Zack into a nearby motel for a quickie. Hell, they didn't even have to get a room. A quiet place in the airport would suffice. Once they were back at headquarters, there was no guarantee they'd ever be able to reconnect again.

Frankie hadn't ever wanted to settle down, but having Zack available for sexual activities whenever they could manage a few hours together might be a workable future solution. She planned to suggest it when they had another quiet moment together after they picked up their luggage.

She followed him down the escalator to collect their bags after the surprisingly short time getting through customs. He'd held her hand like they were a couple still on their honeymoon until stepping onto the narrow metal steps moving downward. He faced forward, and Frankie could tell when he went on alert. He swiveled his head left to right as they descended to the next level. She also looked around, but saw nothing.

No suspicious looks directed their way. No one exhibiting signs indicating they watched Zack or Frankie at all.

Zack stepped off the escalator and paused. She almost ran into his back. He turned and grabbed her elbow.

"What?"

"I don't know. Something just feels off," he whispered. "Stay close." As they marched toward baggage claim, Frankie searched the immediate area for any sign of danger and saw absolutely nothing. Not that she minded being close to Zack.

After several minutes of being hyperalert with no reason, she murmured, "Relax already. We're fine."

He said nothing, but didn't seem to calm down or loosen up his stance.

They collected their bags and headed for the exit near ground transportation. Before leaving on this particular mission, they'd left a vehicle in long-term parking in case they needed one. It was standard operating procedure. Frankie liked having a getaway car, so to speak.

Behind the front license plate there was a secret compartment containing the car key.

Frankie and Zack entered the third level parking structure from the stairwell, opting not to get trapped in an elevator. They walked to the correct row and found their SUV in the expected slot without incident.

She retrieved the key, unlocked the doors, and climbed into the driver's seat. Zack looked around the empty garage once more, loaded their bags into the back hatch, and climbed into the passenger seat.

"I can't believe you aren't going to argue over who gets to drive."

Zack snapped his seat belt into place with a smirk. "You can drive. All the better to keep an eye on you. Head for the Protocol building." He glanced at her cleavage, the corner of his mouth lifting slightly, before drilling a lustful gaze deeply into her eyes.

Frankie cleared her throat and forced herself to break their intense stare. She ignored the shiver running down her spine as sexual tension filled the front seat between them. She moved the gear selector into reverse and backed out of the parking space before she did something publically to quench the desire now pooling in her core.

Before she put the selector into drive to pull forward, she asked, "What would you think about the two of us meeting every so often in an out-of-the-way hotel to relieve our sexual stress?"

Zack's gaze, which had drifted back to her chest, darted quickly to her eyes, and the desire she saw gave her the answer she expected. "Good answer," she said quietly.

A sardonic smiled formed on his perfect lips. "I didn't say

anything."

"Your eyes spoke volumes. I read you loud and clear. Name the time and place."

He shrugged, but the smile didn't stop tugging the corner of his mouth. "I'll think about it."

"Think fast, I'd love to meet later today. I know the four rounds from yesterday should hold me for some time, but I've discovered that I'm very greedy."

Full-blown grin now shaping his lips, Zack didn't have time to respond before the vehicle's engine suddenly shut down. Foot stomped on the brake, she turned the key, but nothing happened. Duh. She put the gear selector into park and tried again. The engine turned over a couple times but couldn't seem to engage.

In the next second, the front door locks popped opened. *What the hell?*

Frankie reached over one shoulder to manually shove the lock down. It didn't budge. Several men with black ski masks appeared as if out of the concrete parking structure walls and from between the other vehicles. They swarmed the vehicle. Zack reached across her body to grab her door handle. "Start the car!"

She twisted the key as one masked man yanked on her door. Nothing happened to the engine. It didn't turn over or make a noise. How were they keeping her from starting her own car?

"It won't start!" She bruised her fingers attempting to get the key to work in the ignition.

Zack's door snapped open and one of the thugs lunged inside. Zack stomped his chest with one boot, but another man pushed his leg into the door frame, aimed a weapon, and zapped him in the neck with a stun gun. Zack's eyes rolled back until she saw the whites. He fell heavily on top of her, but his hand still gripped her door. She reached out and put an arm around his shoulder. Her door was finally wrenched out of Zack's hold. Once opened, the barrel of a real gun instead of a stun gun was jammed painfully against her temple.

"Get out. Now!"

She pushed the panic button on the key chain. The vehicle's horn sounded a blaring noise for about three seconds before she was dragged forcibly from the front seat.

Then the echoing horn noise stopped in mid-blare and the man holding the gun punched her in the face with his empty hand. The force of the blow, which centered near her left cheek next to her eye socket, knocked Frankie's head back against the SUV's door frame, and everything went black.

* * * *

Paul received the news about Frankie's abduction from Ken, who'd gotten the news from Zack when he called in from the airport parking lot after regaining consciousness.

Having been zapped with a stun gun once himself during training, Paul almost felt sorry for Zack. Almost. On the other hand, Zack had been in charge of guarding his most precious agent and now she was missing. He tempered his accusations because he'd read the initial field report of what had happened. The men who'd taken Frankie had moved the vehicle back into the parking space and left Zack unconscious in the front seat. He couldn't assign blame to Zack when obviously someone else had access to his puny fleet of vehicles. Someone had set them up.

The bad feeling that had been churning in his gut all day burst into his chest the moment he heard the news that Frankie had been taken. And why hadn't they captured Zack? He figured he'd been out for at least twenty minutes. Surprisingly, no one else at the airport parking lot noticed the takedown.

"Zack said the five masked men disabled their vehicle like they had a set of keys. How is that possible?"

"I don't know," Paul grated out. "Who the fuck even knew they'd be there?"

Ken shrugged and shook his head. "I don't have an answer for you."

"Where is Zack?"

"On his way here." Ken had an unusual expression that Paul hadn't catalogued in all their time together. Was that worry etched on his tired features?

Paul took a new tack. "What's the status report in operations regarding the files they downloaded from their party host's computer the other night?"

"The analysts are working on it. Breaking the encryption on the sophisticated file they stole takes time. When they have something, I'll get a call."

Paul and Ken retreated to the conference room to plan some sort of strategy, although at this point, he didn't think they even had enough information to form one.

Zack arrived an hour later with little to add. Not even an apology. Not that Paul expected one.

"Any news?" he asked.

"Like what? You were there. Someone took her. You tell me. Any news?" Paul might like Zack, but he was irritated that his agent was missing, and putting Zack with her during the most recent mission hadn't seemed to help protect her one damn bit.

Paul suddenly felt like he was missing something crucial. Like a word being on the tip of his tongue, he knew an elusive fact escaped him. What the hell could it be?

He watched as Zack's whole body deflated from his remark. He parked himself in a chair at the table. "I meant like a ransom note. A lead to follow up on. A person of interest that I can go beat the shit out of to gain important information on Frankie's whereabouts." He flattened his hands on the table as if keeping them there controlled his need to strangle someone.

"No," Ken answered. "Nothing like that."

Ken's phone buzzed, and he answered, "Davenport." He listened for a short while and finally said, "I'll be right there."

His expression said there was another problem. Paul didn't know if he wanted to know what it was. "What now?"

Ken shook his head. "Problems with the download. They hit a snag. I'm going to go kick some asses and get them working again. If you need me, I'll be in the basement."

Paul nodded and sat back down to study all he knew. Mostly a big fat nothing.

Zack started speaking in such a low tone, Paul had to strain to hear his words. "I regret that Frankie was taken. If I'd been conscious, I would have stopped it or died trying." Zack shifted in his seat and put his elbows on the table. His hands scrubbed down his face a few times.

"And that's as close to an apology as I'm going to get, right?"

Zack's lips quirked, but he didn't smile. "What I don't understand is how they got a set of keys to our vehicle. Unless someone in this building is on the wrong side of our agenda."

Paul sighed. "Yeah. Well, I've suspected there might be a traitor for awhile, but haven't been able to prove it."

"Tell me how the Protocol agency works. I already know a little bit because of Colin and Rachel, but not everything. He may have mentioned something he shouldn't have when we were drinking. Rachel had an alter ego named Laurie. And that's who Colin is married to now."

Paul pushed out a long sigh, but then gave Zack a short synopsis of his Protocol spies, the recent history involving a possible traitor and the medical lab where they were converted. He also mentioned the delicate nature of their dual identity. "Most importantly, Frankie and Daphne cannot know about each other."

"Or else what?"

He threw his hands up. "Catastrophic things. Each person is different. At best a minor nosebleed, at worst a total brain meltdown. The system created these spies. And Frankie is a great spy, but she needs the downtime of Daphne and that life to regenerate, if you will."

Zack seemed to absorb the information. He didn't look up, just studied the surface of the table between them. "I care about her," he finally said.

"Frankie or Daphne?"

"Both."

"Just keep in mind what I told you."

Zack nodded. "What's our next move? I hate just sitting here waiting."

"Me, too." Paul pushed out a long sigh. "What do you have in mind? I'm open to suggestions."

Zack's gaze focused on the center of the shiny surface of the table between them for a long time. Paul wondered if he might be running scenarios or maybe simply compiling a grocery list. The silence in the room was unnerving. Finally, his eyes lifted to Paul. "What does kidnapping Frankie accomplish? Who does it hurt?"

"It hurts the Protocol Agency."

"Who wants to do that?"

Paul started to shrug and say something flip, but then stopped. Zack might have hit the nail on the head. Who *would* want to hurt the Protocol Agency? As a group, they worked on lots of different assignments for lots of different agencies. It wasn't as if they had one big bad guy out there that they hammered at. No, something else was at work here.

A mole had managed to integrate and remain hidden for quite a while, suggesting to Paul, and not for the first time, the possibility that he, or she, had an elevated position within their secure building.

Zack straightened in his chair. "Who has the ability to manipulate our recourses?"

"Almost anyone above a level seven clearance in this building. And perhaps a few out of this building." Paul always figured they were never as secure as they wanted to be.

"That might limit our search."

"Or make it exceptionally difficult."

"Why?"

Paul squinted as if in disbelief. "If another director came to me asking if I was a traitor, I'd kick him in the nuts."

Zack sighed. "Well, I wasn't planning on announcing our intentions up front. But I could certainly do some snooping around if you give me a list of names."

"Fine. The list is short. Five names. One is mine."

"I don't think *you* want to bring down your own group. So four names."

"One is your boss, Ken Davenport." Paul didn't really think Ken was culpable, but wondered what Zack would say.

Zack rolled his eyes at first, but then nodded. "I'll have someone check out his movements for the times in question." He pulled out his phone and sent a text message.

Paul gave him three other names. "Matt Timberton, Joel Sanders, and Robert Grayhaus. All three might have the means, but not a motive."

"That you know of."

"The spooks here only share a building. It isn't like we hold hands and sing songs around a campfire to engender camaraderie. Most times we barely interact. We keep our sections private for a reason."

"But occasionally you share personnel resources."

Paul shrugged. "So is a level seven-plus manager pissed because one of my agents didn't do what they were supposed to or did something they weren't supposed to?"

"How should I know? I only want to find Frankie. Whatever it takes."

Paul sent a pointed gaze to Zack. "I appreciate it."

"I'm not doing it for you."

"I know."

His phone rang just then. He answered, "What!"

"Sir, we finally broke through the firewall protection on the information from Brazil."

"And?"

"We have the name of the contact used to deploy a hit on Frankie. We traced it to a phone extension in this building." The operator sounded on edge. Probably not happy that one of the leaders in this building was a traitor.

"So who the fuck is it? Speak, for Christ's sake."

The operator paused and then whispered, "The line traces to Ken Davenport's extension."

Chapter Sixteen

Frankie, pain screaming from every muscle in her body, woke up in a dark place. Not pitch black—a glow of ambient light filtered through the upper part of the room she was in—but not enough to recognize where she was, either. Her last memory was of being in the airport with Zack.

She reached out a hand first to one side and then the other, feeling as far as the limit of her reach allowed. Nothing.

"Zack?" she called out quietly.

She sensed that she was alone in this space.

Carefully, she sat up. The cold stone floor beneath her was sucking the meager warmth from her body. Time to get to her feet.

The space was small, dank, and she smelled rotten potatoes. Must be a cellar of some sort.

Odd place to end up.

She felt around the room slowly and discovered a cot with no bedding and a locked door. The light turned out to be a single bulb hanging just out of her reach, even when she stood on the flimsy cot. Damn.

The last time she'd seen Zack, he was slumped over the center console of the vehicle they were in. One of the masked goons had punched her in the face. She reached up to the tender spot on her upper cheek. The skin wasn't broken, but she'd likely have a bruise. The last thing she remembered was cracking her head against their vehicle. And then everything went black.

Tap. Tap. Tap.

The distant muffled sound of footsteps approaching sent Frankie searching the room for a weapon. She only had the cot. So be it. She lifted it, ready to throw it at whoever opened the door.

Someone fumbled with the door handle for a long while before it finally swung open forcefully. Frankie half swung and half flung the cot at the first person through the door. The moment the wood hit him center mass, he released what sounded like, "Whoof," and crumbled to the floor without another sound.

Frankie leapt over the man now writhing on the floor and exited the door. Unfortunately, the man hadn't come to her room alone. Two of the masked goons from the parking garage waited for her just as soon as she made it through the doorframe.

"Where do you think you're going, sweet thing?" one of the men taunted.

Frankie aimed a hard kick between the speaker's legs. This time, instead of a "whoof" sound, a high-pitched, girly scream came forth.

The hallway wasn't any better lit than the room she'd just been in, but she sidestepped the man now clutching his battered balls and headed back down the hallway.

The remaining man shot her in the center of her back with his stun gun before she made it two steps. Pain radiated across her body right before she lost consciousness.

* * * *

Paul stared at Zack with intensity for several seconds after getting the phone call. Zack's eyebrows raised in question, but it didn't prompt Paul to pony up any information. Zack crossed his arms and waited, impatiently rocking from side to side.

"Are you certain?" Paul asked. "Could it be a frame-up?"

Zack didn't hear the answer, but he could tell that Paul was shaken by whatever information he'd just learned. "Last time I checked, he got a call from you and was on his way down to talk to solve a problem with the download." Paul told the caller.

"What?" His gaze searched the room quickly then landed on Zack. "You didn't call? I see. Well then, send out a team. Find him. Quickly." Paul hung up his phone and got a faraway look in his eyes.

"What's going on?"

Paul twisted his head to one side. "I'm not sure."

Zack snapped his fingers in front of Paul's face. "What the fuck is going on? You look like you lost your best friend."

He stood up and got right in Paul's face. "Did they find Frankie?"

Paul also stood and took a step away. "No. The techs decrypted the information you got from the party the other night. The calls and messages came from a surprising place."

"Where?"

Paul's gaze centered on his face. "Ken Davenport's office."

Zack shook his head. "Not possible. He'd never do anything to hurt a covert group."

"That's what I thought, too, but the techs say otherwise. Plus, they told me he also lied about where he was during both the takedown at the airport four months ago and the bombing of the hospital three months later. The techs have his GPS coordinates for both times in question."

"Also not possible."

Paul huffed. "That he lied? Whatever. You think I always tell the absolute truth about where I am or what I'm doing? Fuck that. It's part of the job to lie. The higher up you are in the company, the bigger the lies that are required."

Zack shrugged. "Ken isn't a liar about things that are important."

"But he lied about his location during two times when someone was fucking with my organization."

"Our organization got fucked with, too. Remember? I got a bullet to the head."

"Yeah, too bad you don't remember who shot you. Based on the scene, you probably trusted the guy who almost ended your life."

"What are you talking about? How do you know that?"

"Back at the airport hangar where you were shot, I had a team of techs analyze the crime scene for sequence of events or at least the probability of what happened and when. You came in through a back office window in the second story. You hid at first. Then someone came in and killed the two kidnappers who had tied up my agent. You entered and released my agent, and then that someone shot you. What if it was Ken?"

"I'll never believe that."

Paul narrowed his eyes. "I don't blame you for your defense of him, but if he didn't have a hand in this, where is he? Why did he lie about where he was before showing up on scene back then?"

"I don't know." Zack pulled out his phone and speed-dialed his boss. After four rings, he heard Ken's canned response to leave a message. "How long has he been gone?" Zack hadn't looked at the clock when Ken left the room.

"I wasn't paying attention." Paul shrugged. "An hour maybe? Right after he got that call. Which he said was from the techs downstairs, but they claim they didn't call him."

Tilting his head to one side, Zack called the tech center. "Are you sure no one from your center called Ken Davenport earlier for any reason?"

"No. But we're finding a glut of information on his secret activities that we didn't have firsthand knowledge of before now. The download we received has been very illuminating. He's been lying on official documents regarding not only his whereabouts, but his phone calls to enemy nations and his statements don't line up either. We sent a security contingent to find him. Tracking his cell phone tells us he's not in the building anymore, but there is no signal at all. He's probably disconnected it. We have no idea where he is."

"I see. Thanks. Let us know if you find him or if he comes back online."

"Yes, sir."

Zack folded his phone in half. He didn't speak and hoped Paul couldn't read the expression on his face because he was pissed and it was hard to suppress his rage. He felt in his gut that Ken would opt to die before he'd do anything like this, but the negative facts were stacking up against him.

Paul's eyebrow rose. "More bad news?"

Zack pocketed his phone and crossed his arms in defiance. "He can't be the traitor we've been looking for all this time. I won't believe it."

"No. I agree with you. Something else is going on."

"What else?" Zack forced himself not to frown.

"I don't know, but we need to figure it out. And fast."

Zack's phone rang again. A text came through. He brought it up hoping that it would be good news. He should have known better. The identity of the caller surprised him, but the message was more bad news about Ken. He tried to guard his expression as Paul was scrutinizing him carefully.

"Is it Ken?" Paul asked.

Zack shook his head and reread the short text message once more.

Back in town for express company
task to help an executive retire.
Call if you want to lend assistance. Jeff

With or without confirmation of Ken's crimes, Jeff's clandestine organization was about to take Ken out and "retire" him. Zack closed his eyes and tried to figure out what his next move should be.

Save Ken and then Frankie?

Or was Ken responsible for her capture?

* * * *

Frankie woke up tied to a chair. Before she opened her eyes, she sensed that someone else was in the room. Every muscle in her body ached with overuse and abuse.

The stale smell of the room was the same as before. It was dank, sour from her own sweat, and musty as if it had been closed up for a long while. Without using big movements, she pulled her arms, widening her elbows as slowly as she could, and noted the bite of the ropes at her wrists. She tested the strength of the bindings and wondered if she could free herself before the other occupant of the room realized she was aware.

"I know you're awake," came a familiar voice.

She opened her eyes, and a man's out-of-focus face came into view. He moved forward and bent closer.

Frankie was so surprised at the identity of her new roommate, she sucked in a short breath. With it came the scents of the dusty, dank, neglected room.

Ken Davenport squinted as he hovered over her. A concerned expression rested on his haggard face.

"Are you hurt?" he asked.

"Were you the one who shot me with the stun gun?"

"No." He stood to his full height. "I was the first man through the door. Remember? The one you hit with the cot."

"No disrespect intended. I was just trying to escape."

"None taken. I was being led here against my will."

Frankie pulled at her bindings with more verve. "What do you mean?" She was trussed up tighter than a Thanksgiving turkey headed for a blazing oven.

"I was kidnapped."

"Really?" Frankie couldn't keep the disdain from her tone. "Then why didn't they tie *you* down, too?"

"Probably because I was still crumpled on the floor in the fetal position after you dropped me with the folded wooden bed frame to my chest. They shot you with the stun gun, dragged you in here, tied you up, and then the bastards left without giving me a situation report. Damn them."

Frankie was used to sarcasm from Paul. She'd never heard Ken use it much. Although, she'd only worked with him once before.

"So you're saying that maybe they were trying to protect *you* from *me*." She snorted in disbelief.

A tired smile surfaced on Ken's mouth. "Perhaps."

"Can you untie me?"

"Maybe. If you promise not to clock me with the cot again."

Frankie narrowed her eyes and gazed at him. "No promises." She didn't know if she could trust him or not. She had a bad feeling about where she was and why Zack's boss was here with her, but couldn't nail it down. Maybe he was a kidnap victim as he purported.

And maybe he wasn't.

Ken gave her a wide berth and moved behind her. She soon felt his fingers brush her hands as he presumably studied her bindings to free her. "Zack was pretty worried about you," he remarked as he tugged at the ropes securing her.

"Was he?" Frankie pulled on her bindings with no results.

Ken continued without acknowledging her efforts. "Last time I saw him, we were trying to figure out how you were taken from the airport. Do you know? Did you see anyone without their mask on or hear a voice you recognized when you were brought here?"

"No." But her subconscious toyed with an idea just out of reach. Frankie hadn't seen anyone she knew, but something bothered her, but she hadn't figured out what it was just yet. It was driving her crazy. Her headache, that had likely started when she hit her head on the SUV at the airport, intensified.

"What's on your mind? I can see waves of heat coming off the top of your head in serious thought."

"Who knew Zack and I would be arriving in DC today beyond a handful? And who would have the means to find out and do something about it?"

"I don't know." Ken rolled his eyes. "But I would probably be fairly high on that list."

"Name another."

"Anyone with a clearance equal to or greater than mine."

"So Paul is another, but he doesn't have motive."

"Neither do I."

"That we know of."

"Trust me."

"No." Frankie didn't want to elaborate, but said quietly, "I'm not quite ready to trust you yet."

"Let me know when you are. I could be an asset."

Frankie sighed. "Who else in our building has the means to pull something like this off?"

Ken tilted his head back and closed his eyes. "Only a couple of others, but they are level seven directors like me and Paul."

"So a couple is two?"

He shook his head. "I can name three of us, not including myself or Paul, who might have the means. But why would they? In the dangerous games that we dabble in, usually we help each other out for God and country and all that."

"I discovered recently that Matt Timberton really hates my boss. I don't think he'd go out of his way to piss on Paul if he were on fire." Frankie remembered the look on his face at the party when she and Diego ran into him. If looks could have killed, she'd be a smoldering pile of carbon on the floor of a Brazilian drug lord's expansive home right now. "Perhaps he's behind all of this."

Ken asked, "Why would he? What's his motive?"

"I don't know. Has Paul done anything to Timberton that he'd be vindictive about?"

Ken shrugged at first, but then squinted as though a thought had just occurred to him.

Frankie pressed. "What are you thinking?"

The sudden rapid gunfire from just outside their door silenced the two of them before he answered. Ken also stopped trying to release her bonds, ramping up Frankie's distrust of him. Was he here only to discover what she knew?

The pervasive dread lingering in the back of her mind since she'd woken up here charged to the forefront of her brain.

The door swung open. Two more men stood ready to enter the room. Both had very familiar faces. Although they both held guns, Frankie felt a rush of relief wash down her body. Her South American contact, Diego, was standing next to his boss, Matt Timberton.

"Get away from her, Ken." Timberton advanced into the room, and Ken moved several steps away with his arms held up and away from his sides. Diego, weapon pointed at Ken's chest, entered the room and moved in position next to her chair. She was saved.

"I wasn't going to hurt her." Ken's hands lifted halfway up his body. He sent a puzzled gaze her way.

"Bullshit." Timberton's expression bordered on rage. "You're the one who engineered her capture, you fucking traitor."

Ken's gaze sought her out again. "I did not. I did not bring you here." He shook his head as if to lend further credence to his words of protest.

"The calls we intercepted from the man known as Valentino traced back to your secure phone line in our building, asshole."

"That is not possible." He glanced at Frankie. "Don't believe it. I'm being framed."

"Framed, my lily-white ass," Timberton chortled. "Explain one other discrepancy to me then, smart man. During the warehouse debacle four months ago, you lied about your location when asked to list your whereabouts during the crime. We checked the GPS coordinates of your phone. You were less than a mile away. So how come it took you so long to show up, huh? Your agent was lying in a pool of blood after saving another and you waltz in half an hour later acting like you came through rush hour traffic."

Ken's eyes slid shut, and he pushed out a long sigh. "I can explain that. My phone was less than a mile away, but I wasn't. It really did take me thirty minutes to arrive."

"And you also lied about where you were when the bomb was set in the secure hospital a month ago after visiting there earlier in the evening. Why did you want her dead?" Matt asked.

"Listen to me." Ken's protests were calmly delivered. "I didn't set that bomb."

Timberton squared his shoulders. "I don't believe you."

Ken also squared his shoulders. An expression of calm rage descended over his features. "I didn't know it was in your purview to believe or disbelieve me, Matt. You can't hold me here."

Timberton and Diego exchanged a look. "We aren't holding you here. We found you after getting an anonymous tip. We came for the girl. She's coming with us." Diego helped her stand.

Ken stepped forward. "No. I don't trust you with her. Don't go with them." His eyes genuinely implored Frankie not to trust the two men rescuing her. Interesting stance.

The gun Timberton held pushed into Ken's chest. "I don't care if you trust me or not. Make a move and I put a bullet in you."

"Frankie, I'm telling you. I didn't do this to you. Please don't trust him."

She stood carefully. Diego's hand was gently wrapped around her upper arm. "I don't care who did it. I just want to leave."

Ken drilled another look her way. "I don't have a gun, Frankie. Look at who's holding the automatic weapon. If I was behind all this, why wouldn't I have at least a freaking pocketknife?"

She shrugged, but the thread of his logic wound around her consciousness and took root. Frankie wasn't in a position to believe or disbelieve either of them. Diego was the one she was taking her cues from right now. He was with Timberton, and they seemed to have evidence of Ken's culpability for more than just this current occasion. She wouldn't have suspected Ken, but she wanted to leave.

"I just want out of here." Her desire to get out of this prison overrode any gut reaction to Matt Timberton. This morning she would have said he was a bastard. Actually, he probably still was, but he was getting her out of here. Ken hadn't. He hadn't really even tried to release her bonds.

Ken glanced at Diego. "Hurt her and I will find a way to kill you."

"Big talk for an unarmed ass wipe who's about to be jailed for being a traitorous mole," Timberton said. He turned his head toward Diego. "Get her out of here. Take her to the room I showed you on the way here. We can debrief her."

Frankie headed toward the door. She glanced over her shoulder at Ken one last time. The look he gave her was one that seemed genuinely concerned. Then again, she didn't trust her instincts right now. The two thugs from earlier had probably stunned the good sense right out of her. And then Ken had been "put" in her prison cell. He'd instigated a discussion where Matt Timberton was a candidate for the person behind all the trouble in the Protocol team. How had she been so wrong about him? Her instincts were not only mistaken, they were "off the rails" wrong.

"Can you untie me?" Frankie asked as she and Diego walked down a stone-lined hallway to yet another dismal room.

"Of course. Let me get you to the debrief room first, okay?"

She nodded. This was almost over. They heard a single gunshot from behind them as they entered the doorway.

"He didn't shoot Ken, did he?"

Diego looked down the hallway. "I certainly hope not. Probably just a warning shot to ensure we mean business."

"What are you doing here? I thought you'd be back slogging through the jungle with your merry gunrunners by now."

"Got pulled late last night for a special task. I guess they found out Ken was the traitor and had Matt find him to take him down." From a pocket in the leg of his pants Diego pulled out a knife to cut her bonds.

"But I didn't think they'd even cracked the code by the time we arrived in DC. How did Matt find out so fast?"

"He keeps his fingers in lots of pies. And he's the supervisor over the analytical section. Any new information is likely shuttled to him first before it goes out to anyone else."

Diego turned her around. She felt him make the first cut with his knife to release her. She was still bound, but the ropes were loosened.

"What are you doing, Jeff?" Timberton asked from the doorway. Frankie hadn't even heard him come in. *Jeff?* Was that Diego's "real" name?

"What's it look like? I'm cutting her bonds."

"Don't."

"Why not?"

"There's been a change of plan." The smug smile on Timberton's face didn't bode well. In that second, Frankie knew he was not only evil, he was Valentino. The traitor. The man they'd been chasing for months. The man who'd tried to kill her at least once, maybe more. The man Zack had trusted and gotten a bullet to his head instead. The man Ken had just tried to tell her was setting him up.

"Why do you want me dead?" she asked simply.

"It started out as vengeance. Today, we have one other item to discuss though."

Diego's eyebrows scrunched. "What the fuck, Matt? I don't understand."

"You don't need to." He turned his gun on Diego. "Are you going to go along, or do I need to put a bullet in you right now?"

"I'm cool. I work for you. And you know I follow your orders." He removed his hands from Frankie's ropes and put his knife back in his pants pocket. "So what are we going to do with her?"

"I need some information. Help me get it and then we're out of here."

Diego shrugged. "Fine by me."

Frankie had trusted Diego. She'd been a fool.

The look of loathing Timberton sent her way froze her to the core. Diego's quick defection to his side made her ill. The puzzled look on his face soon shifted to one of hard determination. He glanced at

Timberton, smiled, and put his finger on the trigger of his Glock nine millimeter. Unfortunately, this time he likely wouldn't save her. Instead, he was here under his boss's direction.

"Put her in the chair." The single chair in the room looked exactly like the one they'd just left. She glanced at Diego, but he wouldn't look her in the eyes. She was on her own.

"Miss Belle has a unique personality," Timberton told Diego. "Sometimes she's a spy, and other times she's not. Paul Kelly runs a very mysterious spy operation, but I know the secret to his success."

"I don't know what you're talking about." A dull headache formed in the base of her skull. She wouldn't give him the satisfaction of seeing her weak.

Sexual satisfaction didn't equal dependability, especially in their line of work. She was so very disappointed by Diego's presence here. Two days ago she might have said she'd trust him with her life. Zack trusted him and by association, she'd thought his reliance was solid. Bad mistake.

Diego didn't once look in her direction. He kept his gaze averted. However, Timberton continued to glare at her. Frankie sent a loathing return gaze.

One thing she figured out. Ken had been innocent of the charges Matt spewed at him earlier. She thought about the gun shot from a few minutes ago. Was Ken dead? She hoped not. One thing was perfectly clear though. She was on her own until help came. Was there anyone left?

Who did she trust besides Paul?

A single name came forth.

Zack.

Was he even still alive after the assault in the airport parking garage?

Chapter Seventeen

Jeff cooperated with Matt's insanity for now. It was his only play. He knew Matt would kill him instantly if he didn't go along. He wasn't sure if Ken was still alive. The unexpected gunshot echoed in his soul. Arresting a fellow agent they suspected of treason was fine. Shooting an unarmed man and leaving him crumpled in a prison cell seemed extreme and not an act he wanted to participate in. As in most all things clandestine, there was a fine line between enemy and ally.

Today's activities put him on the fence. Matt seemed slightly maniacal. In his heart, he knew he might as well be back with the sadistic gunrunners he'd left in the jungle.

Even if Ken *was* a traitor, Jeff thought shooting him like a rabid dog and abandoning him seemed especially coldhearted. Even for Matt, who was acting very strange again. His usual uptight attitude was replaced by one of determined urgency to get Frankie. Why?

Something was not right. He tried to send another text to Zack, but there was no signal here in this underground bunker. Not a wisp.

Jeff couldn't have been more surprised when Matt not only pulled him from his undercover operation overseas, but brought him to this dungeon of a place to be his muscle for a "special duty" as he'd put it.

He wondered briefly if Matt knew about his and Frankie's intimate relationship from earlier in the year back when she called herself Daphne. Her alter ego Frankie had greeted him with delicious results in Brazil.

Had Matt guessed where Jeff's alter ego "Diego" had spent his last night after the party they'd crashed? Probably. Matt had hustled him out of the country so fast last night he hadn't been able to even make any other contact. If he could have, Jeff would have contacted Zack sooner. The cryptic message he'd left over an hour ago couldn't be checked due to the fucking lack of reception here.

However, knowing Matt the way Jeff did, it likely didn't matter whether he'd been sleeping with a fellow spy sans names or screaming them. Matt expected loyalty in all work-related events regardless of his current identity.

"Do you remember me, Miss Belle?" Matt asked with a particularly demented grin.

"Yes. You're the asshole that almost got me caught during an undercover operation two nights ago. No thanks to you, Diego and I made it out just fine. Thanks for asking." She turned to him with fury etched in her expression. "Or do you prefer to be called Jeff?"

Jeff shrugged and smiled over at Matt.

"What a clever wit!" Matt laughed with a little bit too much maniacal humor for Jeff's comfort. "Tell me, Miss Belle, do you remember meeting me before the other night?"

Her brows knit in an almost frown as one slim shoulder lifted. "Should I?" Jeff thought her tone was rather sedate given the circumstances.

Matt produced a very large syringe from his inner jacket pocket. "Well, that is the question of the day, isn't it? I believe you should remember. This will help." He pulled off the protective cover to reveal the thick metal tip.

"What is that?" Frankie's eyes widened just slightly, but her gaze didn't waver from Matt's hand, or more likely, what it carried.

"This is a special medicine to help you remember your other life."

"I don't have another life." Frankie squinted as if a bright light had just been shined in her eyes.

"I believe you do. That's how the Protocol Agency works. They manufacture spies. It's clever, but it shouldn't have been chosen as a worthier project than mine."

What the hell was he talking about? With an eye on Matt and his big scary needle, Jeff carefully reached into his pocket, opened his phone, and texted a message. He wasn't sure if it went through, but his phone would keep trying every three minutes to send it once a signal was available. If Matt noticed and found out, he'd be dead in a second, probably with a needle in his eye, but given the current events unfolding, Jeff didn't exactly trust Matt anymore.

Frankie's eyes blinked rapidly. "You're crazy. I'm not a *created* spy. I'm a trained operative."

"Yes. That's true. And at the same time, you also used to be a file clerk for a man named Benny in Loganville, South Carolina. He acquired something unusual and sent you to deliver it to me. But you fucked up. I guess it wasn't totally your fault. Daphne Kane didn't have the same skills as Frankie the spy."

Jeff had to hold his mouth closed. Frankie was a spy, but Daphne wasn't? What the hell? He glanced down at Frankie. She looked positively gray. He'd consider her spy career later. For now he needed to get her away from Matt.

"She doesn't look so good," Jeff stated the obvious.

Matt shrugged and took a step closer. "She'll be fine."

With Frankie tied to a chair about to be the recipient of a drug overdose at worst or a big fucking needle injury at best, he didn't want to be on the wrong side of this scenario.

She mattered to him.

A glance at his boss gave Jeff a sudden and pervasive idea that would not dissolve. It became unmistakably clear that Matt was as crazy as a shithouse rat. Jeff easily shifted his alliance and vowed to do whatever it took to save a woman he loved.

Loyalty be damned.

As Matt advanced on Frankie, Jeff tried to think of what the hell he could do to help, short of shooting Matt and trying to escape this underground maze. Even tied to a chair, Frankie could take care of herself. She kicked out at the opportune time and knocked the needle from Matt's hand. The syringe clattered across the stone floor, and the expression on Matt's face darkened.

"Not smart, Miss Belle."

"You're an asshole," she replied.

Matt bent to retrieve the needle. While he was turned away, Jeff sauntered to the space behind her chair. A glance down and he saw she still had several lengths of rope tied around her wrists. Jeff wrapped one arm around her shoulders as if to hold her in place for her shot.

"You traitorous bastard," she whispered.

"Sorry, honey, I have loyalties to serve." He stealthily pulled out his pocketknife once more and cut through her bonds as carefully as he could, hoping he didn't slice her skin. "You were fun to hang out with, but now I've got to run with the big dogs."

To her credit, she didn't even flinch or make a move when she was free. He slipped his knife back into his leg pocket and secured his other arm around her loosely.

Matt watched them. "Stand her up. Keep her from kicking me." Jeff urged her upward. Together they slowly moved out of the chair. She kept her fingers laced together. Jeff pushed her forward until he could squat down and circle her thighs with his arms. If Matt wondered why she didn't fight him, he ignored it. The moment Jeff had a good clasp around her legs, Matt moved forward.

Frankie head-butted him in the face. He howled in pain and reared backward with blood spurting out of his nose. Jeff let go of her legs, and she ran toward the open door. Matt gained his footing and flung the needle at her like a dart. It landed in her lower flank. She kept going. Jeff was on her heels out the door and slammed it shut on their way out. He put the shitty, weak lock in place, knowing it wouldn't keep Matt contained for long. Frankie pulled the wicked big needle from her body and threw it on the ground.

They raced down the long stone hallway side by side in almost perfect step. He slipped his arm through hers. She looked at him quizzically, but didn't protest. "Where are we anyway?" she whispered.

"Not sure," he replied as they hung a left at the T juncture.

Ahead was another long hallway. Jeff searched for and finally saw the first white chalk mark. "But we're on the way out. Look for white chalk on the walls. I left a marked breadcrumb-like trail to follow out."

"How did you know to do that?"

He shrugged. "Force of habit I guess. I hate not knowing where I am or how to get out. You're a spy, don't you do things like that?"

A grin started to shape her lips, but then alarm shone in her face. Frankie's steps faltered, and she almost fell down. They didn't have time to stop. "What's wrong?" he asked. "We need to keep running."

"Whatever was in that needle is giving me a spiking headache. Seriously, it feels like my skull is about to split open."

A sudden onset headache was a bad thing, but Jeff looped an arm around her waist and kept them moving. Matt would be hot on their trail.

He saw another chalk mark on the right. At the next intersection they went right. With each step the incline increased. Jeff knew they were underground and needed to ascend to get out. They'd barely taken two steps when she fell to her knees. "Sorry." She spoke through gritted teeth, voice no louder than an agonized rasp. "Need to rest. Head hurts like a son of a bitch."

"We can't stop. Matt will be dogging our heels the minute he gets out of that room."

"Please. Just for a second. My head hurts like hell." And then her eyes rolled back in her head and she fainted dead away in his arms. *Fuck.* He looked behind him and listened. Nothing. No sound. But he knew the calm in their wake wouldn't last. Matt was a determined, vendetta-seeking son of a bitch. Probably even more so now that Jeff had turned on him.

Jeff scooped her up in his arms carefully and continued down the narrow stone hallways. He searched for his chalk marks, hoping to find either the exit out of this dungeon or a hiding place to rouse Frankie.

After a third turn in as many minutes down the same maze of hallways with no hiding places, Jeff saw the light at the end of the tunnel. Literally. There was a window in the door at the end of this passage. Finally, the way out of this stone dungeon.

Once at the heavy, wood-planked door, he clumsily unlatched the rusted apparatus and pushed through into the late afternoon day with Frankie in his arms. He wanted to kick the door shut for another weak obstacle to hinder his former boss, but decided quiet would be better.

Jeff glanced at the sky to get his bearings and turned toward where his best avenue for escape was.

When Matt had brought him here, they'd left the vehicle hidden at the end of the lane in a small clearing surrounded by an unexpected forest. This entrance to the underground cavern was well hidden. He'd been coming to this part of the city for a decade and never suspected there was anything here.

Still cradling the unconscious Frankie in his arms, he made his way down a road with knee-high grass in the center of two narrow ruts. Nothing larger than a riding mower would fit here, and it was obvious nothing with a blade had been here in a long while.

Frankie roused slightly halfway to the vehicles, but Jeff kept moving. There was no cover in this alley, and if Matt came out of the wooden door, they'd be easy targets to pick off.

She stirred in his arms. "Where am I?" she mumbled. He felt her shift. She slipped her arms around his neck and pushed her face into his collar. The scent of her hair curled a wisp of memory around his brain stem. He leaned down and kissed her temple.

"We're still running, honey. Only I'm doing all the work." Jeff kept moving, feeling in his bones that they were about to be caught and mowed down with bullets to their backs the instant Matt saw them running down the lane.

There was a slight widening in the road ahead on the left side. A space barely wide enough to house his frame, but better cover than before. Jeff ducked into the place and leaned Frankie against the stone wall lining the narrow roadway. He checked his phone for messages. Nothing. After sending another short text to Zack, he searched the area for a better place to hide. There was nothing. They were completely exposed if anyone came out of the secret door. Jeff decided quickly that splitting headache or not, they needed to keep moving.

"Can you walk?" he asked. "Better yet, can you run?"

Frankie opened her eyes. She looked around as if with wonder. "How did we get here?" Her gaze shifted to his face.

"I got us out. I carried you."

She put her hand up to his face. "Thank you."

"You're welcome." *Time to go.*

She leaned in and pushed her lips against his with such soft pressure, he didn't expect the touch to even register. *Holy hell.* He *felt* her all right, all the way to the tip of his cock. He wanted nothing more than to lay her down in this overgrown lane, crush his mouth to hers, and make them both forget they were on the run. He licked her lips apart and took a taste of heaven. She responded in kind, and before he realized it, he had one hand down the front of her shirt beneath the edge of her bra, stroking her nipple until it pebbled against his fingertips.

"Where is Zack?"

"What?"

Frankie turned her glistening eyes back to his face. "Is Zack okay? I'm so worried about him."

Shit. Had he just left Zack back there? Matt never said anything about another prisoner beyond Ken Davenport. He turned and looked at the road they'd just come down. He listened for anyone else, but there were no sounds. He cursed his weakness for allowing the distraction of Frankie's kiss to make him forget where he was and what he was supposed to be doing. He must be crazy. They were on the run for Christ's sake.

"What's wrong, Jeff?" The alarm in her tone stilled his heart and almost pained him, but not as much as what she'd said.

Fuck. She'd just called him Jeff.

He brushed a strand of hair off of her forehead. "Daphne?"

She gave him a watery smile. "Yes, of course." Her brows creased in concern. "What's wrong?"

He plastered a grin on his lips. "Nothing." *Absolutely everything.*

Jeff ran a hand down his face. *Really time to go.* "Can you walk, honey?"

"I think so." She leaned away from the wall and took a tentative step.

"Does your head still hurt?"

"A little. Not too bad." She wrapped an arm around his waist. "Are we going to see Zack?"

"Sure." *Not yet. We're getting the fuck out of here.* Jeff figured he'd secure Daphne somewhere and come back to look for Zack.

She frowned as she looked at their overgrown surroundings. "I'm not sure, but I think he might be in trouble."

"He's fine. I promise." He slung an arm around her shoulders and eased them back onto the path towards the vehicle.

"Okay. Good. Where are we anyway?"

Shit. How should he answer *that* question? "On the way to the car."

Jeff calculated the time it would take him to hot-wire the vehicle and where in the world he would take her that would be safe.

All of a sudden, she sagged in his arms again. Was she conscious?

Her eyes opened suddenly. "Where are we?"

"On the run. Don't you remember?"

She nodded her head and then grabbed it as if in pain. "I know. I just didn't remember making it this far away from the dungeon. Must have passed out or something. This headache is a killer. Like something's trying to eat its way out of my brain."

"There might be a first aid kit in the SUV with pain relievers. If we can get there. Can you walk, or do I need to keep carrying you?"

"I can walk. Jesus, I'm not an infant."

Jeff narrowed his eyes. "Frankie?"

"Yes. Who else are you traveling with? Let's go." She stood on wobbly feet.

Freaky. She seemed to be flipping between the separate personalities of Frankie and Daphne. Probably not good. She must have gotten a dose of whatever was in the needle. Jeff pushed that revelation to the back of his crowded mind for later and cinched an arm around her waist. They continued slowly.

They came to the end of the narrow alley and he turned them to the right side. Thirty feet more and they'd be out of here.

"I think we'd make better time if I carried you."

"Screw that. I'm walking on my own."

She took several more quick steps before she collapsed against him.

"Frankie?" Jeff lifted her into his arms. She didn't answer. "Daphne?"

Her eyes opened. "Daphne? Who the hell is that?"

"Someone who reminds me of you. Never mind."

"Put me down. I can walk." She wriggled out of his arms and they walked several more steps. She seemed to be making better progress, and she wasn't wincing in pain with every step. Perhaps she was getting better. She hadn't received the full injection. He shuddered to think what would have happened if she'd gotten a full dose.

The square front corner of the black SUV's hood came into view. Jeff hustled her a little faster, resisting the urge to look over his shoulder. He only had time to think of the question, "Why isn't he after us?" when the answer became completely clear. They weren't alone in the clearing.

"What took you two so long to get here?" Matt asked. He leaned against the hood of the vehicle with another large syringe in hand and an evil smile playing around his lips.

* * * *

Another incoming text message made Zack's cell phone vibrate in his pocket. It was a coded message meant to convey a set of GPS coordinates. But the code was one Zack hadn't used in a long while. The second message was also from Jeff's stateside account.

Zack decrypted the text as best as he could in his head. The first part was easy. An SOS requesting help. The second part was a bitch because his head was still ringing from being zapped with the stun gun earlier. It was a wonder he could calculate and remember his own name. The long string of numbers representing the location coordinates was too difficult to remember in his addled brain. He grabbed a map and a stubby pencil from the glove box to transcribe and record them.

The coded numbers translated to a local GPS coordinate. Zack started his vehicle and quickly fed the numbers into the onboard system. Satisfaction rose inside as the computer chewed on the data with a rotating hourglass to pass the time. Utter frustration bled into a feeling of critical resolve at finally having some sort of direction to point himself in. His short-term plan was to find Jeff, assess the situation with Ken, and enlist his help to find Frankie. If Ken was the traitor they sought, Frankie was likely already with him.

The hourglass on the screen flickered and the destination came up. He put the vehicle into drive as he stared at the screen, ready to race to the location showing.

In a British accent, the GPS chirped, "You have arrived at your destination. Would you like to select another?" *What the fuck?*

The coordinates in Jeff's coded message were for the building he was already sitting in? That couldn't be right. Could it?

Zack recalculated the message. He repeated the agonizing process of putting the numbers in more carefully. And then waited endlessly for the hourglass to stop flipping over only to get the exact same fucking result.

Jeff wanted to meet him in their spy building. He was already sitting at the adjacent parking structure trying to keep from being seen. Zack hadn't mentioned to Paul where he was going. If he didn't move soon and go someplace, they could just wave at each other when Paul discovered him sitting in his vehicle trying in vain to make the GPS say something different.

He put the vehicle in drive again. He needed to get moving. Better to at least drive around the building and feel like he was accomplishing something rather than sit here waiting to get caught.

His car had moved about three yards when his cell phone beeped again with another text from Jeff.

South side of the building. Hurry.

Zack was parked on the north side. And it *was* a big building. He roared out of the parking lot and headed south.

He saw an overgrown road that looked like it *might* lead him to the south side of the complex. Operating on pure gut instinct, Zack gunned the engine and turned down the road, which was lushly bracketed by trees, bushes, and shrubbery. He navigated the narrow road traveling way too fast If he didn't end up wrapped around a tree before this was over, it would be a miracle.

He revved the engine to climb an incline. It ended quickly and required an abrupt left turn that he almost missed. Rear wheels trying to scrabble to gain traction, he almost plunged into a murky, pond scum-covered puddle of water that looked like it would easily swallow his vehicle and he'd never be heard of ever again. Twenty years from now they'd find his skeletal remains still gripping the steering wheel and foot buried in the gas pedal when they cleared the swamp to put up a future shopping mall.

The road along the narrow edge of the pond he tried not to plunge into eventually opened into more solid ground. Through another stand of increasingly thickening woods and the road dead-ended in a clearing.

Another SUV was already parked in the space barely large enough for a single vehicle. He saw two things immediately.

Matt Timberton shot Jeff with the gun he held in one hand and then promptly stabbed Frankie in the chest with the biggest fucking needle he'd ever seen.

Jeff fell forward to the ground and didn't move.

Zack barely got his vehicle into park before opening his door to use it for cover.

"What are you doing here, Zack?" Matt's tone held a certain crazed edge that explained some of what was going on.

"I'm here to get Frankie. That's it."

Matt motioned with his gun. "Then join us, why don't you?"

Frankie pulled the needle from her chest one-handed and promptly shuddered. She fell to her knees, and Zack's insides liquefied in terror. Had Matt killed her?

"What did you just give her?"

"Something to help her remember a certain event from many months ago. She has something that belongs to me."

"You murdering fuck," Frankie slurred. She threw the needle at Matt, who easily dodged it. She turned to Zack. "Get out of here, Zack. He killed Ken and Jeff. He won't hesitate to kill you, too."

"I'm not leaving you alone with him." Zack edged from behind his SUV door.

He threw out his gun, lifted his hands, and slowly moved towards Frankie. One careful step at a time, he watched Matt out of the corner of one eye and got closer and closer to her. Someone had bloodied Matt's nose, and it was still slightly swollen. Zack silently applauded whoever had clocked him one.

The minute he squatted down and wrapped an arm around her shoulder to hold her, blood started pouring out of her nose.

Shit. Hadn't Paul said something about that being very bad?

* * * *

Paul Kelly never panicked. But with today's unparalleled events stacking up, he was nearly frantic. When it became clear that Zack had ditched him, he marched down to the analytical department in the basement to find out if there was any new disheartening intelligence retrieved from the information they'd obtained in South America. He had absolutely no other direction to go to find answers.

If Ken *was* the traitor, then had he called Zack to help him? Did the raid at the airport really happen the way they said, or had Zack simply betrayed her and taken her to Ken? And for what purpose? Was she even still alive?

He approached Matt Timberton's office. Before he got there, someone familiar stepped from a hallway up ahead. Wearing a medical smock, the man looked like one of the medics from the Protocol Agency Med Lab. What the hell? The man never looked back but made a beeline for Matt's office. The man was ahead of him by the length of a car. His lumbering gait was easy to identify. It had to be Alden. The prick.

He slowed, and Paul ducked out of sight in a hallway and peeked out, catching the side of Alden's head.

Alden looked around like he was doing something he wasn't supposed to then ducked into Matt's office and closed the door. Paul approached until he stood before the door Alden had entered. *Matt Timberton, Analytic Supervisor* was on a plaque between the door frame and the window.

Matt's office window had the inner blinds pulled, so Paul couldn't see inside, but knew there was absolutely no reason for one of his Protocol medics to be visiting Matt Timberton.

Pausing at the door for a slow count of ten, Paul suddenly wrenched the knob open and entered Matt's office, resisting the urge to say, "Ah. Ha. Caught you!"

He expected to see Alden giving Matt either secret information, or money exchanging hands, or any number of illegal or morally reprehensible activities, but the joke was on him.

The room was completely empty.

Chapter Eighteen

The pain banging around in her brain was so intense, Frankie could barely open her eyes. Her head pounded as if one thousand head of cattle had just been let loose to trample her mind. She thought her eyes were watering when she felt a drip from her nose then saw a drop of blood fall onto her wrinkled shirt. Not good.

Zack carefully slipped an arm around her shoulders as if to lend comfort to an already appalling situation. She hissed in pain the moment he touched her skin, but he didn't release her.

"Where is the bag?" Matt asked. His seething tone with the forceful bitter edge did nothing to help her headache.

Speaking was agony, but she managed, "What bag?" She wanted to cry after saying two frickin' words.

"The bag you were sent to put in the safety deposit box."

Frankie grabbed her head with both hands. "I have no idea what you're talking about, you sick fuck." The vibration of merely saying that many words together cost her.

Matt huffed as if supremely annoyed. "You're Daphne, right?"

A throb of pain at hearing that single word pulsed across her brain and would have brought her to her knees if she wasn't already kneeling on them. *Oh, god, don't say that name again.*

"I'm Frankie," she managed before black spots of unconsciousness plied her into demanding sleep before any other activity took place. Zack squeezed harder. The dark depths of just letting go lured her with a siren call of no pain, if only she'd succumb. She fell forward. Barely catching herself from smashing her face on the ground by bracing herself with one palm, Frankie moaned as more blood dripped steadily to the grass between her knees. Zack helped hold her, his strong grip keeping her from hitting the grass nose first.

Matt kept his distance from her and shouted out, "Stay with me, now. I need information. You're the only one who knows it."

"What the fuck did you give her?" Zack's angry voice seemed like it came through a long tunnel. The pain was lessening, but she was losing the battle to stay aware. As she slid into oblivion, flashes of memories dotted her waning conscious. But they were like having someone else's dreams stuck in her head. And her brain wanted to purge them.

Frankie fought to stay awake. She didn't want to see the foreign memories. She shifted one hand to Zack's leg in an effort to gain enough strength to rise to her feet again. The moment she tried, a new spike of pain drilled behind her eyes into the center of her head.

Just when she thought she couldn't be in any more pain, the poison of whatever Matt had injected into her chest laughed and dished out even more torture for her to endure.

Zack's face came into her view. "Jesus, God Almighty, I think you've killed her."

"No. I just gave her an extra dose of something she already is well versed with. She'll live. And she needs to flip over to Daphne and start talking. I don't have all day."

Frankie's brain pulsed at hearing that name again. She cried out in pain, unable to stop herself.

"She's fucking bleeding from her eyes." Zack's tone, laced with more than just a hint of fear, also scared her. *I'm bleeding from my eyes? Damn. That sounds dire.*

"Daphne? Answer my question. Where is the black and tan bag? I need to know what you did with it after you put the contents from it into the safety deposit box."

Frankie's head imploded in pain. Memories foreign and familiar assaulted her.

She wanted to die.

* * * *

Paul searched Matt's office carefully for the opening to the secret passage. There had to be one here. He'd never researched the history of this particular building, but given the secret nature of the groups who were using it, the idea of a hidden space wasn't a stretch. He just wished he'd heard of it before now.

Matt was as wily as any in their profession. The lever to open wouldn't be obvious. Or would it?

He looked at the bookcase on the back wall. There were several heavy-looking bookends containing various books on military warfare and tactical strategy for successful assault situations both amphibious and terrain based.

Paul reached out for the bookend closest to the back wall at chest level and tried to pull it off the shelf. It didn't budge. He pushed it and a panel opened next to the shelf. The space was wide enough for two to enter, if needed. Without looking back, he entered and secured the door behind him.

The backup gun he kept on his ankle might be a nuisance on most days of the week, but right this second he was glad to have it. The penlight in his pocket also was much appreciated. He kept the small beam of light pointed low as he made his way down the stone hallway.

After a several yards, he came to a dead end. His choices were left or right. He took a black Magic Marker out of his pocket and made a mark on the stone. If he had to exit back the way he came, it was better to have a marked trail.

Three forks in the road later, Paul put another mark at waist level on the stone. He genuinely hoped he wasn't hopelessly lost in this slightly claustrophobic underground maze. Paul thought he heard a noise up ahead. He paused momentarily to listen. Nothing. He continued on.

Another choice, another mark, another hallway deeper into unknown territory.

Paul definitely heard a scraping noise up ahead.

Where the hell was Alden going?

* * * *

Frankie woke, but kept her eyes closed. She was on her stomach, a hard surface beneath her still-aching body. She smelled dirt. Was she outside? The cool, moist blades of uncut grass mashed into one cheek. She heard voices as if they echoed through a glass tube. It took a few seconds to understand the words spoken. She listened for a few more minutes and realized it was Zack. A burst of tingling feeling resonated through her limbs.

She trusted Zack. He would help her. Protect her. Did she need protection?

He said, "Why are you doing this?"

Another man's voice responded, but she didn't hear what he said. Who else was talking? Was he talking to her?

She tried to remember what had been going on and why she had woken up on the ground. The residual headache had abated some. She searched her memory for a clue as to why she was facedown sniffing blades of grass.

The last thing she remembered was a big needle being shoved into her chest. Shit that hurt. She cast back further and remembered Jeff talking to her by a wall along a narrow, weed-strewn roadway.

She felt moisture on her face. Had she been crying? That hardly seemed like her.

No! Zack said her eyes were bleeding. *Crap.*

All of a sudden, her brain unfolded the long, complicated story of her busy life. It didn't hurt as much as before, but the visions were uncomfortable at best.

Flashes of memory zipped by one by one ceaselessly. She resisted the urge to moan. *Stay silent.*

Not one but two lives were knitting together in her brain to form her complicated past.

She was Frankie.

She was Daphne.

She was a spy.

She was a file clerk.

In fact, she was both of these people at the same time.

Oh, God. Zack! Jeff!

She remembered the salacious weekend from four months ago. She remembered another one from two nights ago. No wonder Jeff was so perplexed that she didn't remember him.

Frankie also remembered the safety deposit box and what she'd put in there. She knew what Matt sought. Her alter ego, Daphne, had liked the oversized bag she'd carried all the way there. She hadn't put the outer black and tan bag inside the box like she'd been told to do. She'd kept it. Hidden it away and then forgotten about it during the exceptionally vivid, sexually liberating weekend.

What she didn't know was why the bag was so frickin' important to Timberton.

Zack's voice became clearer. She listened in and prepared to make her move.

With her shiny new memories all folded together, she waited patiently for a signal, and the best news was that she could be either identity.

A flood of memories had yet to be studied and catalogued, but without a doubt, Zack Mahon, in all his tall and amazingly muscled glory, was the most important of all her imported and combined memories. She loved this man both as Daphne and as Frankie. He'd stepped in front of a gun for her four months ago when she'd been Daphne. They'd spent an amazing weekend together. The last conversation they had that day, before chaos reigned, came into her mind.

Seated in his truck and then standing in the airport parking lot, he'd been reluctant to end their affair. He hadn't wanted to let her go. She hadn't wanted to leave. Now she knew why she was so compelled to go back to her life as a file clerk in Loganville. Frankie the spy motivated her. As a member of the Protocol Agency, she couldn't be Frankie without accepting Daphne as her downtime role.

With the new blended memories, Frankie, she determined, was her dominate personality. She didn't know exactly how she'd move forward from now on, but knew she wanted Zack as a permanent member of whatever life she ended up living.

Zack's curt tone cut through her reverie.

"I don't remember a warehouse. Was that where you shot me?"

"An educated guess. Good for you. Or your boss clued you in." Timberton's voice. A rush of recent memories involving Zack's boss, Ken Davenport, surfaced. Where was *he*?

Hopefully, not dead.

"Ken told me what happened. That it must have been someone I knew."

Matt's maniacal laughter pealed into the air. "The expression on your face was priceless when you realized you'd been betrayed."

Frankie faded a bit. Remembering all this information taxed her strength.

"Daphne!" she heard Matt scream. "Wakey. Wakey. Tell me what I need to know."

She groaned. She couldn't help it.

Before she could strategize the best option of who to wake up as, someone else came into the mix.

"Oh, my god! What have you done to her?" came yet another very familiar voice.

A huge rush of new memories regarding this man crashed across her brain.

And Frankie knew that there was more than just one traitor.

* * * *

"How much of the drug did you give her? I told you to be careful," whined the newcomer in the white lab coat. Zack wanted to pound him one.

"Shut up, Alden. Or I'll shut you up." Matt gestured with his gun. Alden stopped talking. He also hunched his shoulders inward and pushed his glasses up on his nose. In the next second, they slid back down, and he repeated the process twice more before Zack turned away. His blood pressure went up just watching the spineless weasel.

Zack didn't recognize Alden, but he already wanted to rip the guy's glasses off of his face and punch them down his throat. Given the big-assed needle Matt had wielded earlier, it was obvious he'd gotten help from a member of the Protocol's medical team. The white lab coat with the embroidered stitching was a further indication.

Paul had been right about a mole in his organization. He'd just been looking at the wrong pool of candidates. Zack hated treacherous behavior. His fury rose in concert with his frustration of being able to do nothing.

The woman he loved more than reason was currently crumpled on the ground bleeding from disturbing places and unable to center herself to one personality. Ken was still missing and presumed dead. Jeff was down and out. He hadn't moved. Matt held a gun on him. Zack had no doubt he'd use it. Alden wasn't going to help him, and he had no backup on the way to lend assistance.

Alden hunched over more and then moved two steps forward, reaching his arms down as if to touch Frankie. Zack risked another bullet to his person by stepping in front of her. He snarled, "Stay away from her or I rip you apart with my bare hands."

To Alden's credit, he stopped. He pushed his glasses up on his nose. But then the prick turned to Matt. "You said she was mine once you got the information. I want to take her away from here."

"Over my dead, rotting corpse." Zack took another step towards

Alden. Even the threat of being shot didn't deter him from protecting Frankie while she was down.

"That can be arranged," Matt said with a laugh. "Again." He sobered and turned to Alden. "Wake her up and make her talk." He glanced at his watch. "I need the information stored in Daphne's head, and I've got someplace to be."

"How much did you give her from the syringe?" Alden asked, but didn't attempt to move closer.

Zack answered for him. "He stabbed her in the chest and emptied the whole thing into her."

"I don't think that was a good idea," Alden whispered.

Matt frowned. "You said if she got a big enough dose, she'd convert back to Daphne permanently, so she'd never snap back into Frankie again. That's what you said you wanted. You wanted to romance Daphne without worrying about Frankie showing up to kick your sorry, sniveling ass."

Frankie moaned and pushed up onto her forearms. Zack moved next to her and squatted down to help her.

"Stand up, Zack. I don't trust you. Hands in the air or I develop better aim and put one between your eyes. That should keep you down this time."

Frankie moved forward and wrapped an arm around Zack's calf. Her head rested against his ankle. He relished her touch and wished he had a move to keep her safe. Out of the corner of his eye, he could have sworn he saw Jeff move.

Alden bent over. "Daphne? Can you hear me?"

From his vantage point, Zack saw her lift her head. "I hear you. Where am I? My head really hurts."

"Daphne," Matt said eagerly. "Where did you put the black and tan bag?"

"The bag?"

"Yes. The one you carried to the bank." Matt stepped closer. "Where is it?"

She remained quiet for a slow count of ten before lifting her head and saying, "It's under the passenger seat in Zack's truck. I put it there when we left the bank. But I forgot about it."

Matt looked over at the SUV Zack had brought.

Zack said, "That's not my personal vehicle. It's not in there."

"Guess you get to live a little longer then." Matt swiveled toward her. "Where is it? Where is your truck?"

Zack shrugged.

Matt lunged forward half a step and snarled, "Where is it?"

Before Matt could threaten Zack to get him to reveal any further information, a shot rang out from behind them, and Matt flinched. A bloodstain swelled and grew on Matt's shoulder. The one *not* holding his weapon.

And it didn't stop him from aiming his gun at Frankie.

* * * *

Zack felt her hug closer to his leg. He started to charge forward, but before he could say the word no, move to protect her, or even look down to see if she was unharmed, another shot rang out from a different direction. From below him. This time the shooter hit Matt's gun hand. He promptly dropped his weapon and cradled his bloodied fingers in the crook of his arm with a moan.

Over his shoulder, Zack saw Paul, smoking gun in hand, advancing on them with a satisfied smirk on his face.

Beneath him, Zack then saw Daphne holding his backup gun. It was also smoking. She must have procured it from his ankle holster. How in the world had she known it was there? Better yet, how did she know how to shoot it? He thought Frankie was the personality with the spy skills. He'd felt her clinging to him, but hadn't realized Daphne had the ability to shoot the gun out of a villain's hand.

Alden had backed away with his hands over his ears.

Zack nodded once at Paul and then reached down to help Frankie to her feet.

"How did you do that?"

"I remembered where you kept your gun."

He smiled and wiped blood from her cheek. "I don't remember telling you."

"It was four months ago when we were at your house after we met at the bank."

"Huh. So you remember all of that now? Because *I* don't even remember it."

A smile appeared through the chaos of blood on her face. "I remember everything."

* * * *

Frankie Belle peered at her reflection in the mirror as she cleaned up in the protocol lab bathroom. Blood was everywhere. A nice shiner was forming on one cheek below her eye. *Shit*. She was a hot mess. She'd have to spend a week at a beauty spa just to achieve the title of Miss Death Warmed Over.

Matt and Alden had been taken into custody. Ken had been found shot and unconscious in one of the mazes of rooms and hallways beneath the building they'd worked in. Jeff had been transported semiconscious to a secretive hospital to recuperate. He'd been wearing body armor, but one of Timberton's bullets hit right below his protection, and he'd lost some blood. Hopefully, he'd be okay.

Frankie wiped away runnels of blood from her eyes and nose with a water-soaked paper towel before she simply pushed her face into a sink full of cold water.

Dead leaves and blades of grass clinging to her hair and clothes were the next offending things she removed piece by excruciating piece.

Daphne had been much more of a girly girl, and Frankie called on her memories to do a better job of making herself more presentable.

Except for the bloodstains still visible on her clothing, she didn't think she looked half bad.

Her eyes looked terminally bloodshot, but at least all the blood was gone from her face and the rims of her eyes.

She pushed out a long breath and exited the bathroom to endure whatever came next.

"There you are. Finally." This from Paul, who had the sarcastic expression to go with his statement. For all his bluster, she knew he'd been worried.

Zack approached her. "How do you feel?" His gaze searched her face before dropping to the bloodstains on her shirt. "Your eyes look a little bloodshot, but better than actual blood seeping out of them."

"I'm fine. No worse for wear."

"I disagree." Paul zeroed a look on her and approached as well. "Tell me what you know."

"I remember in a chronological order the events of my past. And I remember both lives."

Paul looked into her eyes. "Does it hurt to remember Daphne?"

"Not anymore. But it hurt like a bitch when the memories folded together."

"Will she stay this way permanently or revert back?" Zack asked.

"I wish I knew. The medical staff seems to think you'll stay as you are. If any of your memories get fuzzy, it's possible you can be given a shot to restore to where you are now."

"I'm not sure I'm willing to get anymore shots. Does that mean I can't be a Protocol Spy for you anymore?"

Paul shrugged. "I haven't decided yet pending your medical recovery."

"Well, I have. Listen up." She put a splayed hand on her chest. "I'm Frankie. I'm a spy. It's what I do. Sure, Daphne is a part of me, but I'm more Frankie than Daphne. And big-assed shots or not, I'd like to continue. I'm good at it. Don't kick me out."

"I'll have to assess your skills again. I'm not sure if you're ready.

You'll need a long time to recuperate, and we'd need to watch and evaluate you."

"I'd work with her." Zack slipped an arm around her shoulder.

"Really. Why?"

"Well, for starters, she shot the gun out of Matt's hand from ten feet after a traumatic brain injury because poison from a big fucking needle was plunged into her chest while she bled from her eyes, for Christ's sake. What other skills do you need to evaluate? My god, she's already hard core." He squeezed her tight against his side. She loved being with Zack. All of their memories together had her wishing for him to be in her life.

Paul voiced her fear. "Protocol spies don't have significant others."

"They also don't remember both of their lives, so I guess you can make an exception for that as well. I'm not letting her out of my life."

"She doesn't want to settle down and raise a family."

"Good. Neither do I. I love this life. I've only ever wanted to be a spy. She's the ideal mate for me. Having her at my side while we conquer the world together is perfection as far as I'm concerned."

Paul's mouth twitched, but he didn't actually smile. "I'll give your impassioned thoughts some consideration. No promises."

"Also, I'd like to take some time off." Frankie glanced at Zack. She had a few things to discuss with him.

"Fine. I guess you've earned some time off for discovering and subduing the traitors in our midst." His expression then turned stern. "But you call me if anything changes. Any nosebleeds or headaches, I want to know about them. Got it?"

Both she and Zack said, "Got it."

Together they exited the building and got in his truck. She reached beneath the seat as soon as she entered his vehicle.

"It's not there."

"Where is it?"

"Back at my house. I found it right where you left it after my stint in the hospital. I didn't know where it came from, but there was this intriguing scent clinging to it, and I couldn't seem to part with it."

"Why do you think Matt wanted it so badly he was willing to kill for it?"

"Let's go find out together, shall we?"

* * * *

Paul entered Ken's hospital room with a file folder in one hand and a bag of illegal food in the other. "Don't say I never gave you anything." The smell of grilled onions and saturated fat wafted into the air when he opened the top of the bag. He should have gotten one for himself.

"Thanks. So what was in the black and tan bag that Matt had such a hard-on for?"

"How'd you know about that?"

"Zack told me earlier. He said he retrieved it from his personal truck and turned it over to you for analysis."

Paul crossed his arms. "Figures." He wasn't really upset. Eventually Ken would have been briefed anyway. "Turns out there was a microchip sewn into the lining of the bag. The information was pulled from a small local bank in Loganville. Turns out that they are a subsidiary of the bank in DC where our agents met."

"What information was pulled?"

"Bank routing numbers and the accompanying passwords for several numbered accounts in the Cayman Islands. Once we accessed them, the names on the accounts were also listed. Several accounts had eight figure balances." He handed Ken the list of account numbers. "See any that look familiar?"

Ken studied the list for a few moments before cursing under his breath. "Shit. One of these is a covert slush fund account for my black ops group."

"Yeah. I had one listed on there, too. But don't worry, I removed them from the investigative list. No one knows but us that they were even there in the first place."

"How?"

"I called in a few favors." He handed Ken a card with his new numbered account. "Here's your new account. All your funds are intact."

"Thanks." He relaxed back against his pillow. "Who do the rest of the accounts belong to?"

Paul smiled. "That's actually the best news. Several were traced to a few well-known criminal elements. I guess it was Matt's retirement plan. He wanted lots of money, but our accounts were a personal vendetta. He was angry that the Protocol Agency got funded instead of his proposed goon squad. I'm just glad he failed. And I'm more glad he didn't kill any more of my agents in the process."

"How's Frankie?"

"She's doing very well. The entire medical staff is amazed. I expect she'll resume her duties very soon."

"Good. You've got to love a happy ending." Ken pulled out a double deluxe fat burger from Fat Boy's burgers and moaned after the first bite. A blissful expression along with mayonnaise coating his lips, he asked, "What do you want from me for this burger? I know it doesn't come for free."

"Why did you lie about where you were during the warehouse incident and the hospital explosion?"

Ken's face creased in puzzlement before shifting to resignation. "I'd rather not say."

"Too fucking bad. Spill it. I have an official report to fill out."

"Not telling."

"Not telling? What are you, a twelve-year-old girl? Give it up. You know I'm not leaving without an answer."

A long-suffering sigh came from Ken. "Maybe I was with someone."

"Like a woman?" The incredulous tone escaping his lips was

unfortunate.

"Don't sound so surprised. I'm not a monk. Are you?"

Paul shrugged. "We aren't talking about me." He pulled out a pen and clicked the end and opened the file folder. "And her name? Or are we talking about more than one name here?"

Ken took another bite of the burger and chewed thoughtfully for several seconds before shaking his head. "Just one name."

"Interesting, I never suspected you were seeing anyone."

"Yeah. I know. And I'm not telling you her name."

Before Paul could threaten Ken to reveal her name, a familiar voice from the door said, "Ken, darling. They said you were hurt. I was so worried about you, I had to come and see if you were..." She stopped talking the moment she saw Paul next to Ken's bed.

Paul's mouth opened in utter surprise. His longtime assistant, Stella Pemberton, mirrored his surprise with an openmouthed stare of her own. "Sir, I didn't know you here."

"Obviously."

Ken put the burger down. "Now you know why I didn't explain where I was during both incidents."

Stella blushed. "He didn't want you to find out we were a couple."

"How long has this been going on?" Paul was stunned. He'd never had an inkling that Ken and Stella had a relationship beyond the professional one at work.

"A year," they replied in unison and then stared at each other with goofy expressions on their faces.

Paul shook his head and exited the room.

Nothing would be the same, and apparently nothing had been what he thought it was anyway.

The smile he couldn't stop had more to do with the end of the traitor hunt than his newly found ammunition regarding Ken's love life.

Frankie was off happy with Zack. Ken was probably playing kissy face with his secretary as he walked to his car.

Paul breathed a sigh of relief that no one ended up dead.

* * * *

"I'm not so sure about this anymore," Zack said as the Protocol staff wired him up to one of the chairs they used to flip their spies on and off.

Paul rolled his eyes and paced next to the chair. "Quit being such a baby. It probably won't even work, but if you want a chance at remembering the warehouse incident, this is your best bet."

"Not to worry, Zack. I've been in the chair plenty of times." Frankie ran her hand down his arm, trying to soothe the man she loved. Her memories had returned with even the scents and sounds of minutia most might forget after a while. She relished the combined memories of her time with Zack and Jeff.

And while she'd told Zack absolutely everything she could remember, his personal memories hadn't come back, and he'd been so curious to know from his own perspective the events that brought them together.

Paul offered to let him sit in the Protocol chair and have their special serum administered on the off chance it would help him retrieve his lost memories.

"Fine. Let's get this over with."

Frankie held his hand. He closed his eyes and waited for the serum to take effect.

Zack turned in time to see a beautiful young woman trip over her feet and skid into him. She was carrying an unusually patterned tan and black satchel with something heavy and box-shaped inside. The box hit him squarely in the solar plexus, causing him to grunt before it glanced off his abs only to be replaced by the owner of the sweet, feminine voice he'd heard and ignored moments ago.

She was much softer than the satchel-covered box she wielded. Zack's arms automatically raised and grabbed her to him as if in reflex. He kept her on her feet as she began her appeal, begging the bank manager to let her in.

"Please, ma'am," she pleaded. "I simply must get inside. My boss sent me here in an airplane, for heaven's sake, to make sure what's in this satchel got put inside his safety deposit box tonight. I couldn't find a cab, and I mixed up the address, and I should have been here several hours ago and..." She started to cry as she chattered on, tears slipping easily out of beautiful eyes. "I already missed my flight back home tonight, and I'll lose my job if I don't get this inside for my boss. Please, ma'am, please, you just have to let me in." She ended on a sob, staring earnestly at the bank worker.

"I'm sorry, but—-"

"Aw, come on, let her in," Zack said, wondering why he'd spoken up. "Couldn't you chalk it up to a random act of kindness or something?"

Zack looked down at the soft woman he held comfortably in his arms and then back to the bank worker woman and saw her face soften. She reached up and tucked a strand of hair behind her ear then nodded, looking at the floor. "All right, but we have to hurry. We're doing a bank audit tonight. We can't get started until all the patrons are out." She stepped back from the door to allow the young woman to enter.

"Oh, thank you. Thank you so much," said the soft woman he held, thanking the now very unhappy looking bank manager. Daphne then turned to him and he got his first unhindered look at her face. Wow!

Zack felt like he'd taken another blow to his gut. She was absolutely beautiful. Curly, honey colored hair ran all the way down her back in thick waves and brushed his arm. Sparkling sea green eyes and a luscious wide mouth sporting a big smile now focused directly on him. She brushed a quick kiss on his mouth in exuberant gratitude. He didn't have time to react or participate in it before she leaned back and smiled.

"Thanks for opening the door for me, otherwise I wouldn't have made it," she said and drew away from him, stepping through the door and into the breezeway to the bank with her bulky satchel slung over her shoulder. He almost didn't care about the poker money any longer. He just wanted to follow her in and talk her into one more kiss. His lips were tingling. Damn!

"You've got sparkly pink lip gloss on your mouth," she said.

He brushed a finger across his lips. "There are worse things."

Zack looked at the stern-faced bank manager and said, "I don't suppose you'd let me in to get some cash. I need more than I can get out of the ATM. Although my job doesn't hang in the balance, I just need money for a poker game."

The bank manager looked him over for a moment and tucked another strand of imaginary loose hair behind her ear. "Why not?" she said curtly, stepping back to allow him to enter.

"Thank you," he said and stepped inside the bank. She stuck the key in the outer door and looked outside as she twisted the lock. They walked through the large vestibule to the inner door, and all three went inside the lobby of the bank.

Touching her again, a feeling of intense satisfaction ran through him at the simple pleasure of helping someone out. A random act of kindness for a lovely stranger. He was glad he had needed poker money tonight and wondered if he would even end up at the game. If he played his cards right, he might end up with a gorgeous young thing instead. Zack leveled an interested look her way, vowing to wait for her once he got his cash.

"Are you coming?" the bank worker asked, briskly marching past them.

"Yes," Daphne responded without looking at her. She gave him one last speculative look and sighed, turning away to follow the surly manager further into the bank.

Oh, yeah, he was waiting for her outside when he got done. Her mouth made him think of wicked things he hadn't experienced in a while. If she was interested, he'd take her out and skip poker night altogether. He could think of more satisfying ways to blow hundreds of dollars in an evening. Tonight was shaping up to be much different than he'd planned.

"Henry, we have one last customer for the counter. I'm heading back to the safety deposit vault. I'll be right back," the bank manager told a cashier behind the counter.

The bank was old with high ceilings, decorative carved moldings, and lots of waxed and gleaming woodwork everywhere. It was a man's bank, and that was why Zack liked it. You expected to see an old-time bank president with a big cigar clamped between his teeth counting money under a green banker's lamp.

Zack got more money than he'd planned on, and after thanking the bank teller, he went and stood by the front door. The bank guard told Zack the manager would have to come back with the keys to let him out. Zack waited for the luscious young woman and the potential for a night of wicked possibilities.

He nodded politely and watched through two sets of glass vestibule doors at the darkening sky outside. The streetlights hadn't come on yet. The sun was setting, making the streets dusky and almost dark.

Zack's libido was in high gear as he waited for Daphne to return. He thought about where he would take her and the promise of unexpected carnal activities for the night ahead. Maybe they could go dancing after dinner, he'd thought, and a rush of frenetic sensitivity blasted its way through his body at the image of dancing close to Daphne Kane while he pressed his face into her soft hair.

Moments later, Daphne returned with the bank manager. He turned his back completely to the inner bank doors and put his full attention on Daphne.

"Thanks again," Daphne said and stepped up to him, offering her hand. He took it in his and held on, wishing she would kiss him again. Right here, right now.

"Can I drive you somewhere? Perhaps someplace to eat dinner?" He turned on the charm.

"Don't you have plans?" she asked. "I'd hate to keep you from your poker game."

"Those plans weren't set in stone." Like hell they weren't. "Besides, I'd rather spend the evening with you." Oh, yeah, baby. Dinner and dancing and whatever else she wanted.

"All right, I'd like that." She smiled and winked at him. "I'll have to find a way to the airport on Monday morning to get a flight out."

"I can take you to the airport on Monday morning, too...and whenever you need to go tonight."

"Thank you so much."

Zack couldn't wait to get started on the evening, and his weekend prospects just got better, too.

The best parts of the rest of the weekend unfolded in his mind along with a few things Frankie had told him about. But now he had his own memories.

Zack woke in the chair after only an hour with a mild headache and a smile. There were still some black, foggy patches in his mind regarding those few days, but most of his lost memories had come back. He turned to Frankie. "Did you know that I loved you from the very first moment I laid eyes on you? I thought I'd died and gone to heaven when you kissed me in front of the bank."

Her lyrical laughter sent his pulse racing. "I love you, too, Zack."

Zack's memories were complete. He even remembered something that no one else knew. He'd found the black and tan bag, the one Matt was so hot to acquire, inside his car before they'd left on Monday morning. It had been tucked away beneath the passenger seat. He hadn't pulled it out from beneath the seat. He'd wanted her to forget to take it. He'd failed to remind her it was still there. He'd wanted her to remember where she left the bag after she got home. He'd wanted her to contact him to maybe see about retrieving it. While things hadn't worked out exactly as planned, Zack contemplated a rich, seductive future with Frankie.

The memories courtesy of the Protocol chair detailing their initial meeting only added to their already perfect relationship.

Epilogue

A year later

"Have you been out catching bad guys all week?" Frankie asked the moment he entered their house on Friday night. She'd been on convalescent leave for several days after a perilous mission they'd shared a week ago. She had wanted to join him anyway, but Paul had put his foot down, and she'd remained at home.

"Yep. 'Cause that's what I do best." Zack stopped and took a look at her from the top of her golden head to the tips of her painted toes. Even after a year together, she still took his breath away. She stood at the sink with her hands wrapped around a mug of something steamy. "Well, I'd say what you're best at is a tie between catching bad guys and one other thing, but the good news is that in one more week I can join you."

"Can't wait." He bent down and quickly kissed her lips. She set the cup on the counter and opened her arms to hug him. Apparently, she was looking for a longer and more involved kiss. He tasted sugared peppermint tea as she tangled her tongue in his mouth, licking and exploring until his cock made its presence known against her leg.

Zack slipped his arms around to hold her tight until he was nearly mad for her. Burying his face in her hair, he murmured, "Something smells good."

"And you're stunned because, as we both know, I'd burn water."

"Well, I was talking about your perfume, but yeah, something else smells good, too." He inhaled and caught the scent of something spicy in the air. "Besides, you *know* how to cook, you just don't like to. Daphne is in there somewhere, fighting to get out and prepare a meal. I know she is."

"Don't count on it. I've suppressed whatever homemaking skills were ever in Daphne's memory. Lucky for us, Jeff is in town to shoulder the cooking responsibilities."

Zack hadn't seen a rental car in the garage. "Is he here?"

She nodded. "He showed up in a taxi late this morning with three bags of groceries in hand and then spent the last couple of hours cooking. He's downstairs resting up for future sex and what he's calling, *a threesome without equal*. If you're interested, that is."

He smiled. "Oh, I'm interested all right."

"Good. He offered to bend me over the kitchen table and do me if you were grumpy or tired when you got home." She retrieved her mug and took a long sip.

"So generous of him." Zack laughed. "How does he look?" Jeff usually came back from undercover work looking like a survivalist who'd been left in the wilderness to find his way home after first enduring a long winter hibernation.

"Scruffy and tired. So naturally I'm jealous. I'd rather be out kicking ass and taking names instead of sitting at home waiting for a man to come back." She placed her mug in the sink, crossed her arms, and sighed with supreme exaggeration.

"You'll be back in the game soon enough. In the meantime, go wake his ass up. I want some *threesome without equal* sex."

She grinned. "Or we could go down to his play room and get started ourselves. He'll figure it out and join us when he wakes up."

Zack returned her smile. "Let's go." He paused. "Unless you wanted me to bend you over the kitchen table and do you first."

She eyed the table. "Tempting, but I sort of had my heart set on rolling around on the surface of Jeff's huge bed with the navy silk sheets."

He slung an arm around her neck and they descended to the next level. The door was slightly ajar. "He must have heard us. The door was closed when I came through here from the garage earlier."

"Please enter the pleasure domain," Jeff called. "And let the threesome without equal sex begin."

Zack pushed the door open, and Frankie entered ahead of him. Inside, Jeff was already dressed for the party. He wore only a scratchy-looking, three-day-old beard, a raging erection, and a big grin. Arms open wide, Jeff wiggled his fingers and motioned for Frankie to join him. She walked into his arms. They kissed passionately as Zack watched. His cock came to stiff attention. Without breaking the kiss, Jeff began taking off Frankie's clothes. Zack removed his jeans and shirt in record time, slid a condom onto his already thick cock, then came up behind Frankie to help with the last of her clothes.

Once she was completely naked, Jeff kissed a path from her lips to her breasts as Zack pressed his lips repeatedly to the sensitive spot on the back of her neck. She moaned as if with sweet desperation as Jeff descended further down her body, fell to his knees, and buried his face between her thighs. The minute his tongue hit her clit, she shuddered, and Zack's cock responded in kind against her butt cheek.

Zack slid his hands around to play with her nipples and hold her up as Jeff ate her pussy with gusto.

"Thank you for not shaving," she murmured. Her right leg lifted onto Jeff's shoulder, widening her thighs so he could feast easier. She writhed in Zack's arms, and it didn't take her long to climax, shrieking.

The center of her back laced with perspiration, Frankie slumped against his chest when Jeff finished lapping up her juices.

Suddenly impatient to be inside her body, Zack turned her and bent her over the corner of Jeff's bed. He didn't have a footboard, and it was the perfect height for what he wanted to do. Jeff rounded to the other side and nudged his cock against her mouth. Zack almost lost it before even getting his cock near the inside of her body.

She latched on to Jeff's cock and sucked him deeply into her mouth as Zack pushed his dick as deeply as he could into her tight, wet pussy.

Together they found a good rhythm. Jeff fucked her mouth, and Zack stroked his cock in and out of her body with such zeal, he hoped not to propel her off the end of the bed. He slipped a hand beneath her hips and found her clit. Rubbing her hot spot as he powered thrust after thrust into her nirvana-inducing pussy, Zack didn't think he'd last very much longer.

Jeff grunted, suddenly sounding as if he was surprised by his own orgasm. But Zack knew Frankie had a wide and very talented mouth. She sucked him dry.

Frankie suddenly squirmed against him, pushing her ass against his groin, and moaned with Jeff's cock still stuffed between her lips. Jeff soon pulled his cock from her mouth and promptly fell backwards onto the bed a couple feet away from them. He put a hand to his chest and panted.

Zack doubled his efforts and thrust even harder. The ripple of her pussy squeezed his cock with indefinable pleasure and most likely signaled her next climax.

He grabbed her hips and thrust his cock as deeply as he could. She was moaning and pushing against his every stroke as if to take him even deeper into her body. The spiraling sensation of release ignited in his balls first before plunging down his cock like a stampede of bulls. He fell over the edge of oblivion and into an exhilarating orgasm, the likes he hadn't felt since the last time he'd had sex with Frankie.

Pleasure riddled his body from chest to knees as an unstoppable growl erupted from his throat. He bent in half and kissed the center of Frankie's spine.

"I love you," he murmured. "Love you." As if saying the words only once wasn't enough to express his devotion.

"I love you, too," Jeff said, still flat on his back.

Frankie giggled. "I love you both. This is absolutely perfect."

Jeff rolled to one side and faced them. "It's the threesome without equal. Am I right?"

They were still intimately connected when they answered, in unison, "Yes!"

THE END

WWW.LARASANTIAGO.COM

ABOUT THE AUTHOR

Lara Santiago is the bestselling author of over twenty-five books. She's a WisRWA award winner for her bestselling novel, *Menagerie*, an Ecataromance award winner for *The Miner's Wife*, a Passionate Plume finalist for *The Lawman's Wife*, and has garnered a coveted four and a half stars from Romantic Times Book Reviews for her novel, *The Blonde Bomb Tech*.

From her futuristic and science fiction novels to her contemporary romantic suspense books, she's known for her independent heroines and those compelling alpha males we all adore.

After turning in her twelfth manuscript, she came to the realization that this writing gig might just work out after all. She continues to dream up stories, keeping no less than ten story ideas circulating at any given time.

Also by Lara Santiago

Siren Classic: Prequel to *The Wives Tale*: *The Prosecutor's Paramour*
Siren Classic: The Wives Tales 1: *The Miner's Wife*
Siren Classic: The Wives Tales 2: *The Executive's Wife*
Siren Classic: The Wives Tales 3: *The Lawman's Wife*
Siren Classic: The Wives Tales 4: *The Mercenary's Wife*
Siren Classic: The Tiburon Duet 1: *Just a Kiss*
Siren Classic: The Tiburon Duet 2: *Just One Embrace*
Siren Classic: The Tiburon Duet 3: *Kissed By Fate*
Siren Classic: Blind Date After Dark 1: *Mr. Right*
Siren Classic: Blind Date After Dark 2: *The Perfect Tool*
Siren Classic: Blind Date After Dark 3: *The Mistletoe Mistake*
Siren Classic: The Double Recall 1: *The Forgetful Spy*
PolyAmour: Tasty Treats 11: *Range War Bride*
PolyAmour: Galactic Gunslingers 1: *Rogue's Run*
PolyAmour: Dark Colony 1: *Sex or Suffer*
PolyAmour: *Menagerie*
Siren Classic: *The Blonde Bomb Tech*
Siren Classic: *Little Red Rides the Wolf*
Siren Classic: Siren Classic: *The Sins of Their Fathers*
Ménage Everlasting: The Lost Collection: *Annie Gets Her Gunmen*

Also by Elle Saint James

Ménage Amour: Badlands 1: *Mail Order Bride for Two*
Ménage Amour: Badlands 2: *Two Wanted Men*
Ménage Amour: Badlands 3: *Double Chance Claim*
Ménage Everlasting: The Double Rider Men's Club 1: *Unbridled and Undone*
Ménage Everlasting: The Double Rider Men's Club 2: *Unbridled and Unbroken*

Available at
BOOKSTRAND.COM

Siren Publishing, Inc.
www.SirenPublishing.com